*By Jane MacKenzie*

Daughter of Catalonia

Autumn in Catalonia

# *Autumn in Catalonia*

JANE MACKENZIE

Allison & Busby Limited
12 Fitzroy Mews
London W1T 6DW
*allisonandbusby.com*

First published in Great Britain by Allison & Busby in 2015.



A CIP catalogue record for this book is available from
the British Library.

First Edition

ISBN 978-0-7490-1937-2

Typeset in 10.5/15.5 pt Sabon by
Allison & Busby Ltd.

The paper used for this Allison & Busby publication
has been produced from trees that have been legally sourced
from well-managed and credibly certified forests.

Printed and bound by
CPI Group (UK) Ltd, Croydon, CR0 4YY

*To my good friends and readers Maureen and Jenne, with endless thanks for all your help and support*

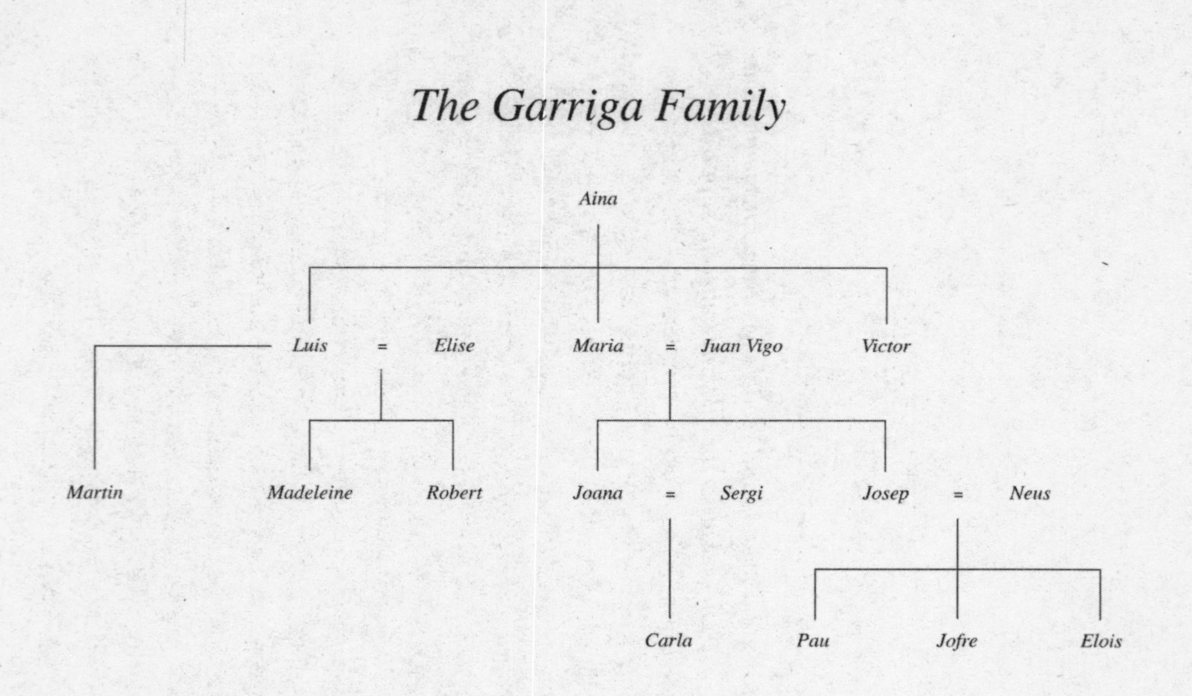
The Garriga Family
Aina
Luis = Elise
Maria = Juan Vigo
Victor
Martin
Madeleine
Robert
Joana = Sergi
Josep = Neus
Carla
Pau
Jofre
Elois

# Chapter One

Barcelona, 1962

It was the first day of November, and Barcelona was decking itself with chestnut stalls, and cake stalls, and dressing up its children for All Saints Day. A long weekend beckoned, warm still as the autumn sunshine held good in unclouded skies, and the streets were already quite full as Carla emerged from her student hostel and made her way to Luc's apartment.

She stopped to buy sweet chestnuts, too hot to touch and smelling of sugared autumn. Everywhere smelt of sugar. She passed by another stall selling *panellets*, the little, round cakes, covered in pine nuts, which were the traditional dessert today, but she didn't buy this time. She and Luc were invited to lunch at Uncle Josep and Aunt Neus's house, and Aunt Neus made the best *panellets* in Barcelona. She couldn't arrive at their home carrying street-bought cakes. The chestnuts were for Luc, just to keep him going until lunchtime.

It took longer than usual to make her way through the crowds on the Rambla to where she turned off towards Luc's little backstreet. It would be even busier this evening, when still more of Barcelona's citizens would come out to stroll and enjoy the festivities. Even a group of Civil Guards on a street corner looked more amiable than usual.

But once she was off the Rambla, in the narrow little residential streets behind, the hubbub ceased, and she was able to stretch into her usual rapid walk. She opened the street door to Luc's block, and set off up the five flights of stairs to his tiny room way up at the top of the building. Luc would be waiting for her – he was always early, always methodical, Mr Steady with his few shirts always neatly ironed, and his shoes always polished. Only his features weren't so well ordered – his knobbly face only beautiful if you loved him, and his hands large and too clumsy for the tiny space he lived in.

She reached the top of the stairs in a rush, a bubble of excitement pushing her up the last few steps. Today she was going to introduce Luc to Uncle Josep and Aunt Neus, her first presentation of the man in her life to anyone in her family. And next week they were going to spend the weekend with Luc's parents. Things were getting serious!

She knocked on his door and it opened immediately, inwards unfortunately, since as it did so it always hit the side of the bed, and never failed to pin Luc's left leg, because he didn't step aside in time. The attic room contained just this bed, a tiny desk and chair, and a small chest of drawers, and in one corner, on the floor, was a portable gas stove. On the landing below this room was a shared bathroom. As 'apartments' go, it was practically non-existent, but it was private and quiet and had become their haven. Carla's girls' hostel was a no-go area for Luc, male visits being banned, so any private time they had was spent here.

And beyond the tiny room was the balcony, which made the room really special for Carla. It was the smallest balcony imaginable, really more like a ledge outside his window, but from it you could see over the Barcelona rooftops and the warehouses beyond to the sea, which was just a misty blur behind the jumble of cranes. It was this old harbour area that Carla always felt was the lifeblood of Catalonia. Economist and accountant Luc might talk about the new factories and tourism, about foreign investment and the new Spain, but Carla loved the old docks, with their piles of tyres and wooden crates. They would sit on the floor of the balcony, facing out to sea, letting the sun soak into their faces, and drink cheap coffee brewed on the stove, or sometimes real coffee and sandwiches bought from the café in the street below.

And they would talk – endlessly they would talk. About the past, about the battles of the present, and about the future their Spain needed, that they had to help deliver for her. But also about music, and poetry, which Carla had always studied very formally, but which Luc approached with almost hedonistic pleasure, quoting love lines from Lorca to her in a humorous voice which ill-concealed his adoration for his favourite poet. He would declaim lines from Lope de Vega too, and was endlessly singing – verses of Catalan folk, or pop music, or even opera, in a fine baritone which Carla appreciated more, perhaps, than his neighbours did. It wasn't silliness – it was just freedom, and gradually Carla was learning. Could you learn spontaneity, or did you ingest it by osmosis? It didn't really matter, but she had never been so happy.

And now she was taking Luc to meet Josep. He'd taken extra care over his appearance this morning, she noticed with amusement. He'd brought out his newest shirt, one rarely worn for university or for the campaign trail, and was wearing a tie. Well good! She'd made an effort herself, bringing out a dress and jacket set that she hadn't worn since the summer, of a deep Mediterranean blue and flowing wide from a narrow waist, giving her some curves and swishing around her long legs. It was an outfit her mother had chosen, not the most elaborate or the most expensive in her wardrobe, but not normal student wear either, and she'd surprised herself this morning when she'd wanted to wear it for Luc. She didn't normally dress too fine to go to Josep's house. Josep and her mother might be brother and sister, but they lived in different worlds, and it always felt senseless to flaunt silly trappings of another life when visiting Josep.

But she'd succumbed today, and she felt all the pleasure of success when she saw the little appreciative gleam in Luc's eyes.

'Beautiful,' he murmured, as he drew her to him for a kiss.

'*Idiota*!' she protested, but she was absurdly pleased. 'I brought you a mid-morning snack. I thought you might not have had more than three or four rolls for breakfast!'

'Yay! It's the *Castanyada*!' Luc grinned, for All Saints Day was all about eating chestnuts. There would be chestnuts at Uncle Josep's, too, freshly roasted after lunch, but this little paper cone of sugar was just what Luc loved, and he ate through the packet within minutes as they left his little room, and made their way out towards the newer part of town where Josep and Neus lived. It would barely dent his appetite, she knew.

Uncle Josep lived in a 1950s block of family-sized, utility apartments built around a central, open courtyard, which the residents had turned into a communal space for themselves and their children. It was rare in Franco's Spain for neighbours to create such a community. People still watched each other, and were scared to speak openly, and so many had flooded into the cities from different villages, looking for work, that your neighbour could be from anywhere, and woe betide you if you trusted him too easily.

But in Josep's building most of the apartments were occupied by men who worked for the same engineering company, workers who took the same bus together each morning and had even dared to create a small workers' union. They were flexing their muscles very cautiously, but they stood together, and inside this building everyone spoke Catalan, and joined together for festivities, and their communal courtyard took the place of the old village squares which had been the meeting places in another life.

As Luc and Carla entered the courtyard, it became quickly clear that this was a day when the little community all planned to eat together. Children were running around everywhere, in their best clothes, looping between three long communal tables, which were made up of all the household tables put together, with an assortment of white and flowered tablecloths covering the whole. On a long, low wall that bordered the yard a small group of men were already sitting with glasses in their hands, while their womenfolk finished laying the tables. Charcoal grills had been set up, on which the chestnuts would be roasted.

Luc loosed Carla's hand as they walked into this scene, and she realised that he was nervous. She had butterflies herself, but she waved at one or two of the neighbours as she led the way in, and seeing that neither Josep nor Neus was present here, she moved with her usual quick-footed pace towards their apartment in the ground-floor corner, and as she reached the open front door she turned to wait for Luc, ushering him in with a reassuring smile.

Inside, the apartment was functional and square, with modern furniture bought cheaply, Carla knew, when Josep and Neus had moved in with their young family just five years ago. But there was flowered paper on every wall, and photos everywhere, mainly of the children, but also some of grandparents and older generations.

They entered on a surprisingly peaceful scene, contrasting with the activity outside. Neus was just coming out of the kitchen with a huge tray of *panellet* cakes, which she laid on a large sideboard ready to be carried out to the tables. Josep was sitting with the three boys, tying their ties before letting them go outside. Glasses had been laid out on the floral runner on the coffee table, alongside a bottle of chilled red wine and a dish of olives.

It was Neus who saw them first, and she came hastily forward to greet them, kissing Carla and then taking Luc's hand in both of hers.

'My dears, you're here! Come in, come in!' Her huge, welcoming grin beamed warmth at them. 'Don't mind all that going on outside – we'll be going out to eat with them shortly, but it's early yet, and we want a little time with you first. They'll be at the *aperitiù* for a long time before they think about eating! You must be Luc! How happy we are to meet you. Come sit down here. Pau, make way for the young *Senyor*!' This to her youngest son, whom she shooed to a corner of the sofa to give Luc pride of place in the centre.

Josep had risen at their entrance, and stood waiting in his quiet way for Neus to finish talking. As she drew Luc towards the sofa he stepped forward and reached out his own hand.

Carla watched them both, each of them tall, roughly even in height, although Luc was like a bear in comparison to Uncle Josep's slender build. Josep was the fairer, his blond curls defiantly un-Catalan in colour, and for a moment you could almost have thought he was the younger. He had a young face for his thirty-seven years – just like Mama, thought Carla. Brother and sister were a good-looking pair.

'Luc,' Josep was saying, 'Welcome to our home. Carla has told us something about you, and we have been looking forward to meeting you.'

'Me too, *Senyor.*' Luc's deep tones came out as measured as usual, and then, as he saw Josep's smile, he smiled in return.

Josep looked over at Carla and winked. 'I've just been wanting to meet the guy who had the balls to take you on, little niece!' he said, and as Neus protested, gesturing at the children, he grinned and pulled Luc down to sit next to him.

They were destined to be good friends, Luc and Josep. Over an initial glass of wine they were already laying into the regime. And several hours of non-stop talking later, accompanied by several glasses of *moscatell* and far too much food, the world had become rosy, the harshest elements of the regime were being eroded, and Spain was en route for a brighter future. After lunch with the neighbours they sat a little apart in the shade, watching the children playing, while some of the men carried on feasting noisily, and their women, in this macho culture, withdrew indoors. Luc and Josep were deep in debate, glass in hand, and the rest of the world had receded from them.

Neus, pragmatic and tolerant, left them late in the afternoon to visit her parents' graves, traditional on this day of remembrance of the dead. Carla settled down with her glass of *moscatell* in her hand to watch her men from the sidelines. She wasn't in the least abashed by their company, but by nature she was more reserved, and by upbringing more wary. Silence had often been Carla's greatest defence, and it made a sheltering blanket from which to watch the world.

But Neus's departure brought a more sober mood to Uncle Josep. He watched his wife leave, following her with his eyes until she was through the outside door, and then turned to Carla.

'You know Carla, I don't believe in all that tradition about the day of the dead, but one of these days I must ask my mother where my father is buried. He's here in Barcelona, but I don't know where. I'd like to pay my respects, somehow.'

'Your father is buried in Barcelona?' It was news to Carla – her grandfather was buried here?

'Why, yes. And don't ask me why, but after all these years here I am finding myself thinking about him more and more.' His voice was thoughtful but not melancholy. 'I think it's been creeping up on me since you came back into our lives here, and since Mama left the village and there's no one up in the old house anymore. I've been thinking more about the past.' He shook his head as if to shake away ideas. 'I'm getting old, I think.'

Luc was curious. 'I thought that your family all came from Sant Galdric, up in the hills. That's what Carla told me.'

'Well yes, she's right, except that my early years were spent here in Barcelona, and then my mother went back up to the village after father died. I was about nine years old, maybe ten, and I grew up in Sant Galdric after that, became a real village boy. But I was born in this city.'

'Your father was from Barcelona?'

'No.' Josep ran his hand through his blond hair with a rueful grin. 'Where do you think I get this colouring from?

My father was from the south, although even he couldn't explain how he came to be so fair! He was a journalist, working here in Barcelona.'

'And he met your mother?' The question was valid. Village girls didn't just come to Barcelona on their own forty years ago.

'He worked with my mother's brother. My Uncle Luis was a journalist too, a bigger one than my father, by all accounts. He was the great success of my mother's family. Anyway, Luis and my father were great friends, and so introductions were made, and my father ended up marrying Luis's sister!' He disappeared for a few minutes into his own reverie, and then added, with a sigh, 'They were great days, here in Barcelona, with just father and mother, and me and my sister Joana – that's Carla's mother, you know – and Uncle Luis hanging out with us all the time. Different times.'

It was the first Carla had ever heard of her mother's family living in Barcelona. She knew nothing! It was astonishing. She wanted to ask questions, but her mind was too much of a jumble, so she let Luc carry on putting them for her.

'Was this during the Republic?' he asked, and Josep nodded.

'So your father, Carla's grandfather, was a Republican journalist?'

'Yes, he and Uncle Luis ran a newspaper here until 1934, when it got closed down after the November uprising and everyone was arrested. Uncle Luis got away, but my father was thrown into gaol for a while. It damaged his health in there, and he died not long after they let him out.'

'Poor Grandma,' said Carla, finding her voice at last.

'Yes, it was tough for my mother. She'd lost her husband and her brother, and had no means to live, so she took us back up to the village, to where the rest of the family still were, and the rest, as you might say, is history.'

Carla looked long at Uncle Josep. It explained a lot about him, and about Mama, to know that their life hadn't always been lived in Sant Galdric, with its sheep and goats and dusty houses. Josep was a good product of a village school, but he had a broader view of life and the world than most villagers, and was a voracious reader when he had the time. And Mama? Carla felt the usual frustration when she thought of Mama, tailored and manicured, and increasingly brittle and hard-edged, swanning around Girona in her Mercedes with chauffeur Toni at the wheel. Mama was beyond the reach even of Carla, and she certainly didn't fit into any picture of Sant Galdric. It was hard to imagine her as a village child, playing in the dirt with all the rest.

Carla caught Luc watching her, his face a query, and raised her hands at him to show her own bewilderment. 'This is all news to me! I can't believe I never even heard of it before! All I knew was that Mama got herself out of Sant Galdric by marrying one of Franco's men after the Civil War. I kind of understood that from Papa's sarcastic comments about her humble origins over the years. And I just assumed she must have worked hard to turn herself into that elegant government wife she's become.' She turned to Uncle Josep. 'How old was Mama when you left Barcelona?'

'When our father died? I guess she must have been about twelve or thirteen – something like that. She was very much my big sister! She was very bright, you know, always brilliant at school, and she loved to sit with the journalists and listen to them talk. She absolutely hated it when we had to go back to the village – she never really accepted life there, unlike me, being younger.'

'So when Papa offered to take her away . . .'

'Yes, I guess she just grasped at the offer, and of course life was pretty grim just after the war ended. Lots of people had lost faith in the Republican cause.' Josep's faced clouded. 'But still, I never thought she would betray the whole family – everything we stood for – just to get away. It came as a shock to everyone. She kind of simply disappeared one day, packed her bags and she was off, and the next thing we knew she was married to Sergi Olivera. No one could believe it.'

There was grieving in his voice, and it struck Carla that he must truly have loved his sister. And after she left he'd never seen her again. Life was very strange.

A silence had fallen over them all. In the background there was the murmur of voices from the courtyard, with occasional bursts of laughter, but it didn't touch them. Carla couldn't tear her mind away from the image of Mama in Sant Galdric, frustrated and angry, and seeking a way out. Carla's parents had a summer home in the hills above Sant Galdric, and you had to drive through the village to get there. Her mother, Joana, always kept her gaze straight ahead as their Mercedes made its way between the stone houses, skirting the square in front of the old church, and then on out again into the wooded country above.

Toni, her mother's factotum and driver, was from the village, and his mother had also worked for them – she'd run the summer house for a few years before her health broke down. Both of them would talk to Carla about the village, and their family and friends. But Carla had never once, in all of her twenty-three years, been allowed to go there herself. She'd known she had family there herself – her grandmother, her mother's uncle, her great-grandmother even – but Toni and his mother were servants, they had their jobs to protect, so the information they gave her was sketchy, and in the face of complete silence from her parents she'd learnt not to ask questions.

Only when she left home for university in Barcelona had Toni told her about her Uncle Josep, living now with his family also in Barcelona.

'You could visit him,' Toni had suggested. It seemed impossible, but gradually, as she basked in the freedom of a life away from her parents' home, she'd finally come to believe that she could, and, using Toni's directions, she'd one day found the courage to knock on Josep's door.

She looked across at Uncle Josep now, and found him watching her. She reached for his hand. 'You lost a sister,' she said to him, with more than an edge of bitterness, 'but she lost much more. God knows how Mama could feel that what she now has was worth losing her family for! She could have got out of the village the same way you did – by working her way out. Instead she prostituted herself!'

Luc frowned. 'That's harsh, Carla.'

'Perhaps, but what else can you call it when a girl from

a staunchly Republican family and village walks into the arms of the enemy in exchange for a soft life in Girona?'

Luc's gaze went to Josep, sitting across from him, his forehead knotted in distress, and he shook his head at Carla. She nodded, penitent. Whatever her own battles with her parents, to persist in this line with Josep was cruel. What was important was the discovery of her grandfather. An eminent journalist at the heart of the Republic! It was like a gift from the gods to have such a share in history laid at her feet. She gave her uncle a smile and squeezed the hand she still held under hers.

'If Grandma tells you where your father is buried, I'd love to come with you to see his grave,' she told him. 'After you've been yourself, of course. Do you know where you used to live in Barcelona?'

'Roughly,' was the reply. 'My mother told me we lived behind the cathedral. It was important to my father to live in the centre.'

'Not far from where Luc lives, then! Find him, Uncle Josep! You've given me something to be proud of, something else than my own father's politics!'

Josep still looked grieved. The day of the dead hung over him, with its memories and its ghosts, and it took Neus's return, with her brisk plans and comforting smile, to lift the trouble from his face. She brought extra sweets for the children, and surrounded them not only with their own three boys but all the neighbours' children as well, and with his arms around his sons Josep became again the easy-hearted, family man who had helped to change Carla's life.

They took the boys with them, later, as they all headed out into the streets of Barcelona to walk among the holidaymakers and drink coffee near the port. We're just normal Barcelona citizens, Carla thought, a family and two young lovers out to enjoy the evening. Every person around them had a history, every family here had its own complex story, but tonight was a holiday, and with Luc and Josep and Neus she could almost feel she belonged at last with the milling crowd.

# Chapter Two

## Barcelona, 1934–1935

*Josep played as quietly as he could at the end of the long balcony. If he made any noise he would be sent inside, and once inside he wouldn't be allowed to wave his sword around for fear of damaging the furniture. He was a medieval warrior, and there was a dragon lying dead on the floor beside him. There was another hiding just behind the wall, on the neighbour's balcony, and it would come out any moment. He was poised and ready.*

*Behind him, at the far end, Joana was sitting, also keeping quiet, watching as Papa and Uncle Luis sketched out on paper the outline of tomorrow's newspaper. She was listening in to their conversation about politics, and later, when they were in bed, she would repeat it all to Josep. Sometimes he had to pretend to be asleep to stop her.*

*The balcony was warm, soporifically warm, with no hint of a breeze to cool the summer's morning, and the scent of jasmine and passion flower hung around them from the plants which Mama watered so lovingly every day. Below them the Barcelona street was two floors down, and they could hear all the people going by, and smell the coffee from the café opposite. It didn't affect Papa and Uncle Luis, though. They had their heads down so intensely over their papers that the neighbours passing by went unacknowledged, and even a lazy bee droning around the table between the plants couldn't make them look up.*

*Mama came out onto the balcony with coffee, and finally the two men stopped talking. Joana slipped out of her seat to help Mama serve, and Josep left the dragons and came towards the table. There would be biscuits on the tray.*

*Joana was placing a cup carefully by Uncle Luis's elbow, and he reached out his arm and pulled her to him.*

*'Thank you,* carinyo,*' he said, as he hugged her around the waist. He gave her his biggest smile, and reached behind him to pluck a single passion flower from Mama's precious plant. He tucked the flower behind her ear, sweeping her hair back as he did so.*

*'How is my princess today?' he asked, as he did every day.*

'Gràcies amable Senyor, *thank you kind sir, I'm well,' she replied, with a mock curtsy. Joana always liked to play these games with Uncle Luis.*

*Luis turned round in his chair. 'And you, young man? How is my Josep?'*

*Josep came forward to be hugged, and Luis slipped an extra biscuit into his hand.*

*'Him?' Joana answered, dismissively. 'All he thinks about are his stupid games!'*

*'Yes, but that's a mighty fine sword!' Uncle Luis countered.*

*'Papa made it for me – from one single piece of wood!' Josep boasted, and got a broad grin from Papa before the two men turned back to continue their debate.*

*'What do you think is going to happen to the unions, Maria?' Papa was asking Mama. He always included Mama in their debates, even if some of his colleagues didn't like it. The Republic had given women suffrage, he would say, and in this house women would be heard. Joana would lecture Josep that everyone had to respect their Mama, because she was not only Juan Vigo's wife, she was also Luis Garriga's sister, and Uncle Luis was the greatest journalist in Barcelona, who had even lived in Paris! Just smell his French eau de cologne, she used to tell Josep!*

*Mama was taking her time to answer Papa, wrinkling her nose in thought before she spoke. It would get boring now, Josep thought, and moved back to the other end of the balcony, stuffing one of his biscuits into his pocket for later.*

*'The right wing are cracking down,' he could hear his father saying. 'All in the name of democracy, of course.' He sounded very troubled, which was strange. Juan Vigo was the most carefree of men, and viewed life as the happiest of adventures, so when he was serious you had to pay attention.*

*'Have we come all this way in the Republic to give it all up now?' he was continuing, in his crazy Andalucian accent, which Joana could mimic so well sometimes, and*

*then Papa would chase her round the chairs.*

*Mama finally answered, speaking in her usual thoughtful way, but just then the dragon emerged from hiding, breathing fire, and Josep forgot all about the grown-ups at the other end of the balcony.*

*He couldn't really exclude them, though – he knew that. There were strikes all over Spain against the new government, and threats of some kind of uprising in Barcelona. Papa and Uncle Luis became more and more busy, and often weren't around, and then one day Joana and Josep came out of school and found Mama waiting for them. She took Josep's hand, and ushered them through strangely empty streets to the house, which Maria locked up behind them, securing them inside with all the shutters closed. There was nothing happening that Joana and Josep could see, but Mama told them that there was going to be a major confrontation with the central government – a real battle, Josep thought, half excited, half terrified, with guns and bombs.*

*'And where is Papa?' he wanted to know. Maria shrugged, helplessly, and produced juice and cakes which Josep ate with scared eyes, and which Joana couldn't even touch.*

*That night they could hear the guns just a kilometre away. By morning it was quiet, with just a few sporadic shots from time to time. They waited, and waited, but there was no sign of either Uncle Luis or Papa. And it wasn't until night had fallen again that one of their friends came to tell Maria that her brother had fled arrest, and her husband was in gaol.*

* * *

*And after that there was no laughter in the house, and Mama spent her days visiting officials, trying to see Papa, who was somewhere they weren't allowed to visit him. All the politicians and the fighters had been arrested too, it seemed. Joana asked lots of questions. How could it have happened when Papa had always told them things were going to be all right? It was Mama who had to explain everything now.*

*'They all forgot about democracy, my dears,' she told them both. 'They all just wanted their own way. And what your Papa and Uncle Luis had been arguing for, debate and consensus, and the right to strike, and freedom of expression, well all of that has been forgotten for now. But we still have a democratic constitution, and we can vote these people out again one day, and Papa will come home.'*

*'And Uncle Luis?'*

*'Well, we don't know where he is. He has probably gone back to France, and he'll be fine in Paris, but he'll come home too, just you wait and see. And Papa will be home before you know it. Many people are working to have him released. He wasn't involved in the fighting, and the Governor knows that.'*

*And after a long winter Papa did come home, but he wasn't the same Papa any more. He'd been ill in prison, some kind of lung infection, Mama said, and he coughed, and wheezed, and had to pull himself out of his chair, and he no longer laughed and played with Joana and Josep. Mama told them to be patient, and Papa would get better, but one day Mama and Josep found him slumped in his chair, his face all the wrong shape, and Papa was dead.*

* * *

Josep lay in his bed in Barcelona with Neus by his side, unable to sleep. Should he have shared that with Carla this afternoon? Would it do her any good to know about her family's past? Well it might not be doing him any good either, but it was as he'd said to Carla, since she'd come knocking on his door she had brought Joana back with her, and with her came all the other memories. When was it that their father had died? It must have been in the spring of 1935. And they'd moved up to Sant Galdric. Funny, but he had no memory of that move, only of already being there, in their grandmother's house, and helping Uncle Victor with the sheep, and playing football endlessly with the other boys. It had been a good life for a young boy, and he hadn't really felt any change in their schooling, for example, though he knew Joana had.

Joana! What a dynamo she had been! And how she had hated being immured in Sant Galdric. It dawned on him that she must have missed their father dreadfully, and Uncle Luis. She'd idolised them both. His thoughts went back to the final time they'd seen Uncle Luis. It must have been a year or so after their move back to the village, and a left-wing government had been elected again, so Luis could come back to Spain.

*The boys looked up in unison from their game of marbles as the big black car glided slowly past them along the street. It was so seldom that a car came to Sant Galdric that all eyes were fixed on it. From where he sat on the side of the road Josep could only see the passenger, a woman wearing a black hat with some kind of lace over it. The car moved away, and as one the boys rose, watching as it made its way along the street and turned the corner into a side street. Together the boys ran to the corner to see where it was going, and as they reached it Jordi called out to Josep.*

*'That's your house it's stopped at! Look!'*

*The car had indeed stopped outside grandmother's house, and the driver, a man, was ushering the lady in the hat inside the house. Josep stood watching, wondering what to do, but then like a bullet behind them came Joana.*

*'Quickly, Josep, come quickly! Uncle Luis is here! It's him driving that car!' she gasped, and grabbed his arm as she carried on running.*

*He followed her, not really taking in yet what she had said. Outside the house they both stopped, suddenly shy, and after staring into the car, gaping at the shiny upholstery and leather-covered steering wheel, they entered the house almost timidly, on tiptoe, as though they'd been caught out doing something wrong.*

*They entered directly into the living area of the old village house, and sure enough, there he was, Uncle Luis, standing with a huge grin on his face, while Grandma Aina held him helplessly by both hands, and Mama stood by, twisting her apron in her hands as she waited her turn to touch him. Next to him stood the most elegant woman Josep had ever seen, fair and genteel in a simply cut skirt and jacket, and that funny confection of a hat, and with her hair curling over her peaches-and-cream face like the posters you saw of Hollywood actresses. She was so different from all the women Josep had ever seen in Spain that he wondered what she could be doing here.*

*'Maria!' Luis was saying, holding Mama tight, and then he turned and saw the children and his face broke into the smile he'd always kept for them, and they ran to him.*

*'Look at you, little Josep, grown so big, and as for Joana, what a beauty you've become,* vida meva*!' Luis exclaimed, and she blushed beetroot red. It brought a wave of memory back to Josep, because he was speaking in that caressing tone Papa used to use. Much as the village boys might run stupidly after her, it was against all their mother's principles to pander to vanity, so no one in this house ever told Joana she was beautiful. Papa would have told her, but Papa wasn't here.*

*He felt all choked up, and noticed that Mama was crying, and he wondered if she too was feeling as though something terrible was lost in this little room.*

*Luis was introducing his wife to them, and it took a moment before Josep realised that the person called Elise that he was talking about was the smart woman by his side. Uncle Luis was married? But he'd never been married! Josep stood staring stupidly until Mama called him to order, and then he stepped forward with Joana to shake the wife's hand. Elise smiled at them, and Josep caught Uncle Luis's look of pride as he watched his new wife. He was watching Joana for some kind of lead, but she was no help – she looked stunned, and kind of gutted, and her eyes looked all liquid too. For a young boy there was just too much emotion in this room, and too much to understand.*

*And then the adults were at the table, sitting, while Maria made the inevitable coffee, and Grandma tried to calculate what was in the house to serve them for lunch, and all the while Grandma kept talking. She had three children, did Grandma – Uncle Luis was the oldest, and then there was Uncle Victor, away right now with his sheep, and then there was Mama. Josep had never really thought too hard about his family, but it dawned on him now that Uncle Luis was Grandma's darling, the older son who'd done great things.*

*'Now you can come home,' the old woman repeated again and again, fluttering around Uncle Luis, and around Elise. 'You don't have to run away anymore. But keep away from politics now. It does no good, and these Republicans, they just want to close our churches, and nothing is any better than the old days.'*

'No, Mòmia,' *Luis's voice caressed her as he disagreed. 'Don't be fooled into thinking that way. That's what the right-wing parties in Madrid want you to believe. No real Republican will ever interfere with your religion, but they want the people to run the country, not the clergy and the army. We'll make mistakes in the Republic, but they'll be honest ones, and we will always put people first, and Catalonia first.'*

*'He always spoke like that,' Grandma told Elise, who smiled, though she didn't look as though she understood much of what they were saying in Catalan. Grandma Aina touched her son again. 'He was always so passionate and so political! Maybe one day you'll be proved right, my son. Your brother seems to think so, but all I can say is, it didn't do your sister Maria any good, all that politics.'*

*A shadow crossed Luis's face. He turned to Maria. 'Tell me,' he said. 'Felip in Barcelona told me Vigo died. He was ill? But Vigo was never ill!' He was talking about Papa, and the room went quiet as Mama answered.*

*'It was the prison.' Maria sighed, 'He contracted a lung disease there, and it affected the heart. He seemed to be getting better after a while, but then one day we found him dead, just where he was working, eh Josep?'*

*Josep nodded, his throat tight as it always was when he remembered that moment. Mama wasn't telling Luis how awful it had all been, but Uncle Luis's face seemed to suggest he'd understood. He looked desolate.*

*'He died at home, then, at least?'*

*'Yes, in his own chair.'*

*A silence fell after this, and then Maria asked, 'Where have you been yourself, Luis? Did you go back to Paris?'*

*'Yes,' he answered. 'Ironically it was Vigo who insisted I should get away, because he believed there was a strong chance I wouldn't even make it to prison if one or two people got hold of me.' He waved a frustrated hand. 'So I ended up back in Paris. I could write there, of course, and hopefully do a bit of good, but it was damnable to be away in exile among people who largely didn't give a damn for Spain. But I met Elise,' his face softened. 'And then we moved down near to the border. We live in Catalonia again now – French Catalonia – just over the border. It has felt closer.'*

*'And now you can come home.'*

*It was a statement rather than a question, again coming from Grandma. Maria said nothing, but to Josep it seemed as though they were all somehow in suspense. He looked across at Joana again, and saw that she was holding her breath. Uncle Luis was married to a Frenchwoman now. Would he come home?*

*'Yes,' Uncle Luis said, and Josep saw Joana breathe again. 'My newspaper bosses in Paris want me to write for them from Barcelona – they're keen to have an inside view. And Elise,' touching his wife on her shoulder, 'my lovely Elise wants to make a go of life here if we can, and she's even learning Catalan! We just need to wait for a few months – Elise is pregnant, and we'll wait to have the baby in France. But after that, we'll come home, and you Maria, and the children, you'll come to live with us in Barcelona.'*

*There were endless exclamations after that, and fussing over Elise, and protestations from Maria that she couldn't live off her brother, but Josep heard it only as background noise. He didn't have much interest in babies, but it seemed Uncle Luis wanted them to go back to Barcelona. He turned the idea over in his head. What would that be like? The tall, blond, tousle-haired, laughing man that was their father would not be there. And he would have to leave behind all his friends in Sant Galdric.*

*Joana looked incredibly excited. Her eyes were fixed on the group at the table, and on Uncle Luis's new wife, who was listening serenely to the three Catalan voices all raised excitedly in unison. They must be completely undecipherable to a new learner of the language, but she didn't look fazed – she looked quite content. She looked nice.*

*'Do you hear what they're saying, Josep?' Joana whispered, under cover of all the adult voices. 'Can you believe it? Uncle Luis's wife is happy for us to live with them in Barcelona! We can go back to our old school, and have proper teachers, and I can learn French again and I'll be able to talk to her!'*

*Suddenly Joana moved towards Elise and stood just in front of her chair. Josep wondered what she was going to do.*

'Madame,' *she said, screwing up her face as she tried to remember the French she had learnt before Sant Galdric. Uncle Luis turned round to look at her, and the room fell silent.* 'Bienvenue en Catalogne et bienvenue dans notre maison,' *Joana continued, forcing her lips round the French words. Then she kind of gave up and spoke in Catalan again, so Josep could understand it. 'We are very happy that you will come to live with us.* Merci.'

*And to Josep's surprise (and perhaps to Joana's too) she gave a little curtsy, as Uncle Luis broke into applause, magicking from his pocket a little bedraggled passion flower, which he tucked behind Joana's ear like he always used to, as he pulled her into his embrace.*

The memory was surprisingly strong, and bitter-sweet, because they'd never seen Luis again after that visit. Just a few months later Franco and the other generals had declared war on the Republic, and Spain had descended into Civil War. Catalonia became a militarised zone, and Luis's French wife must have felt it was too dangerous to come and live. They'd had the odd letter from Luis, saying he was raising money for the Republican army in France, and would come soon, but he didn't come, and Josep soon forgot him. Life was Sant Galdric, and he was content. And Joana was the prettiest girl in the village, with all the boys after her, and he'd thought she was content too.

# Chapter Three

Carla came out of the university the following Thursday floating on air. Her most recent essay had received high praise from her tutor, the only tutor she truly respected among the government-appointed, antiquated clerics who dominated the history faculty. In front of the full tutorial group he'd told her that she had written something researched, intelligent and thought-provoking, and that if she continued in this vein she would finish top of the year on graduation day next summer. It was heady stuff, and it was hard to refrain from gloating as she received the congratulations of her fellow students after class.

She wanted to tell Luc. He was consistently top of his year in accounting, and it was the first time she'd been able to equal him. Somehow girls didn't seem to get the same marks as male students, even though their work was often visibly better. They were accused too often by the exclusively male tutors of being irrational in thought. Well not this time! One up for me, Luc, she thought, with a grin. She'd buy them both a drink this evening to celebrate.

She walked through the town towards her hostel, buttoning her jacket as she went. The sunshine of last weekend had gone now, and there was an edge to the autumn air. She would make coffee when she got home, and eat that cake she hadn't been able to finish at lunchtime. She was frugal despite her allowance – she was saving her money, and had tucked the half-eaten cake into her bag for later.

As she neared the hostel she was surprised to see her mother's Mercedes parked in the street outside. She saw Toni at the wheel, and walked even faster towards him, as curiosity tinged with unease nipped at her senses. As she neared he got out of the car, and she walked right up and gave him a hug, as befitted a childhood playmate.

'Well?' she queried, as she saw the slight frown on his forehead. 'What have they sent you here for, Toni? Is there anything wrong at home?'

He shook his head. 'He wants to see you, Carla. Don't ask me why but he's hopping mad about something. He told me to come here and wait outside the hostel until you appeared, and to bring you to Girona straight away.'

Carla was surprised. The last time she'd seen Papa was in July, and relations had been strained as usual, but merely because her presence chafed at him, and she forgot to be always deferential. He'd been pleased with last year's grades, in as far as they interested him, and had been happy to see her disappear back to summer school in Barcelona, so that she didn't have to go up to the hill house with them for the summer holiday.

'What on earth does he want?' she exclaimed.

Toni considered for a moment, and then asked, 'Have you been doing something political? I thought I heard him mutter something about Bolsheviks. Would that be right?'

Carla froze. Oh help, had Papa heard about the student marches she'd been on? She'd never played a committee role, not like Luc, but she'd played a bit part in the various student actions this autumn, partly in support of the workers' strikes, but mainly demanding changes to bring the university into the twentieth century.

But how could Papa know about that? She hadn't been among any names reported to the authorities, or photographed in the papers. She was sure of that. With growing unease she went inside to collect some overnight things, and left a message in case Luc should ask for her. She was going to miss their evening out tonight, but there was no help for it. Papa paid for her studies, and she would have to go with Toni and appease him.

They occupied the two-hour drive talking about familiar things, catching up with family – his mother's health problems, his sister's problems with her husband, and from Carla's side, all the latest news from Josep's family. But as they neared Girona they fell silent, and Carla found her breathing going funny, as it so often did when she had to face Sergi Olivera in his angry moments. It was made worse by not knowing exactly what she was going to face, or how much he knew about her life. And the big question was how he knew about it at all.

It didn't take long to find out. She was let into the big, four-square, old-fashioned house by the maid Mireia, who ushered her straight into the main sitting room, and there she found her parents waiting for her. They had glasses in front of them, and looked as though they'd been there some time, and from the look on her father's face he'd been gnawing at what he wanted to say to her over more than one cocktail. Mama was usually the drinker, but tonight she had a glass of water in front of her, and a coffee cup in her hand. Was it in honour of her coming home, Carla wondered, with irony, or was Joana just taking care to avoid inflaming Sergi's anger still further?

She greeted her parents, careful to show no sign of anxiety. 'Toni said you wanted to see me?' she said, with just the right tone of query in her voice.

Her father rose. 'Oh yes, Carla, I wanted to see you. And, no, you needn't bother to sit down. I'll have you right there, thanks, where I can see into that deceitful little face.'

It was friends of her parents who'd spotted her, back in August, during a small demonstration outside the university chancellor's building. Such a petty demonstration, that one, and ironic that it should be the one which set Sergi onto her. Since then he'd been having her watched. She shivered at the thought that he'd been tracking her movements – not every day, thankfully, but whenever he got wind of a march being planned, or any student action, of which there had been many this autumn. He'd had her followed, and even knew she'd been visiting Uncle Josep. 'Your mother's scumbag family,' he called him, and as his insults flowed he grew more and more angry.

Carla stood silent in front of him and tried to breathe normally, with her feet planted squarely on the silk rug, and arms held as if casually by her sides. Behind the folds of her skirt her right hand was clenched in a tight, nervous ball, but hopefully her father couldn't see this. She knew her face was tight but she stopped her forehead from knotting, using the control reflexes she'd built up over years of confrontation, as her father's anger engulfed her in torrents of outraged abuse.

'I should never have let you go to that stupid university. You're making a mockery of your family, and I won't have it. Do you understand? I won't have it.'

The tirade went on. She was to leave university, right now, and come home, since she couldn't be trusted to behave herself when given the freedom to study. Didn't she realise how privileged she was? How generous her parents had been in even allowing a daughter to study away from home? And yet she had to mix herself up in politics, make friends with a bunch of troublemakers who were just using her to get at her father. She was stupid, just stupid, and naïve if she thought any of that crowd of hers actually cared one iota for her. But it was just like her – she had no thought for her family, or for their position. She was without loyalty, without respect.

She let the words flow around her, and tried to detach herself, but Sergi's solid frame stood just a couple of paces from her, and the naked ferocity of his anger made detachment difficult. Parents all over Spain might be having such conversations with their children right now, but surely not with the same fury. It made his face turn purple, and as his anger grew she wondered if he would contain himself, or if he would lose control and strike her, as he had so often before. She tried not to flinch at the thought.

Behind Sergi, perched on the corner of the expensive leather sofa, Mama sat still and silent, slender and elegant as always, her face rather pale, but carefully turned away from Carla, studying the coffee cup with apparent concentration. Help me, Mama, Carla wanted to say, but there was no point – she knew better.

As the tirade blew on, she realised that Papa was serious – that he really intended to take her away from the university. This was not some fit of anger which would fizzle out once he'd had his say. He was in deadly earnest, and intended to remove her immediately from her studies. Her blood chilled at the thought. All that she'd been working towards hinged on that degree. Papa didn't know it, but for a long time now she'd been planning never to return to his life. It was why she saved her allowance so carefully, and why she worked so hard. She wanted her degree, and then she would go her own way.

She'd been very careful recently when home for holidays, just getting by with her parents and hoping to finish her studies without major flashpoints. But she'd been spotted by some stupid family acquaintances, and now she was facing the ultimate flashpoint, and didn't know how to get out of it.

Sergi was staring at Carla, and she realised suddenly that he'd stopped, and was waiting for an answer from her.

What to say? She longed to hurl her own anger at him as she had when she was a teenager, but there was too much to play for now, and she was no longer sixteen. If I can be conciliatory without giving everything up, then maybe it will be enough, she thought desperately, and made herself begin talking.

'Papa,' she said, and heard her voice quiver, then pulled herself together to continue more strongly. 'Papa, it isn't quite the way it has been painted to you. I haven't done anything wrong, really I haven't, and nothing that could create any problems for you. There's a strong student movement just trying to make the universities more up to date, and allow us more access to the libraries, and to change some of the old staff. It's not exactly subversive politics, and you know yourself that even the newspapers are beginning to talk about change, and modernising Spain. Students are just young, and want to be part of that change.'

Never had Sergi looked less convinced. 'Rubbish!' was his response. 'You're just proving how naïve you are! These new student unions are in cahoots with the communists and the anarchists, and you're all being manipulated by anti-government forces that you haven't got the common sense to understand. I've heard some of your ringleaders – what's his name, Pujol, a dangerous subversive if ever there was one.'

'But I've never even met Pujol!'

'No, but don't tell me you haven't joined his rallies! I know, Carla! They've got you well and truly indoctrinated. There's only one thing for it, and that's to get you out of there. What do you need a degree for, anyway? It was only that daft teacher of yours who convinced me to let you go.'

'Yes, because you thought it would make me more marriageable!' Carla couldn't stop herself.

Sergi's face loomed even closer into hers. 'The only thing that will make you more marriageable is to teach you your place, you stupid girl.'

She forced herself not to back away, and looked into his eyes. 'I haven't done anything,' she repeated. 'Nothing you have to worry about, honestly.' She kept her voice calm. 'But you can't force me to leave university. I'm less than a year away from graduation, and I'm not a child, I'm twenty-three years old.'

'I can take away your money, girl, that's what I can do. You have no means to live, and nothing to pay your fees with.'

A silence fell, and he stood back, with a smug expression on his face that made Carla want to strike out herself. She thought of her room in the hostel, paid monthly by Sergi, the tuition fees for her course, her generous quarterly allowance, which paid for food and all her living costs. A chill came over her as the implications of his words came home to her. She looked across at her mother again, in desperation this time.

'Mama, won't you tell him I've done nothing? I need to finish my degree!'

Joana looked up at her this time, but her eyes were veiled. Carla thought she saw an imperceptible shake in her mother's blonde curls, but no more. It was Sergi who thundered, 'Leave your mother out of this.'

So where do I go from here? Carla wondered, thinking

hard as her heart seemed to thump against her left lung, interrupting her breathing. Without her degree she had no future, or none outside her father's narrowest plans. But nothing she could say here was going to change her father's mind, that was clear. Could she find money to finish her studies without him? She couldn't think straight – no one else in her family had any money, that was for sure.

Could she maybe stay with Uncle Josep if she lost her father's support? Her mind was reeling and she didn't know. His home was already crowded with three young boys. But somehow surely she could manage? Even if she had to sleep on someone's floor and clean houses, or even defer her degree for a year while she earned some money. And she had her savings. That thought steadied her, and her mind came clearer. I will get my degree, she thought, with a return of courage, and she looked up into Sergi's eyes with her old defiance.

'All right, then I'll pay my own way through the rest of my studies.'

Sergi's lip curled. 'And how then, little princess, without your precious allowance and all your fees paid? You know the second instalment of fees is still to be paid for this year?'

She nodded, and resisted the impulse to withdraw her eyes from his. She could see his brain working, trying to decide if she was serious, contemptuous of her but also deeply frustrated, as so often before, by this daughter who wouldn't fall easily into his world of total control.

Her silence forced him into speech again. 'This is all just stupid Carla, and you know it! You'll go with Toni now and collect your clothes from that hostel. It's over, do you understand? You're not a student anymore.'

She shook her head, again not saying anything. To speak would mean she had to defend her position, and what she wanted right now was just to leave, without surrendering, and find her way into that outside world where she could work out what to do.

'Damn me, I've a good mind to lock you in your room!' Sergi's face had become alarmingly red again, and she realised he might even do so, in a fit of temper. It had been a favourite ploy of his when she was a child, but even he must realise that he couldn't shut her up now, at least not forever, and that as a grown woman she could walk out of here if she wanted to – if she was prepared to give up her parents' whole world. She braced herself to be seized, or shaken, but it didn't happen. He was staring at her as though trying to work out where to go next, and she decided to make it easier for him. I want him to let me out of here, she thought, without any further struggle.

'Papa,' she began again, in the gentler voice she'd used earlier. 'You can't just keep me chained up, you know that. And I am going to finish my studies. But don't worry, I'll do it on my own, and I won't make any waves, or cause you any embarrassment. I won't even go on any more student marches. I'll be the quietest student in Barcelona, and you have nothing to worry about.'

She stepped back and turned to pick up her handbag and the overnight holdall she'd brought with her following his summons. She shot him one more look, and he was standing rigid, disbelieving.

'If you walk out of that door now it's for good,' he said. 'You'll never enter this house again!'

She didn't answer. She shot one more look at her mother, sitting staring at her, her face completely void of expression, and then she made her way towards the hallway and the exit, trying not to look rattled or distressed. The maid Mireia was standing beside the telephone table in the hallway, bobbing nervously, her uniform strangely stark against the flock wallpaper, which looked to Carla suddenly more absurd than any decoration she had ever seen. She nodded at Mireia, determined not to cry, and stepped towards the door. Behind her came Sergi's voice, one final bellow, like an angry boar.

'Watch what you do there in Barcelona, my girl. I'll be watching you, all the time! You're a shame to my name and I wish you didn't bear it. But while you're known to be my daughter you'll toe the line or I'll simply make you! Don't forget it. If you ever overstep the line I'll come for you, and next time you won't walk away so easily.'

# Chapter Four

Carla walked away from the house as quickly as possible, looking back just once at the high stone wall with its carefully guarded gate, hiding the house where she had grown up, and played with friends in the garden with its old swing – long removed, and part of a distant past which only the child in her could still view with pleasure. Tears were hot at the back of her eyes, but she was determined not to give in to them. It was no hardship to say goodbye to the house – if she never set foot there again it would make her very happy, and she'd been alone in it for years. The focus now must be on working out how to survive and finish her studies.

She wanted to see Grandma. Suddenly it was all she wanted, and she turned off the manicured, residential street into the park, empty at this hour of the mothers and their playing children, inhabited only by pedestrian commuters scuttling home, and by one old lady trailing a bag of shopping. Ahead of her rose the magical old town of Girona, medieval and Roman stone buildings side by side, dark now against the deepening blue of a lovely November evening.

She turned onto the busy thoroughfare that led past the old town and towards Grandma and Uncle Victor's apartment. New utilitarian buildings juggled here for space alongside older, more gracious facades, which had lined this broad boulevard for nearly two hundred years. They were darkened now by years of grime, so that they looked better in this evening light than in the full light of day, but they bore witness nonetheless to more elegant times, when men in top hats had held parasols for long-skirted ladies as they promenaded towards the park.

As she turned off the boulevard and made her way through the sprawling network of backstreets all vestige of elegance faded. So many of the poor from the villages who had poured into Girona in the last twenty years were crowded together here, in mean tenements with washing hanging from every leaky window. When Uncle Josep had first brought her here to meet her grandmother, she had been shocked to her bourgeois core by the squalor and neglect, worse than any of the areas she knew in Barcelona, but now she walked through without even looking.

She turned in at Uncle Victor's building, and climbed the narrow stairs to the apartment, knocking and then entering without waiting, calling out a '*Holà*' as she shut the door behind her. Nobody was expecting her here, but in a way, as she knew, she was always expected.

Hugging her travel bag to her she went down the narrow corridor to a small living room. There was a bare, brown-tiled floor, walls covered with a worn, patched floral wallpaper, some ill-assorted chairs, a sideboard, and a central dining table covered with a beautifully ironed, flowered cloth, and all around were Grandma's knick-knacks, her small treasures brought from a previous life, crowding every available space. And of course the picture of the Mother Mary in pride of place above the table.

Over by the sideboard Uncle Victor was bent over an ancient radio, trying to get better reception through the crackle. He didn't seem to have heard Carla coming in, and she took the time to study his gentle, lined face, cocooned and content after his day's work, fully concentrated on his task. There was no sign of Grandma, but a rich, savoury cooking smell pervaded the entire apartment, and Carla guessed that she was in the tiny little kitchen which led off from the living area.

She stood waiting until Uncle Victor raised a tune from the radio – a lively piano piece which Carla vaguely recognised, and which had hints of flamenco in it. Victor would know it, she was sure. After a moment he looked up, and took in Carla's presence with a little surprised shake of the head.

'Carla! My dear! Welcome, dear child. *Com estàs?*'

He came across towards her as he spoke, and she dropped her bag to step into his arms. It was typical of Uncle Victor that he didn't even ask her why she was there. It was a simple, embracing welcome from a man of few words, who had spent most of his life in the silence of the hills. Carla held him and breathed in the soap smell from his neck, newly washed before Grandma would let him sit down to eat.

'Maria!' Victor called, from just above her shoulder. 'Come see who is here!' He would hand her over to Grandma for questioning, Carla thought, with a half smile. And Maria emerged from the kitchen, rubbing her hands on a cloth, and stood still for a moment watching them as Carla slowly drew back to face her.

'Carla! *Carinyo*! What are you doing in Girona?'

She bustled forward and took Carla by the shoulders, looking anxiously into her face.

'*Avia*!' was all Carla answered – Grandma. And surprised herself in a flood of unbidden tears. Grandma said nothing, and just held Carla close until her tears subsided, which wasn't long. After a few minutes she shook herself and raised a rueful face from Grandma's shoulder.

'I'm sorry!' she said. 'That was stupid! I just had a bit of a bruising encounter with Papa!'

Grandma smiled at her, and drew her forward to the table, pushing her gently into a chair.

'Bring the child some brandy or something, Victor,' she said over her shoulder, and then took a seat opposite Carla. She was like her brother Victor, darkly Catalan in colouring, with high cheekbones and clear, amber brown eyes that watched the world from deep within her. The age lines around them only drew your gaze to them more, Carla thought, but there was nothing challenging about those eyes. They were intelligent but tranquil, and you felt they saw you without judging. And there was a serenity about her which clad her every movement.

Carla reached out her hand to stroke back some grey strands that had escaped from Grandma's flowered scarf, and then took the glass which Victor was holding out to her.

'I don't need this, really I don't!' she protested, but took a sip anyway. She nearly choked on the rough brandy, and put the glass down in a hurry.

'Phew! No more of that or I won't be able to think!' she expelled. 'I'm all right, really I am! I just needed somewhere to come after getting away from Papa, and I need to get my head in order. I've just been disowned, and I don't even have anywhere to sleep tonight!'

Grandma muttered what might have been an oath in anyone else.

'Heavens above! You poor child! But you certainly have somewhere to sleep, for as long as you need it, and in this house we haven't disowned you, *carinyo*. You'll tell us all about it, but first we'll eat. Dinner is ready, and you look as though you need it.'

Grandma was always trying to feed Carla, fretting at her natural leanness, and now Carla let herself be waited on, sitting between Grandma and Victor as a huge bowl of pork and beans was placed before her. She set to and ate as greedily as Uncle Victor, as she realised just how famished she was.

And while she ate she talked, compulsively. 'He didn't mention Luc,' she said. 'Thank God, at least he didn't mention Luc! He doesn't know about us, because if he did there would have been no holding him back.' She took another spoonful of beans, fretting all the time at what

Sergi had said, to extract what he knew. 'He knows about me seeing Josep, because he told me I'd been seen visiting, but he didn't mention you, *Avia*, or Uncle Victor. He can't know that I come here to see you in Girona.'

Grandma responded placidly. 'But, Carla, how would he know? You haven't been to visit us since you went back to university for summer school, and you say he only started having you followed at the end of August. We haven't seen you since! And anyway, even if he knew, what further harm would it do? If he didn't want you to know your mother's family, then as soon as you made contact with Josep the damage was done. Josep could give you some rebellious ideas – but you're unlikely to find any here! We're not people your father would worry about!'

'He's been worried enough to exclude you from my life all through my childhood.'

It was Victor who interjected here, with unaccustomed bitterness. 'If it was he that excluded us, and not our own Joana.'

Carla grimaced, gripping hard onto her fork. 'Do you know, Mama just sat there throughout Papa's whole tirade, and never said a word – not one word! And when I appealed to her she just stared through me.'

'Do you think she was scared?'

'No, Grandma, I don't think so. She was just cold. There wasn't any emotion there at all – no feeling for me, that's for sure.'

'Oh dear, what has happened to her? If there was one thing that used to reassure me, when you were little and we couldn't see you, it was that Toni's mother always said you were well cared for. She told us Joana was so proud of you!'

So Grandma and Victor had followed her progress as a child? And cared what happened to her? Carla's throat knotted tight.

'I don't know whether she was proud of me, but I was certainly proud of her! You know *Avia*, I used to worship her, when I was a child – she was always so beautiful, in her lovely dresses, and kind of caressing, and she would look at me as though I mattered. All my school friends admired her, and it did make me proud that I had such a mother, especially when I was so, so scrubby!'

Grandma tut-tutted, and shook her head, but she let Carla continue.

'But I was! You don't know, Grandma! I was always kind of gangly, and my hair wouldn't curl, and Mama would buy me pretty dresses which hung off me, and then I would tear them and stuff! Papa hated it. He would call me in to curtsy to his visitors, and I would be all a mess, and never know what I was supposed to say! Mama was good to me then, though, and told me not to worry, because I had Papa's brain.'

It was Victor who interceded here, musing. 'Well he certainly had that, did Sergi. I wouldn't have thought it, when he was a young man, but he proved us wrong, the way he climbed his way up in politics. He runs a huge department now, doesn't he? Well, there was nothing in his own father to make us think that of him.'

'You knew Papa when he was a child?' Carla was surprised.

'Not really, not well, anyway, because his father left the

village when he married, and Sergi was raised in Girona, but he used to come back to see his grandmother, and hang around with the village boys. Nobody liked him much, even then. He had a swagger to him, and thought he was better than everyone because he lived in the city. But his father was nothing, meagre and shifty, and kind of crafty, if you know what I mean. We all felt sorry for the old grandmother, because her son was such a little prick.'

He used the word *cabró*, which was brutal to Carla's ears. She tried to conjure up an image of her grandfather, Papa's father, who had died when she was young, but all that came to mind was a little man, smaller than Papa, well dressed in a showy kind of way. Papa was showy too, but he was imposing, and had money and an excellent tailor. He impressed, and prevailed, and his assurance was unshakeable. Carla shivered.

'That's enough talking about the child's family like that, Victor!' Grandma moved quickly to sweep up the plates, and disappeared into the kitchen. Victor looked apologetically at Carla, and she smiled.

'It's fine, Uncle, I'm not under any illusions!' she reassured him, and placed a kiss on his full head of greying hair before carrying the remaining dishes to the kitchen.

There Grandma was laying out fruit and making coffee. 'Now child,' she said, as she stood waiting for the stove-top cafetière, 'never mind for today worrying about why your parents are how they are. What matters now is making sure you can finish your studies. How much money do you think you will need?'

Carla named a sum which made her grandmother blink.

'It's the fees,' she explained. 'Papa hasn't paid the second instalment yet for the year. But I can use my savings to pay the fees, if I've got enough – I need to check how much is owed. And then I can manage otherwise, I think. I'll have to leave the hostel, of course, but if worst comes to worst I can sleep on someone's floor.'

'You'll move in with Josep,' Grandma said, decisively. 'He won't have it any other way – and don't protest! Among family there is always room.'

Carla didn't protest. If Josep would have her, she would be only too grateful to have one problem removed. 'I can work,' she said. 'I can give tuition to schoolchildren. Some of my friends already do it, but of course I didn't need to while my rich father was paying for me. You can normally make enough money to pay for food and so on, so I'll be able to give that to Josep and Neus. It's the fees that worry me. I'll need to find out if I've got enough saved, and if I can get an extension to pay, if needs be.'

'Well all the money you earn can go towards your fees. Josep won't take your money, *carinyo*, so if you can earn some money gradually and pay off any remaining fees, then maybe the university will give you some time. You don't think your father will try to get you removed from the university by other means? He couldn't have you expelled?'

Carla gulped – this hadn't occurred to her. But on reflection she thought she was safe there. Sergi Olivera had huge influence in the regional government, with the police and even the militia, but the venerable University of Barcelona, with its centuries of history, was a bit beyond his reach. Intellectual people made him feel uncomfortable, she knew, and she doubted very much that he would approach the senior university staff who could have his daughter removed.

'He could have me arrested, though!' she told Maria. 'Not that he'd want to – his daughter in prison isn't the package he's looking for!' She felt suddenly really hopeful, and positive that she could make things work. 'I'll just have to be careful not to show myself politically from now onwards.'

Both Grandma and Uncle Victor concurred with that. For most of their adult lives they had lived in fear of the Franco regime. People in Spain had learnt not to talk, not to blink at the regime for fear of arrest, and now that things were opening up a little, and the younger generation was flexing its muscles, their elders held their breath in sober foreboding.

'I've done nothing much,' Carla reassured them. 'And from now onwards I'm not going to get involved at all! And anyway, if I have to earn my living as well as studying then I won't have time for all that! Did I tell you my best tutor thinks I'm going to graduate with top marks? It's all that matters now.'

She slept with Grandma in Grandma's bed, and rose at dawn to get the first bus back to Barcelona. There was no time to waste in sorting out her life. To her surprise she found Grandma packing a little bag to come with her.

'I'm going to make a visit to that son of mine,' Maria told her, 'and I want to see your young man as well! It's all very well my Josep having vetted him, but if you're planning a life with him I want to meet this Luc for myself!'

It was clear she was determined to be involved, and to make sure Carla was all right.

'What about Uncle Victor?' Carla protested. 'You're going to leave him to manage for himself?'

'What do you think he did when he first came down to work in Girona? I was still looking after our own mother then, up in the village, and he was on his own down here. Well I'm not saying he did a good job, but he didn't starve! There's stew left in the kitchen, and when that's finished he'll go out to the local bar. No, *carinyo*, I'm coming with you, just for a couple of days, and we'll see you settled with Josep and Neus before I leave you there in Barcelona!'

So bang goes the weekend with Luc's family, Carla thought, but with some amusement. They would do it another time, and meanwhile Luc had better set about charming her grandmother. If he did so then she would adopt him with her usual serenity, but for now Grandma was less serene than determined.

Well, at least Josep would now be able to ask Maria where his father was buried, and perhaps fill some of the gaps in those nagging memories of his. It was funny to think of Grandma going to busy Barcelona, and even stranger to think of her living there in the past, young and grave and in love with a passionate young journalist, supporting his work, seeking him out in prison, negotiating his release, holding on resolutely to her young family as bad turned to desperate. She looked at Grandma, her face still surprisingly young despite the lines around her eyes. It was unassuming women like Maria Garriga who had kept families going throughout the tough years after the war, and you miscalculated their gentle stoicism at your peril.

'Come with me then, *Avia*,' she said, picking up Grandma's bag to carry it through to the corridor. 'Come and help me with the hostel so they don't take too much money from me when I leave. And come and vet my young man. And I'll tell you what – if the university stands in my way I'll send you to see the vice chancellor himself!'

# Chapter Five

It had been a tough four months but Carla was holding together, and, even better, was forging forward towards her final exams. It was the miracle of family which had got her there, and though her savings were exhausted, by living frugally she knew she could finish the year.

She had no idea if Sergi was still having her watched. She'd stayed away from all public demonstrations, telling Luc to work twice as hard to represent them both. And as far as the world was concerned, she hoped her relationship with Luc had become invisible. She visited him still, but never heading to his flat directly from home, and always checking that his street was empty before she entered his building. They had the occasional coffee together in the canteen, but no longer went out on their own together in Barcelona.

Their fellow students seemed to understand – it had long

been known that Carla's father was a threat, after all. No questions were asked, and Carla thought that most of them were quite simply relieved that she'd withdrawn from their activities. She envied them their insouciance.

When they won the student elections in March she celebrated with them over coffee, safe in the canteen, and stayed at the opposite side of the table to Luc. Luc himself was surrounded by his beloved campaign team, and lost to all else but the joy of success. Manel sat beside him, Manel whom they'd finally succeeded in getting elected to the student union.

It did feel like democracy, like hope, even to Carla. You could still believe, after all, even if you were straitjacketed. She watched Luc, happy and smiling – that smile which brought his whole knobbly face into harmony and made him, for Carla, the most beautiful man in the world. There was her real hope – it resided with Luc.

He looked across at her. 'Catch!' he said, and tossed half a doughnut across the table. It landed on the edge of her coffee cup, sending splashes of hot, black espresso all over the table. Carla pushed her chair back in a hurry, while across the table Manel was dabbing furiously at his sleeve.

'You oaf!' he swore at Luc. 'Look what you've done to my shirt!'

Carla had to laugh. Luc was looking bewildered, as if he couldn't understand what had gone wrong. But we all know, she thought. You're a hopeless big lump!

'Amateur!' she crooned at him, and flicked the flat doughnut expertly back across the table so it landed beside his plate.

He grinned. 'Did I splatter you?' he asked.

She shook her head. 'Not a stain on me. It's Manel who caught it. But you spilt my coffee, and I can't afford another, so you owe me!'

'That's fine, then. Waiter, another espresso for the lady, please.'

'And my shirt?' Manel was indignant.

'Chivalry, my boy, have some chivalry! The lady is fine so all is fine! Give it to your landlady to wash. Are you sure you don't want this half doughnut, Carla? No? Manel, then? It's not quite your grandmother's Easter *bunyol* but it's the best this canteen can offer.'

'But it's not even Easter!' Manel protested. 'Not for weeks! If you throw *bunyols* around from now till then I'll need a whole new wardrobe! And now I'm an official I need decent clothes!'

Luc waved an oversized hand in dismissal. 'Do we care about your clothes? We've just made history, for heaven's sake! It's not just you, Manel. We actually got Roc Pujol elected as regional president! I still can't believe it, and I doubt if the authorities can either!'

'If they let the result stand,' a negative voice sounded from the corner.

Six voices shot him down. Sure they would let it stand! Hadn't they already won freer access to the library, new books, even won some concessions on the Catalan language? This is a new era – Franco is seventy, for goodness' sake – and it's not just us, all over Spain things are changing – have some faith, man!

Carla sat silent, listening to the exultant voices. They're

right, she thought. Things really are changing and they can't put the genie back in the bottle now that we've let it out. The students were right to feel buoyant. She might have personal worries, but people like her father couldn't stop the movement of change.

She looked across again at Luc and caught him winking at her. She smiled back, and a little flare of the old happiness hit her. Life was complicated, but Luc was not. Huge, kind Luc, who took life methodically, and never gave in to irrational fears, or worried about what couldn't be done, or what might never happen. We'll have finished our studies by July, she thought, and then we'll go away, far away, where my father won't think to look for us. But there was a cloud – something she needed to tell him. Something new, she thought, groaning inwardly, in all the complications I bring to him.

'You coming, Carla?' Luc asked her, and she realised with a jolt that the others had all stood up, and were preparing to leave. She grabbed her woollen jacket and joined Luc at the door. The whole group burst from the canteen and erupted out of the campus and onto La Rambla, twirling their new delegate Manel around remorselessly between them in the spring sunshine. The trees were putting on leaves now, and even some of the awnings were out in front of the cafés. It was too early in the day for the cafés to be full, but late enough for people to be on the move, and as the students headed down towards the port, and then veered off towards the cathedral, their capering drew smiles from the strolling couples, and frowns from some of the men in grey raincoats, all urgently heading somewhere, their trilbies dipped over their foreheads.

The destination for the students was a little café on the corner behind the cathedral, where they headed not for the terrace but to the deep inner recesses of the dark, panelled bar, where jazz music played all day, except when owner Andreu brought out his *gralla*, playing old Catalan tunes while his customers sang along with enthusiastic disdain for official disapproval. Carla went inside hesitantly with the group, hoping that no one was following her.

Their boisterous entrance brought grizzle-haired Andreu out from his little kitchen. He gave them a forbearing look. 'A celebration, my little ones? Coffee, perhaps?'

'Cava, Andreu! Bring us cava! This is no ordinary day!'

A bottle appeared, and glasses, and Luc proceeded to pour. Carla shook her head at him.

'Not for me,' she muttered, flushing. There was no money for wine, only a few pesetas from her tutoring job to get her to the end of the month, but Luc waved his hand at her. 'On me,' he mouthed.

'Again?' she protested, but he simply grinned and passed her a glass.

'To the new Students' Union!' a toast was proposed.

'To our Manel! Our own private union official!'

'You know what your first job has to be, Manel? Stop all this talk of giving an honorary degree to Franco!'

'Yeah, right! What would that be for, I wonder? For reaching the age of senility without any more education than you started with?'

Around the table flew the seditious chat, and Carla looked around, checking that there was no one who could hear them. Two men sat just inside the doorway drinking coffee. Surely she'd never seen those two here before? Were they known to Andreu? She saw him coming towards them, a slight frown on his face.

'Careful, boys, careful!' she murmured. Luc looked up at Andreu, smiled irrepressibly, and raised his glass for one more toast.

'To Andreu, who runs the best bar in Barcelona, and who puts up with some of the rowdiest, most nonsensical students in the city!'

Andreu smiled, and a moment later the two men paid their bill and left. She'd overreacted as usual, Carla thought. But she was relieved, nonetheless, when the party broke up, an hour later, and the students all headed for home. They emerged into the advancing chill of early evening, and Luc looked invitingly at Carla.

'Coffee at my place?' he asked, and she nodded.

'I don't have to be back for dinner for a while. Uncle Josep won't be home from work for at least an hour.' She thought about the risk, but there was something she needed to tell Luc, and they needed to be alone.

'Mmm, nice!' Luc replied. 'Well my dinner will be whatever the corner café is serving up tonight, so I'm not in any hurry!'

'Not too hungry, after you only ate three *bunyettes* this afternoon?'

'Less of your cheek – I gave half of one away, remember?'

Carla insisted that they take separate routes to his flat. No one was following her, she was as sure as she could be of that, but she felt relieved nevertheless when she closed the door of Luc's room behind her. She stood watching the sun set over the rooftops as Luc made coffee on the gas canister. When he came out to join her she leant back against him, and held his arms around her. A smell of baking bread came up to them from the street below.

'Doesn't that smell make you hungry?' she asked.

'Not for food!' he said, his chin nuzzling into her hair. 'Remember the three *bunyettes*!'

She turned in his arms to face him, and he studied her face, his grey eyes looking deep into hers.

'You've been quiet today,' he said. 'Not quite with us, if you know what I mean.'

Her face twitched, and he said, 'What is it, Carla? Is it your family?'

She leant upwards to kiss the curved tip of his oversized nose. 'No, not my family, but . . .'

'But?'

'Luc, I'm late. My period, I mean. I've been waiting and waiting, but nothing. I thought it was just that I'm stressed, but no, it's more than that.'

She looked up anxiously into his face, waiting. He said nothing, and his eyes were unreadable, but she was never scared with Luc, never wary. He was too free of fear and convention himself.

Since she'd met him she'd always wished she could be more like him. But their upbringings were so different. She thought back to the visit to Luc's parents, which had finally been paid a couple of months ago. If she closed her eyes it all came vividly before her, the run-down old villa on the edge of Terrassa, just a couple of hours' journey away, with its grounds given over to vegetables, and its faded interior overrun by books and papers, and pottering around inside it, Luc's easy-going, unhurried parents.

Luc's father had worked with the Republicans during the Civil War as an army medic, and had been first imprisoned by the Franco regime, then banned from working as a state doctor. He'd responded by setting up a private practice offering alternative therapies. Harried endlessly through the years by the authorities, he had nevertheless built up a small, faithful clientele, and did rural work to reach villages which no doctor bothered with.

They'd spent the day trekking through the Sant Llorenç hills, Carla, Luc, his mother, and his equally huge, bear-like brother, picnicking in the winter sunshine and returning to find two neighbourhood policemen on the doorstep, brought by complaints about the leaves drowning the drive. Luc's mother had sighed. 'We have no help,' she'd explained to the policemen, with a conspiratorial smile that almost had them smiling in return. 'But of course while I have my sons here we will clear the drive and the pavement outside.'

They'd all cleared the drive together, Luc's father even emerging from his study to chase swirling leaves in exasperated futility.

'We'll do all this, my dear, and then when the boys go away more leaves will blow our way, or the neighbours will find some other irritation to complain about.'

He looked ruefully over his round-rimmed, wire spectacles at Carla. 'We don't have many friends here in Spain,' he explained, rather unnecessarily, 'but we are blessed by a wonderful group of friends overseas, and some have even been to visit us in the last few years. We bumble along, you know, we bumble along. Nowadays it's just those harmless, boy policemen who come to see us, not the Civil Guard, like in the old days.'

Long may it stay that way, thought Carla. She had been less surprised, after that visit, by the casual freedom of thought which characterised Luc, and which made her gulp at times. Right now his reaction could be interesting, but it was unlikely to be orthodox. He'll handle this a whole lot better than me, she thought, as she scanned his face.

The silence stretched between them, just seconds perhaps, though it seemed more, and then, without saying a word, Luc drew her to him and led her through to the little room, pulling her down onto the bed beside him. There he curled her and crooked his arms around her from behind, cradling her close, whispering into her ear.

'And my chamois thinks it's bad news?' His voice hugged her, reassured her, and defied her, as he always did, to be anything but happy. What to say? He didn't have her family, her past. She couldn't be happy-go-lucky like him. Yes, it was bad news because they weren't free yet. Because she wanted to escape first, and work beside Luc, and build a future, not to burden him with a child when they had nothing. He called her his chamois because she was all brown hair and brown skin, but also because she was slight and svelte and tall and athletic. A woman who was alive, alert, who could work, who could contend with anything. A mountain goat could pass anywhere, skip nimbly through difficulties, leap upwards away from danger. A pregnant human was another thing altogether, it seemed to her, and a baby was something she didn't have the place to protect, not yet, not till she was free.

She told him, and he listened, propped on his elbow so he could see her face. He didn't belittle her fears. He knew how real they were. She had plumped up the pillows behind her so that she was almost sitting up. The bed served as their sofa in Luc's tiny room. She pulled at a fray in the bedcover and waited for his reply.

'We have to think,' he acknowledged, after a while. 'You're pregnant, and we're going to have a baby. That's a given. It's also a given that I want to marry you, and you know that very well. Even without a baby we were going to marry, *vida meva*, and if we're going to go away together in the summer we have to be married anyway before we go, otherwise how would we get lodgings, or register for work?'

'We've never talked about how we were going to manage things.'

'I know, we've been stupid. It's March already, and by July we'll have finished all the exams and hopefully have graduation documents. My brother's been working on getting me into his company, in their accounts office. It would be a start.'

'Is Lleida far enough away?' Carla was doubtful.

'Is anywhere far enough away? Talk to me, Carla, now. Tell me really how far your father will go to control your life. If you disappear and change your name, will he really scour Spain looking for you?'

'I wish I knew the answer to that myself,' she sighed. She cast her mind back to that last meeting with Sergi Olivera. What was it he'd said to her? 'You're a shame to my name and I wish you didn't bear it. But while you're known to be my daughter you'll toe the line or I'll simply make you.'

Did that mean that if she changed her name and no one knew who she was anymore he'd let her go?

'He needs to be in control,' she tried to explain to Luc. 'I think he hates me in a way just for being a girl, since I'm the only child. His brother has a son in the officer corps, and he would have loved that, some fine young man to show off to his political connections. I wasn't even cute as a child, and that must have disappointed him too, because to him women are there to adorn his life and to caress him, and to keep house and keep quiet. That's what my mother does. She can be as sharp as hell with everyone else, but when she's around my father she defers to him all the time, and when he gets angry and hits her she says sorry even when she's done nothing wrong.'

'Does he hit you too?'

'Oh yes, sometimes.' Carla stroked her cheek in remembrance. 'Especially as I got older and became difficult. I just couldn't be the frilly little girl he wanted, and I had my nose stuck in a book the whole time. At one time he even banned me from reading, and I had to hide in my room and keep my books under my bed. Even when he agreed, finally, to let me study he made me change my choice of degree from law to history, because no woman could ever make a real lawyer. He's crude, and basic, and has manipulated his way to the top, and I hate him, Luc. I hate him so much I just can't hide it, and so he hates me even more, and wants to control me more, and keep me down, and down, and down.'

Luc shifted his position on the bed so he was beside

Carla on the pillows, and took her into his arms.

'Don't cry, *carinyo*,' he said quietly, into her hair.

'No,' she answered, blinking back the tears, and taking a deep breath. 'Sorry! That's why I don't talk about him, because it gets to me like that.'

'But that doesn't answer the question,' he brought her back to the main issue. 'Will he take his need for control far enough to track you if you disappear? After all, he has already disowned you!'

'It will depend whether he thinks I could damage his name in any way, I guess.'

'Like by marrying the son of an outlawed Republican medic?'

Carla grinned, and dropped a kiss on the hand that was hugging her close. 'Exactly, and even more so if he has led a student revolt!'

'I've been nothing in the revolt, really, but I do take your point! But you know, your father won't want you to marry some high-up official either, because from what you're telling me he would never believe you would behave yourself! I can't help thinking if you just quietly disappear he would be quite relieved!'

'He might. You're actually quite possibly right. As long as he doesn't learn about you, though.'

'There's no reason why, not when you've been so careful. I have to admit I thought all the subterfuge was excessive, but now I can see you were right.'

'Of course I was, and from now on we take even more care. We finish our studies like good little students, and I go home quietly each night to Uncle Josep's, and let my father's spies watch me to their hearts' content. No more visits here, even, and not even Uncle Josep must suspect I'm pregnant. I'll just be the studious Carla Olivera, with my only concern to get my degree.'

'The studious Carla Olivera indeed! All right, for the next while you'll be like Lorca's hidden treasure to me. But then,' Luc leapt up from the bed and dropped to one knee. The bed creaked alarmingly and a pillow fell to the floor. 'But then,' he repeated magniloquently, 'once the exams are over, Carla Olivera, will you consent to be my wife, and disappear with me into the night?'

Carla rescued the pillow, and hugged it to her. 'Only if you promise not to break all the furniture!' she replied, sternly. 'But yes, my clumsy idiot, when we finish the exams, then I'll disappear with you to wherever you want to take me!'

But three months later, when Carla stood at the railway station with her suitcase, waiting for Luc, he didn't appear. And when she and Uncle Josep went fearfully together to the attic flat, the door was bashed in, and the bed had collapsed, and it certainly wasn't Luc who had broken them.

# Chapter Six

Carla struggled along the broad Girona boulevard towards Grandma's little side street, and paused for a moment to put down her shopping bag and ease her tired muscles. Just a few weeks now from giving birth, it was getting tougher to carry heavy loads, and the weight she'd lost since Luc's disappearance didn't help.

The thought of a sit down and a coffee made her pick up the bag and plod on – just a few metres to go and she would be home, and Grandma would have lunch cooking. Carla had no appetite, but the smells which came out of Maria's tiny kitchen turned their shabby apartment into the homeliest refuge in Girona.

Carla had been in Girona for nearly four months now, having fled to Grandma and Uncle Victor's arms soon after Luc was taken. It was the closest she could come to solace.

As she turned the corner she was just in time to see Toni

step out of her mother's Mercedes. He had drawn up right outside Grandma and Victor's house, and the car looked absurdly incongruous in the tight little street. The last time she had seen Toni he had come looking for her in Barcelona. Her blood chilled at the thought that he might also have come looking for her here today.

She stopped to watch as Toni stepped towards the rear of the car, reaching out a hand to open the back door. The door opened before he could get there, though, and a young man got out whom Carla didn't recognise. Toni stepped back from him, and then moved towards the front door of the apartment building. Oh my God, Carla thought, could Toni be taking one of her father's men up to the apartment? They must indeed be looking for her! But could Toni really be helping one of her father's men against her?

She hurried towards the car, calling out as she went. 'Toni, what are you doing here?'

Both men stopped in their tracks. The young man turned, and she vaguely noted that he was about her own age, but her eyes were fixed on Toni. And Toni was gaping back at her, an expression of pure shock freezing his face.

'Carla!' was all he said, when he found his voice. But the single word was wonderful to hear.

'You didn't know I was here!' she said, and felt her nerves relax a fraction.

Toni shook his head, still staring incredulously at her. He hadn't been told anything by her father, that was for sure. If he was on a mission from Sergi, he was flying blind.

She kept her eyes on his. 'And you didn't know I was pregnant either?' She rubbed her huge bump.

He shook his head several times, as though taking the time to absorb what he was seeing. 'No,' was all he managed.

'So you haven't come here because of me?'

'No, but Carla . . .'

'Yes, I know. It must be a shock. Lord, the last time I saw you was a year ago, and I wasn't pregnant then! Well things happen, Toni, including pregnancies. You're still with my father, obviously.' Her gaze took in the car and his uniform.

'With your mother, at the moment, up at the hill house.'

Carla was amazed. 'She's still there in October?'

'Yes, this year she didn't come back down to Girona with your father. In fact he hardly stayed there this summer. She's on her own up there.'

'My God! She must have a lover or something, to maroon herself up there all this time! And she didn't send you to find me? No? So you're looking for Grandma? How strange!'

It was Carla's turn to shake her head. A jumbled vision crowded her head of the hill house, mountain skies, and her mother sitting on the wide veranda, looking as elegant as ever, probably with a glass in her hand. It was a painful little picture, a barrier to coherent thought, and she tried to pull her mind back to the present. Toni had come to Girona, but not looking for her, so that meant Joana didn't know she was at Grandma's. Not that it changed anything, because her father knew exactly where she was, and was watching her more closely than ever. But for now, this visit by Toni had not come from Sergi. So who was the young man with him?

She became aware of herself, of them all, standing there agape like frozen effigies in the street, and as she looked again at Toni she allowed herself a moment of emotion. She put her shopping down on the ground again, took a step towards him, and wrapped her arms around him.

'It's good to see you, Toni,' she said, and was surprised to hear her voice shaking. She felt daily more isolated, and Toni's was a friendly face from different days.

Toni hugged her gingerly and then eased her gently away from him, looking down at her bump. 'It's good to see you too, Carla, but . . . is your husband staying here too?' His voice was deeply troubled.

'No, Toni, there's no husband, although there should have been – was going to be until my father stepped in. Listen, Toni, I can't explain about my pregnancy, not now, not here and not like this. But please, don't tell my mother about it. Or anyone at all, come to that, and don't even mention that you've seen me, all right?'

She fixed her eyes on Toni's face, his hands held in hers. Toni's bachelor life had been sheltered so far from complications such as hers, and the troubled look lingered on his face, but eventually he nodded, and she gave him another hug.

She turned towards the young man who had stepped from the car. 'Is this a friend of yours, Toni? Tell me why you are both here. I'm completely at a loss.'

'I don't know.' Toni's shrug was dismissive. 'He's been up seeing your mother, and she told me to bring him here. She said he was some kind of relative who wanted to see your grandmother.'

'A relative?' Carla was startled. She had no relatives of her own age, unless he was so distant as to be irrelevant. She looked a question at the stranger.

'Your second cousin,' he nodded. 'My father was Luis Garriga, your grandmother's brother.'

'Indeed?' she said, keeping her voice neutral while her mind flew back to what Josep had told her about his Uncle Luis, the journalist who'd gone off to exile in France. This young man was French, his funny way of speaking Catalan gave him away straight away. But Toni seemed to mistrust him, and he'd been with Joana. What had he been doing up there?

'Have you come with some kind of mission from my mother?' she shot at him.

'Not at all,' was his quick reply. 'I only met your mother yesterday because I asked for Luis's family in Sant Galdric, and no one there knew where my Aunt Maria and Uncle Victor were living, so they sent me up to your mother for directions. I've come from France. I have nothing to do with your mother.' He seemed to sense it was important to make this understood.

And the answer was reasonable, as far as it went. Carla bit her lip and made a decision. 'You don't need to tell me you're from France – it's pretty obvious that you don't come from around here! And if that's so, then I guess it's unlikely you're in cahoots with them. You'd better come upstairs, anyway, and meet Grandma.'

She turned to Toni. 'Come and see Grandma too. Come up and have coffee. She'd love to see you.'

Toni refused. 'She gave me errands in Girona,' he

explained. 'I have to buy some provisions before her favourite shop closes at one o'clock, and it's nearly twelve now. I daren't stay.'

Carla nodded. It wouldn't do for him to fail in an errand for her mother. She released Toni's hand reluctantly, and stepped back to let him go.

'Give your grandmother a hug for me,' he asked her, before he got back into the car.

'For sure. She will be sorry not to see you. And give our love to your mother. How is she?'

'Not too good these days, but she'll be glad you were asking for her.'

'Give her a kiss from us all. And Toni?'

'Yes?'

'No word to anyone about me, promise!'

'I promise, Carla. And take care of yourself.' He gestured awkwardly at the bump.

She grimaced. 'I'll try, Toni. I'll try.'

Carla waited until the Mercedes had pulled away before turning again to the young man.

'Come then,' was all she said. He picked up her shopping bag from behind her, and followed her meekly up the two flights of stairs. They entered the second-floor apartment, and Carla led the way down the narrow corridor to the living room.

From inside the kitchen Grandma's voice called, 'Is that you, Carla? Did you get the bread?'

'I did. I also picked up a young man, *Avia*! Come out and meet him. He has come to see you.'

Maria emerged from the open door, a faded apron

protecting her old black frock, and with her flowered headscarf covering her hair. She held a kitchen cloth in one hand and there was a little bead of sweat on her forehead.

'A young man? What young man?' she asked, puzzled.

Carla pointed to him and heaved a tired sigh as she sat down on a wooden chair. 'Here, here he is. He says he's your nephew, Grandma. He's come from France to see you, via Sant Galdric and my mother's house. Toni brought him, and I met them outside.'

Maria stopped short, working out Carla's words.

'My nephew?' she repeated.

Carla nodded. 'He says he's Uncle Luis's son.'

The old lady looked long, very long, at the visitor, and recognition and astonishment gradually registered in her eyes.

'You are really Luis's son?' Maria asked finally, almost shyly.

'Yes, *Senyora*.'

There was another pause, and then a smile spread across her face, an infinitely tender smile, and tears sprang to her eyes as she surged suddenly across the room and took his hands in hers. She held him so, and scanned him, still a little shy, as she repeated again and again, incredulously, 'Luis's son, Luis's son. Oh my God, Luis's son!'

The young man had tears in his eyes as well. Neither of them moved, and Carla watched from her chair, feeling as though she was witnessing something intimate which she shouldn't be sharing. The two seemed to be on a different plane from her, and she felt like an intruder. Grandma, dear, sweet *Avia*, had never stopped thinking about Luis, her adored older brother, and now his son had walked into her home. Carla hoped and hoped again, for Grandma's sake, that he was genuine.

He certainly looked uncannily like the Garriga men she knew from photos, unmistakeable in his broad cheekbones, if nothing else. They all had these prominent cheekbones, the Garrigas, and they were striking, good-looking men, planed and olive-skinned and wide-shouldered, with aquiline noses and eyes that dominated the company. They had a potent appeal and by all accounts women loved them. Uncle Victor was a very mild version of this, but the pictures of Uncle Luis, and of his (and Victor and Maria's) father, gave an unmistakeable impression, even in faded black and white, of the Garriga charm.

This young man was the same, although his face was broader, and his frame was a little stockier. And he looked nice, although she couldn't help reserving judgement. We'll wait, she thought, and then caught Grandma's eyes and thought again. Carla might wait judgement, but Maria had found a nephew, and in a life which had seen too much loss and sorrow, his place was ready prepared.

'What is your name?' Grandma asked.

'Martin,' was all he replied.

'*Martí*!' Grandma used the Catalan form of the name.

There were endless questions over lunch. They ate together at the little table, and the whole while Maria sat next to Martin, often touching him, and while she served up their meal of black rice she kept him close, in the tiny space of the kitchen, getting him to pass her the utensils, the dishcloth, the plates – anything to make contact, and to make him hers.

There was so much she wanted to know. Where had Martin come from? How had he got here? What had made him come here? And, more urgently, was Luis still alive?

He shook his head. 'No, I'm sorry. Luis died in 1944.'

Carla watched Grandma, and thought she had gone far away, back to an earlier life. Some moments passed before she spoke again. She shook her head as if to shake off wraiths from the past, and asked him simply, 'Will you just tell me? How did he die? It was in that same area of France that they were living in, in North Catalonia?'

Martin nodded. 'During your Civil War he wrote for the French newspapers, and helped Spanish refugees. Then in 1940, when the Germans invaded France, he started working for the Resistance, and then in 1944 the Germans found his camp and he was killed.'

Maria made the sign of the cross. 'And you still live in this village where he settled?' she asked.

'Yes, I've lived there all my life.'

'So all this time Luis's family has been living just across the border – so close to here!' Maria's voice was incredulous. 'We didn't know! We didn't even know you existed! What made you come down to Spain after all this time?'

'Old friends of my father in our village told me how he came to visit his Spanish family in Sant Galdric in 1936. They knew he had a brother and a sister – you, Aunt Maria – and your children, living with his mother in Sant Galdric. I only learnt about the existence of his Spanish family a few years ago, and as the years have gone by I found myself wanting to know more about where my father came from. My mother,' this with a shake of the head, 'was very unhappy about me making the journey. But I made it to here unscathed. I told her that I'd just be another tourist to Spain, but she thinks nothing has changed here, and she's heard too many bad stories. She thinks the police are just waiting on every corner to arrest people here in Spain!'

'I remember your mother well from that visit,' Maria said, with a smile. 'She was such a beautiful woman. It's good that she decided to stay in the south after Luis died. She was from Paris, originally, wasn't she?'

Martin froze, and an odd haunted expression came to his face. Carla wondered what on earth for. She looked across at Grandma, whose head was turned full towards Martin. Her simple question hung in the air between them, and acquired an unintended significance as the minutes went by.

And then the young man breathed in a large gulp of air, and seemed to launch himself into his next words.

'You met Luis's wife Elise in 1936,' he said. 'Well, Elise and Luis had two children, but during the war she had to flee France with them, leaving Luis behind. She never came back to France after that, and my sister and brother grew up in England. Elise died there.'

He had Carla's full attention now, as well as Maria's. 'And you?' Carla asked.

'I was born later, in 1944,' he answered, swallowing hard. 'Luis had an affair with my mother during the war, after his wife had left. He never even knew my mother was pregnant, and he died before I was born.' He looked at them both with a plea in his eyes.

'I only found out when I was thirteen that he was my

real father, and I've been trying to make sense of it since then. I came here . . .' He stopped, the words seeming to run dry in his throat.

Maria closed her hand over his on the table. 'You came here to find your family. And we saw Luis in you. You are a Garriga through and through, and you are the nephew who came to make Luis live again for us.'

Carla was still staring, taking in his story. So he was Luis's son indeed, but a bastard son that Luis never even knew existed. But he was a Garriga, just as Grandma said. Luis's blood flowed through his veins, just as Luc's blood would define the baby now kicking inside her womb, however illegitimate.

She looked over to where Maria's hand still enfolded Martin's, and couldn't help laughing.

'If you have my grandmother on your side, Martin, then it seems like you are definitely one of us. How old are you? If you were born in 1944 you must be nineteen, no more! Well you look a whole lot older, but it seems strange that my Great Uncle Luis should have a son who's younger than me.' She eased herself out from the table. 'Do you drink coffee, cousin Martin? Well, if I sit here any longer my back will seize up, so you stay here, and talk to your new found aunt, and coffee you shall both have. I think you two have a lot more to say to one another!'

# Chapter Seven

They lingered over coffee. The coffee Grandma and Victor could afford was always as bitter as hell, despite the sugar they added in spoonfuls, but it was the one thing which Carla seemed to be able to swallow easily, and it burnt a path through her gullet and the sugar and caffeine kicked her tired body awake. God knows what it was doing to her nerves, but they were shot already, and Carla loved its assault on her senses.

As the coffee warmed her she nodded at her new-found cousin. 'I can tell you one person who will be delighted to meet you,' she said, 'and that's Victor. Just wait till he comes home! He gets fed up living with two women, and he'll be dragging you off to drink with him, I'm sure! But he'll never accept calling you Martin. You'll be Martí to him – just like you already are to Grandma.'

Martin smiled. 'My mother calls me Martí sometimes.

Not when she's angry, though! And she was pretty angry about me coming here!' He corrected himself. 'No, that's not fair – she was just worried for me, that's all. It's why I mustn't stay too long.'

Carla studied his face, which was serene and happy. He was a medical student, he'd told them, and his mother had the local café in their village. He was the adored success of the family, for sure. She could guess that he was his mother's darling. All of a sudden she felt desolate.

'How wonderful to have a mother who worries about you!' she said, and found that her voice would hardly bring out the words.

'Carla, my love!' Grandma protested. 'Don't feel like that. You know we've discussed how your mother loved you.'

'When I was a child! When I was happy just to admire and adore her! What about later, when I really needed her? She was too busy dressing up for my father to go with him to their society parties, to worry about a troubled teenager! When my father hit me, did she stop him? When I wanted to get away, did she help me? And when they came to take Luc away, where was she then?'

'Luc?' Martin asked. This extra name seemed to throw him.

Maria came to his rescue.

'Luc is Carla's fiancé. Early this summer he was arrested, just before they were due to get married. The Civil Guard came and took him away in the night.'

Martin looked horrified. 'What had he done?' he asked, in a whisper.

'Nothing!' Carla's voice was scornful. 'My father found out about us, that's all! Luc was a student activist, and his father was a known Republican in the Civil War. My father would have moved heaven and earth to stop me marrying Luc. We kept it secret from my parents, but what fools we were to think they wouldn't know! I knew my father was spying on me, but I thought we'd been careful enough! More fool me. I underestimated my father. He disapproved of everything I did, and we didn't speak, but he wouldn't let me ruin his name by marrying an activist.'

'But if he knew about the baby . . .'

'Of course he knows about the baby! He'll be planning to have it taken off me at the hospital. That's what they do to single mothers here, you know. One more bastard baby given away in Spain. Who's to care?'

'They force you to give up the child?'

'You never see the child after the birth. They just tell you it's dead. End of story.'

There was a pause while Martin seemed to digest what she was telling him. If you didn't live in Spain, Carla thought, you would never believe it, would you? Fascism, relentless despotism, profiteers like Sergi, and all the powerlessness that went with it for ordinary people – it took all of these things to make her situation possible.

'And Luc?' Martin spoke again. 'Do you know where he is?'

'Not a clue, dear cousin, not a clue, although I suspect he's in the Barcelona men's prison. They can keep him hidden away without trial forever if they have someone like my father behind it.'

'And your mother knows about all of this?'

'Oh yes!' Carla looked at him in gentle derision. 'Luc was taken in July, when my father and mother were together at the hill house. She would certainly have known.'

Martin looked thoughtful. 'She hasn't been in Girona since, though, has she?' he said, after a while. 'She may not know you're pregnant.'

'And you're naïve enough to believe she would care?' All Carla's pent-up anger and frustration came pouring out as she answered him. 'She certainly seems to have got round you, up in that damned house. Was she so sweet to you, then? Gracious? Friendly? Did she mention her family at all? The family she has abandoned! The people she has betrayed! And you think she'd care about Luc's baby?' Her voice rasped in her own ears. She got up as tears gagged her, and began to clear the table.

Martin was silenced. He looked towards Maria for guidance. She gave him a smile but her eyes were troubled, almost bereaved.

'My daughter has made some questionable choices in her life, Martí. Since she married Sergi Olivera I have never been sure that I knew her. Something changed in her, and she has led a life which abandoned us all. Until a couple of years ago I had never even met my own granddaughter. Only when Carla went to university and was able to make her own decisions could she make contact with us. No,' she sighed, 'I can't tell you what Joana is capable of. I don't know myself, although she has just sometimes helped us when we needed her, and I have always thought that at least she cared about her own daughter.'

A silence fell that Carla could physically hear as she moved around the kitchen, washing dishes. As she came out to clear the coffee cups she caught Martin's eyes, and what she saw there gave her a moment's compunction. What they'd thrown at him was too far outside his experience. She thought about Luc, stuck in a gaol somewhere, in conditions she dreaded to imagine, desperately worrying about her and cut off from all communication. And herself, weeks away from giving birth, powerless and desperate. It was a situation beyond Martin's scope, and she touched him lightly on the shoulder as she passed, in tacit understanding.

Grandma was still sitting beside him, almost restfully. She had the gift of tranquillity. Martin looked more nervous by nature, in spite of that air of self-possession beyond his years. Did he get that from Great Uncle Luis? She knew Luis had been forceful and passionate, and driven to action, where Victor and Maria were gentle and enduring. His son Martin was harder to read.

From a world far away, almost dreamily, Maria continued to talk about her daughter. 'Joana was the apple of your father's eye. And of her father's. They were the closest of friends, you know, Luis and my husband. And Joana is her father's image.'

There was too much melancholy in the air, too much reminiscence, and sadness, and loss, and Carla moved quickly back to the tiny kitchen with the cups. After a second Martin followed her.

'Is there anything I can do to help you?' he asked Carla.

'Not here, no,' she turned her head and gave him a

quizzical grin to lighten the mood. 'Do you help in the kitchen at home?'

He gave her a half grin back, and shook his head.

'I thought not! Well you won't here, either. But you can walk with me, if you will, after I finish here. Grandma will have a siesta now, but I need to walk. As long as I don't carry heavy bags, walking does me good. If we go up on the old city wall we'll get some air, and I'll be able to put this creature to sleep for a while.' She rubbed her stomach as she spoke.

It was the end of confidences for the day, and Carla thought that everyone was relieved. That afternoon she and Martin walked across the footbridge over the River Onyar, and through the beautiful, if rather undercherished, old town, past the cathedral and on up the hill to the ruins of the Jardí dels Alemanys, and from there they climbed up to the remnants of the old city wall, and walked along its short, crumbling length in a stiff breeze that shook out Carla's hair and smoothed the tired lines on her face, so that she looked again like a young woman.

She found herself telling Martin the whole history of Girona, from Roman to medieval times, trying to impart her love for it, and pointing out the parts built by the Romans, by the Carolingians, and by medieval warring princes. The dilapidated buildings came to life for her as she spoke, and her problems dwindled to a mere transitory blip in history. And Martin grinned, and exclaimed in all the right places, and laughed and asked questions in that funny French Catalan of his.

Occasionally they would pass by other couples walking,

and she would hold a finger to her lips to stop him speaking until they were past. She was astonished to hear that he had been beaten for speaking Catalan at school in France.

'I thought you lived in a democracy!' she exclaimed.

'Yes, but not a Catalan democracy. We're all supposed to prove how French we are.'

'And we thought you were so free!'

'Not at school! They say we can't learn proper French if we are constantly talking Catalan. And it has its effect. Among my friends we mostly speak French now. It's not just because of our teachers, though – it's subtler than that. It's the influence of the outside world – films and tourists and so many people coming to live in the south from other parts of France who only speak French. Everyone wants to be sophisticated, and they've got us brainwashed that speaking Catalan is for peasants.'

'Well it's not true here! Here they can beat you or even arrest you for speaking Catalan, but it just makes people angrier. And the Civil Guard may try to intimidate us, and lots of them are brought in from other parts of Spain, but our local police all speak Catalan at home themselves! There was a group of young men the other week who surrounded a couple of policemen and harangued them in Catalan, asking them what they were going to do about it! The poor policemen were so scared! But you wonder whether the men may have received a visit later on from some rather more forceful policemen.'

Martin grimaced. 'Well I don't think I'll risk challenging any one at all. I'm here without full papers, you know. My mother wouldn't agree to me travelling, and since I'm under age I'm supposed to have her permission. I need to keep a low profile so I don't get you people into trouble.'

'Don't worry! As long as you keep your mouth shut in public there's not much can happen. The neighbours in Grandma's street keep themselves to themselves – nobody wants anybody looking too closely, even if they haven't done anything wrong. So unless you really know your neighbours, most people just keep their heads down and only mix with family, which for us in Girona means nobody. And you won't be staying long – you won't want to, believe me! You'll be sharing a bed with Uncle Victor and he snores louder than anyone I've ever known!'

They met Uncle Victor as they returned to the house in the early evening. He was getting off a bus a block or so away from the apartment, an average-looking man in factory overalls covered by a dark tunic, one among a stream of workers heading for home, all dressed very much the same.

They waited for Victor just outside the apartment block. He smiled as he saw Carla, and came towards her with his hands outstretched. Carla was aware of Martin stiffening beside her and, looking over, saw excitement mingled with apprehension on his face. He was gazing intently at Victor, and Carla wondered if he was looking for a resemblance to Luis. Well there was one, but Victor was homelier than any photo of Luis that Carla had ever seen, and deep lines in a leathery skin bore witness to a life of outdoor labour. His bush of hair was grey too. Luis hadn't lived long enough to go grey. Seeing him through Martin's eyes, Carla noticed more strongly than ever how worn Uncle Victor was, but the smile with which he embraced her brought a shadow of youth back to his face, and she couldn't wait to tell him about Martin.

She took him to one side to tell him, urgent and alight in anticipation of his reaction, and was rewarded by the look of astonishment and delight which flooded him. She led him up to Martin, and he took his new nephew's hand, and held it. An incredulous smile was splitting his face. He said nothing, though, and led Martin into the building, up the stairs and through the door to the apartment before he spoke. Then he threw his arms around Martin in a very manly hug.

'We don't worry those people out there,' he said, shrugging his shoulder towards the outer door and the world outside, 'with the kind of good news we have been brought today.'

Yet another smell of cooking was coming from the kitchen. Aunt Maria's headscarf peeked out from the kitchen door, and Carla went towards her and threw her tired body into a chair as Maria fussed over her. The tiny space was filled with family, and as Victor patted his back again and again, Martin looked almost dumbstruck in their midst.

Looking at their world again through his eyes, Carla thought how well he'd coped with them all. In the space of twenty-four hours, he'd met and won over Joana, it seemed, so that she'd provided her own car to bring him to Girona, and he'd charmed Maria, brought the biggest ever smile to Victor's face, and, to be honest, given even her own prickly self every reason to be glad she had a cousin. She repeated to herself what she'd thought earlier on. Martin was nice. It wasn't a big word, but it was an important one, and for nice things to happen was too rare in their lives. He wanted their kinship too, and the look of appeal in his eyes was like a call to discovery. She smiled across at him where he stood next to Victor, and he gave her a tired but happy smile in return.

'Come,' said Uncle Victor, moving away to a small cupboard. 'I don't often have a companion for a small glass of wine. I need to wash, and change these clothes, and then we'll go down to the café for the *aperitiù*, you and me. But for now, we'll have a small glass here, and see if these two ladies will make a toast with us.'

He smiled at Maria as she made a gesture of refusal, and shook his head. 'Oh no, Maria, you don't get to refuse, not this time. My brother Luis is with us this evening, and you know how he was. Luis would have insisted, and you, my sister, at his invitation you would always accept!'

# Chapter Eight

*It was a cloudless summer afternoon in Barcelona, the air heavy with a heat more sleepy than oppressive. Carla stood on the tiny balcony of Luc's studio flat, languidly watching a plane going goodness knows where, full of tourists heading home. It left a long white trail in the deep blue of the sky.*

*'It's going to London,' Luc said behind her.*

*'Rubbish, it's heading for Paris. I've always wanted to go to Paris.'*

*'For the Moulin Rouge,* vida meva*?'*

*'Not at all, you buffoon!' Carla elbowed Luc in the ribs. 'If I wanted that kind of titillation I could join the tourists on the Costa Brava! No, I want to watch the artists in Montmartre, and visit the Louvre, the Champs Elysées, Notre Dame, Orsay, the Eiffel Tower, oh everything!'*

*'Then we'd better go for a month! A month in Paris for you, and a month in London for me!'*

*'And where else?'*

*'Wherever you lead me, little adventuress!' Luc said, low into her ear. '"I want you, pure, free, irreducible you",' he murmured, 'and before you ask me, that was Pedro Salinas, and he lived in Paris once, so you ought to appreciate him!'*

*He curved around her, his whole frame enveloping hers as he leant against the balcony rail. Carla could feel his breath on the nape of her neck as he bent to kiss her throat, and then his cheek against hers as he pulled her backwards so she leant against him.*

*She closed her eyes and protested, 'It's too hot for that out here.'*

*'Then come inside! Come into my parlour and let me cool your heart.'*

*She had to laugh – he was full of so much nonsense! If man could live from tomfoolery alone, she thought, then Luc would be a millionaire! But his voice was melting, and his breath was hot against her skin as his arms moved up her body.*

*She gave a sigh. She had never in her previous life dared to imagine such happiness as this, something so simple and natural and untainted. They moved together into the bedroom, through the makeshift curtain, which shielded the room from the afternoon sun. Luc's arms stayed locked around her body, and she giggled as his feet caught the sill. He wasn't looking, and he nearly stumbled, and bubbles of laughter took her forward into the room.*

*But as the curtain fell behind them, her father was there. Stocky, stubby Sergi, beautifully dressed of course, flanked by two thugs in uniform. His sneer said it all. What do you think you're doing? You can't get away, you can't be free. Did you imagine you had the right to be happy?*

Carla woke up, tears starting to her eyes as so often before. The dreams were different in detail, but always the same in essence. She could remember so vividly her moments on that tiny balcony with Luc, and in the little room, their secret place from where the Civil Guard had come to get him. Nowhere now felt safe. There were no secret places in her father's Spain.

She lay still, choking back her anguish, waiting for the dream to subside. Next to her the bed was empty. Grandma was already up, and she could hear her moving around in the kitchen, preparing Victor's breakfast before his day at the factory. Carla lay, unrefreshed by sleep, listening listlessly to the sounds through the thin wall. She heard Victor heading for the bathroom, and wondered whether to get up herself. But there was nothing she could do, nothing she could contribute to their morning routine, and with her huge belly she always felt that she occupied too much space in this small apartment, among all the rickety chairs, and the clutter of Grandma's trinkets, the salvaged relics from another world.

The baby shifted inside her. It could no longer do somersaults – it was too tight now. Panic gripped her as she counted the days to giving birth – not much more than six weeks now, surely. She'd come to Grandma in search of shelter and nurturing, and together they were going to try to manage the birth at home, but what if something went wrong? Luc's baby – nothing must happen to Luc's baby. One day he would make it out of prison and come looking for her, she knew, and she and the baby had to be waiting for him. Even her father couldn't keep Luc forever, could he? But he could keep him for a very long time. All he needed to do was emphasise the political threat, and suggest that Luc was planning violent protest. That would be enough to keep him under lock and key for as long as Sergi wanted.

Politically I'm just as radical as Luc, thought Carla. She wanted to go and scream it in her father's face. Take me too, if you have to have him. But Sergi didn't want his daughter arrested, he only wanted her controlled.

She waited until the sounds outside indicated Victor was leaving for work. Normally she would get up to say goodbye, but today she couldn't face his smiles. He had stayed up late last night talking to Martin, teasing out the boy's character, looking for Luis. He was happy this morning – she could hear it in his voice as he spoke with Maria. She couldn't handle that right now. Martin's coming was a diversion, but in the end a diversion always left you inexorably back on the same dark road as before. She knew that she was often sharp, angry, unpleasant at the moment. It was the view along the road which left her in such hostile despair.

Eventually she rose wearily, and washed and dressed in the same old clothes, which Luc would have thrown on to the nearest fire. Another day, and another sixteen hours or more before she could again seek out her bed, and the fragile dreams of Luc.

They went out together that morning, Carla, Maria

and Martin, brought along to help carry a heavy load of washing. It was as they returned that she saw the black car, sitting on the corner of the street, with its two male passengers carefully not looking in their direction. She said nothing to Grandma or to Martin. Perhaps the men in the car wouldn't think too much about the presence of a young man with them. It had been a while since she'd seen the black car with its black-suited driver, sometimes alone, sometimes with a companion. They were here to monitor her pregnancy, she knew. Sergi might know she was pregnant, but he couldn't know exactly how far, and he wouldn't want to miss the birth. He would have all the local hospitals and clinics primed, she was sure, but he would be watchful nevertheless, in case she slipped away.

As she walked past the car she fixed her gaze on the men inside. She didn't know either of them, but they didn't look like policemen, at least as far as she could see. Did Sergi have his own private army? A personal driver, like Toni, but one she didn't know? And another – who was he? She smiled at the two men, a sweet smile of defiance, but they looked determinedly ahead.

It was later that day, after another afternoon walk with Martin, that she saw her father. This time her heart stopped. Never before, to her knowledge, had it been her father who trailed her. It was the silver Mercedes she spotted first, and at first she thought it was Toni driving. Both her mother and her father had a Mercedes, each one a 'gift' from the German entrepreneurs who were currently ploughing up the Catalan coast for their new tourist resorts.

But then she caught a glimpse of a tailored beige suit and

her father's clipped, greying hair, and she knew it wasn't Toni. He cruised slowly towards them, and as he got closer his eyes swept over them both. She caught hold of Martin's arm.

'Martin, we have a problem.' she said.

He looked an enquiry.

'Look to your left, a little ahead. That's my father in the Mercedes.'

He looked startled, and shot a quick look in the direction of the car, then averted his eyes.

Now that she had got over the first shock, Carla felt a soaring anger at the man whose gaze grazed so contemptuously over them.

'There's no need to pretend you haven't seen him,' she told Martin. 'He's making no attempt to hide himself, is he?'

'What is he doing here?' Martin's voice was understandably nervous.

'Checking you out, I think. I didn't say this morning, but two of his henchmen were in our street today, watching us. I didn't think they would pay much attention to you, since you look like pretty much any young guy from around here. But my father is paranoid about who I might meet, and I think they went back and told him there was a young man with me, and lo and behold, here's my loving father turning up to see us.'

The car had come to a near halt now, crawling past them as Sergi studied Martin from head to toe. Carla took a step towards the car, but it just glided past. She fixed her eyes on her father's face, but he wasn't even looking at her. All his attention was on Martin.

'He thinks I'm your boyfriend?' Martin's hand gripped her sleeve convulsively.

Carla was almost amused. 'Possibly, yes, and holding on to my arm won't do anything to dissuade him!'

Martin withdrew his hand as though she had burnt him. The car had passed them now, and they stood and watched as it reached the end of the road and turned onto the main avenue. Neither of them moved. Carla felt suspended in time, continuing to gaze after the car long after it had disappeared from view. What might he do, she wondered? What would Sergi do now? There was a tight knot in her chest and her thoughts wouldn't come clear.

She became aware of Martin by her side, nudging her urgently. 'Should we go inside?' he asked. 'He may come back round again. I think we should move.'

Carla nodded. Her surge of defiance had faded, and she felt cold and afraid. She wanted to hide, from her father and from the world. All she wanted was to feel safe. But she never felt safe now, not even in her dreams.

They found Maria at the table mending one of Victor's shirts. Beside her lay a pile of socks for darning, but when she saw the two white faces coming into the room she laid it all aside and came to greet them, an anxious question in her eyes. She held out her hands and Carla put one hand into them.

'Little one?' It was a term Grandma rarely used these days.

'We just saw my father.' She could never bring herself to call him Papa now, not since last year. 'He drove by to check us out. I think he wants to know who Martin is.'

She sank into a chair, and leant her elbows on the table, reaching for a sock and winding it around her fingers. A little nerve throbbed at her temple, twitching her left eye. Martin sat opposite her, and she noticed his hands working in the same way. Shock, she thought. We're both in shock. If Sergi could create this effect merely by driving past in his car, then what else could he do? Well she knew, didn't she? Luc was behind bars.

Maria disappeared into the kitchen. She didn't bother with exclamations or questions. Instead she reappeared a few minutes later with two cups of hot chocolate, dark and bitter, and placed these in front of Carla and Martin, neither of whom had moved at all.

The hot drink slid down Carla's throat, and reached that cold knot in her chest. Her tight muscles eased, and she found she could think again. Grandma came to sit between them at the table, and her body seemed to give off a warmth as well.

'So, my children?' she said.

It was Martin who told her, how Sergi had slowed down to examine him, taking his time, scanning him with that raking stare, crawling past in the sleek Mercedes.

'He's an impressive man,' he ventured, tentatively. 'Commanding, if you see what I mean.'

'Yes,' said Maria. She looked at Carla. 'What did you make of him this time?'

Carla looked at the wall, thinking back to Sergi, sitting so disdainfully behind the wheel of the car, checking them over. He'd hardly seemed to look at her, and yet she was sure he had noted everything about her, from her gaunt face to her shabby clothes, to the bump he was seeing for the first time. She wondered if it gave him satisfaction to see her brought so low. He'd certainly been angry enough the last time they'd met, but the eyes that had skimmed her over just now had been clinical rather than vindictive. He wasn't acting against her so much as to protect himself.

She brought her gaze back from the wall. Grandma was still watching her with troubled eyes.

'I think he may well assume that Martin is a new boyfriend,' she answered at last. 'It seems mad, when you see my condition, but he's not to know we've only just met. Maybe he thinks I'm so desperate I'll seek any man's protection. It's the way he thinks about women, anyway.'

'So what will he do now?' asked Martin.

'I don't know. Since you're not staying more than a day or two he may get the message not to worry. I guess he'll have his henchmen patrol around here pretty regularly over the next couple of days, watching us. Once they see that I'm back on my own again he should leave us in peace, don't you think?' Peace! Now there's a strange word to have used, she thought.

'Well, no. No, I'm not so sure,' Martin said, taking his time.

'What do you mean?'

'Well, I know I'm new in on this situation, but I can't see that he'll just let it go. If I disappear, won't he just assume that he's frightened us and I'm making myself scarce? He won't necessarily think I've gone for good, and he'll still think I'm around somewhere as a threat to his plans.'

Maria nodded her head. 'I'm afraid I think he's right,

Carla. Your father is the most distrustful of men. Martin can leave us and he'll be safe, but I have a terrible fear now that your father won't any longer leave things to chance where you're concerned.'

Carla knew what was coming next. She knew, too, that they were right.

'You think he'll take me away,' she said, and was surprised at how matter of fact her voice sounded.

'I fear so. He doesn't know when the baby is due, but he has seen for himself today that it's not too far away. He'll want you somewhere secure and under his control for the next weeks, far from me and Victor, and far from any young man who may have taken up your cause.'

Damn him, damn him! Sergi's iron-hard face came before her again, and she felt such a wave of hatred that it was frightening. He can't make me so helpless! I won't let him!

'So I'll go away too!' She put her cup jerkily down on the table and some dregs of chocolate splattered the tablecloth. 'I'll go away to Barcelona. There must be someone who'll hide me down there.'

'Who, my love? Who can hide you that Sergi doesn't know about? And who can hide you when the baby comes?'

Carla met her grandmother's eyes and read such a sombre message that she was filled with dread. 'So what can I do?' This time her voice would barely come.

Maria reached out and took her hand. 'I don't know, child. I don't know. Perhaps Victor . . .'

'Victor?'

'I just thought maybe he might know someone who can

hide you in the hills. One of his friends with sheep. It's not what I would want, with the baby coming, but maybe I could go with you, and together we might manage.'

Maria's voice was hesitant, anxious, and Carla looked at her in despair. To have the baby in a mountain hamlet, or even a hillside shed? She gazed into Grandma's troubled face and thought, she's frightened, as frightened as me.

It was Martin who broke the silence.

'There may be something else we should try.'

'Something else?'

'I think I should go back to see your mother.'

Neither Carla nor Maria spoke. Carla wasn't even sure what he was saying. He continued, his voice growing stronger and more persuasive as he gathered momentum.

'I don't think your mother knows that you're pregnant or what your father is doing to you – not all of it, anyway. I think she needs to be told, and I want to go up there and tell her. You don't think she'll help you, but no one has given her a chance, and you've run out of other options.'

He held Carla's gaze, and his eyes were alive with conviction. Her own brain felt dead in comparison. She didn't agree with him, she knew that, but she was beginning to respect his intelligence, and she had no response to his conviction. But still she couldn't answer him, and Maria stayed equally silent. It didn't stop him, and he ploughed on persuasively.

'If I go up there tomorrow by the earliest bus, I should get to the house before lunchtime. And if Joana lets Toni bring me back I can be here by evening. Do you think your father will feel he needs to work so fast that he'll raid this apartment? I can't see it – he could only do that with the police, surely, and he'd have to have you arrested, wouldn't he? I think he'll try to do something less embarrassing to him than that if he can, and maybe lift you in the street – the street was so empty today that a couple of men in a car could pull up and bundle you inside before anyone noticed.'

Carla shivered, and Martin grabbed her arm across the table. 'Yes, but that's good news, in a way, Carla! If that's the easiest way to remove you, then for now you'll be safe as long as you just stay indoors, and that gives me time to go up and see your mother.'

'And if she refuses to help?' It was Maria's troubled voice that broke into his onslaught.

He paused, but not for long. 'If she refuses to help us, we can look at other options. Not some mountain hideout, though – we can do better than that. My sister – Luis's first-born – is married to a Spanish exile in France, and before I left home he gave me the address of his family by the border with France, in La Jonquera, and if we need to I could take you to them, and then get you out to France afterwards. We must be able to get you out somehow.'

'No!' Carla was surprised by her own cry. 'I won't run away to France! I could never come back, afterwards, and then what will happen when Luc gets out of prison? I have to be somewhere where Grandma can find me.'

Martin was silenced, but his ideas were taking root nevertheless.

'They won't take your baby away from you in France,' Grandma said.

'And when Luc is freed we can get him to France as

well,' agreed Martin. 'But first will you let me go up to the hill house?'

Carla thought back to the last time she had been to the hill house. It would be two summers ago, and relations between her and Joana had never been more strained. Sergi had been there with some friends, for the hunting, and his daughter's mere presence had annoyed him. What on earth is that girl wearing, he'd asked her mother? What kind of specimen is she? She's not even half a woman!

She'd clashed with one of his guests too, when he'd asked her why on earth she wanted to get a degree. Mama had agreed with the guest.

'It would seem that an education is doing nothing to improve my daughter's manners, Señor, and I apologise on her behalf. Carla is the product of a spoilt background, I'm afraid.'

Later that night Sergi had struck Carla hard, twice, snapping her head from side to side, and Joana had stood by and watched him. He'd threatened to take her out of the university, and after that first threat she'd learnt to toe the line, and stay in the background whenever she was with them.

What on earth was it that Martin had seen in her mother that made him think she would want to help? She asked him, and all he could reply was that Joana had vulnerable eyes.

'She's got you besotted,' she protested, exasperated. She didn't want to ask her mother for help!

But she was too desperate now to be proud, too frightened to refuse even the remotest possibility of assistance.

'You won't get any joy from my mother,' she told him eventually. 'I know you won't, but you're right that as things stand I have nothing to lose. By all means, cousin, go up there tomorrow and see what she says. I'll stay indoors and we'll lock the doors. But Martin?'

'Yes?'

'Take care what you tell her! She's spent her life dong whatever my father wants, and she could even turn your visit against us, and make trouble for us.'

'More than we're in right now?'

'No,' she said finally, admitting defeat, 'Nothing can be worse than the trouble we're in right now.'

# Chapter Nine

The autumn day had grown warm and very still, and not a hint of a breeze stirred Joana's afternoon peace on the vast veranda. In the parched heat of August such stillness would have been uncomfortable, and the hill house was designed to capture the summer breezes to cool its dark rooms and shaded terraces. But now, in October, this airless Indian summer was a blessing. It held off the sharp mountain winds of winter, which whistled relentlessly around the house and reminded you that it was meant for summer living.

Joana leant back on the cane sofa and lifted her bare feet from the cold tiles. She placed a cushion behind her head and closed her eyes. Even from the depths of the veranda where she lay, she could hear the chirping of the mating crickets in the wild grasses that surrounded the house, burying their eggs before themselves dying off in the winter cold. And from somewhere nearby came the drone of a bee drinking from the autumn crocuses. Soon Gabriel would come up from the village to harvest this year's honey from the hives, and the drone bees would die to keep the queen alive. Joana twitched the cushion behind her and shifted position restlessly, then gave an angry shake. It was all too inevitable, too peaceful, too inert.

Reaching out her hand, her eyes half closed, she found her glass of champagne and raised it to her lips. The bubbles trickled slowly down her throat and seemed to ease an itching just behind the vocal chords. She relaxed again and dozed gently, excluding the world from her shaded niche. Beyond the veranda the hillside lay becalmed.

Paula shuffled out from the house and lifted the empty glass from her hand. Joana didn't move. The half slumber was too precious to let it slip away, and while she appeared to sleep she was safe from Paula's grumblings. Her soft hair tickled her cheek, and it felt like a caress. She still had beautiful hair, she knew, despite her forty-one years. She had been courted for those golden curls, once upon a time, but it felt like a long time ago.

Joana smiled in her near sleep, remembering those days of innocence and hope, before the war came home to them and all was lost. It was Sergi who'd rescued her then. Sergi who also loved her, who wanted her so badly. She lay on Sergi's chair, on Sergi's veranda, and tried to keep the picture.

Paula shuffled back out onto the veranda with a pot of coffee. Smelling it, Joana opened her eyes. Paula was only trying to make her drink something else than her after-lunch champagne, but the coffee smelt good nevertheless.

Sergi always had the best coffee in his houses. He spoke of a supplier in South America – Columbia, he said. Joana suspected it came as a free gift from some local importer in need of Sergi's favour.

Putting the pot down on the long table, Paula looked over the wall to call Toni in for his coffee. Suddenly she held up her hand to shade her eyes, looking far down the hillside.

'Is Toni not around?' Joana asked.

'Not that I can see. But there's someone walking up the track towards the house, down there.' Paula gestured away down the hill.

'Gabriel?'

'When did old Gabriel ever walk up as far as here?' Paula scoffed. 'He waits for Toni to fetch him, does our Gabriel. No, this is a young man, I'd say. I think it's that same French man that came here the other day – the one who called himself your cousin.'

Her curiosity piqued, Joana rose from the sofa and crossed to the wall. Sure enough, about a kilometre down the track a young man was walking towards them, slowly making his way up to the hill house, and it did indeed look like her new cousin Martin.

He'd appeared out of the blue three days ago, wafting with him currents of air from another world, from France, where her Uncle Luis had made a life, and a family, far from the harsh realities of the Spain he'd abandoned. For a long time as a teenager she had hated Luis for his broken promises. It had taken her own abrupt and frightening emergence into adulthood to make her understand how war could rupture relationships.

And Martin had brought Uncle Luis back to her. The lights in his eyes, and his energy, and his intuitive intelligence were Luis. The reticence in him was not. The boldness of the journey he was making had perhaps made him sober, and the space between their lives was one which you had to explore very lightly, to find the links behind. So they'd reached out very tentative hands towards each other, and found they touched a chord.

Most things she didn't ask – what had driven him to come looking for his roots, what had happened to his mother, whether he had brothers or sisters? She didn't want to know. A shade of Luis had appeared, the connection was made, and the rest was irrelevant. They toasted cousinhood in champagne in a simple acceptance, which was no less eloquent for what went unsaid.

They'd been companions for a few hours, and then the following morning she'd sent him down to her mother and Victor. Very reluctantly she'd let him go. He felt like her friend, her discovery, and she'd watched the car drive away with a sense of mourning, because from now onwards his view of her would be tainted. That moment when all judgement was suspended, and all difficult questions were in abeyance, was over. She had been a mere stopping point on a longer journey, and she never expected to see him again.

And now, just two days later he was back. What could be bringing him back again so soon? Joana felt a frisson of excitement coupled with anxiety. Whatever it was, it was something very practical this time, some serious trouble.

For the second time he had made the cruel six-kilometre hike uphill from Sant Galdric. He hadn't come for nothing.

'Toni,' she shouted, and a voice answered her from behind the house. 'Toni, take the car down the track and meet my cousin Martin – he's on his way up here to see us.'

'Yes, *Senyora*,' came the completely incurious reply, and within a few minutes Joana heard the sound of the car engine gunning. She watched as the car came round the corner of the house and headed at a slow pace down the track. She leant over and saw that Martin had stopped, and was waiting for the car to arrive.

'Paula, bring another coffee cup,' she called, and took her seat again on the cane sofa to wait. 'And bring more champagne, and a tray of food for my cousin. He'll have missed lunch.'

Her mind shifted over all the reasons that might have sent Martin back up here again. When Paula showed the young visitor wordlessly back onto the veranda, she rose with unusual haste to greet him.

There was something different about Martin since he'd left two days ago. His eyes were strained, and something about the set of his broad shoulders seemed too rigid. Was such tension because of her? What terrible things had they been telling him?

'Martin? What is the matter, *el meu cosí*?' She held out her hands, and he put his own into them involuntarily. He didn't answer, and seemed to be searching for some words to say. She reached up and kissed him on both cheeks, and he softened and half smiled.

'That's better,' she said, and closing her right hand more

tightly over his she drew him forward to the couch, and coaxed him to sit down. 'Something has happened, and you have come to ask for my help. But first you must have some coffee. You have walked all the way from the village?'

'No, not all the way. The shopkeeper in the village found me a lift up to the gate to your land.' His voice was tight, so much tighter than two days ago. Joana smiled her understanding, willing him to smile back. He seemed older all of a sudden, but his hand was strong and smooth in hers, the hand of a doctor, she reminded herself. She freed her hand to serve his coffee. As she handed it to him she caught his gaze on her, and his expression was inscrutable.

'I'm glad to see you again, Martin,' she said simply. 'Tell me why you are here. You found my mother well?'

He nodded. 'Your mother and your uncle are both well.' He paused, and looked away into the shadows as he asked, 'Did you know your daughter is also with them?'

'Carla?' The word was expelled from her throat as she looked at him in amazement. His head turned and relief lit up his eyes and brought colour to his cheeks.

'You didn't know where she was!'

'Why no!' Her daughter's dark, slender form swam into her mind, marching, as she always imagined her, in a group of students holding banners demanding student rights. Middle-class intellectuals, all of them, with too much money and not enough to do. All it did was to put Sergi's political life in jeopardy. The thought hardened her, and she looked a challenge at Martin.

'Has she got herself into trouble, then, with those friends of hers?'

'In a way, I suppose – she is certainly in trouble. Listen, Joana, have you heard of a young man called Luc Serra?'

She shook her head. 'Is he one of her political friends?'

'No, he's her fiancé. They were going to be married in the summer, but he was arrested just before their wedding.'

'Then he doesn't sound like an ideal fiancé – indeed it sounds as though he was definitely one of her unsavoury political friends. If he has been arrested, then he must have been up to no good!'

'No, Joana, there have been no protests for some months now, no arrests this last while among the students. Luc was lifted from his apartment for no reason in the middle of the night, and just taken away the day before they were due to leave Barcelona together.' He watched her with anxious eyes, and continued. 'Carla says her father, your husband Sergi, was watching them and had Luc arrested to prevent them getting married.'

That could be true! Joana thought back to the summer months, to August, when Sergi had brought some foreign industrialists up to the hill house to shoot wild boar. She'd asked him if he had any news of Carla. Surely she should have graduated by now? Would she see sense and come home? Would he allow her to? And Sergi had laughed and said yes, Carla's studies were indeed over, and as for those friends of hers, she wasn't with them anymore. He seemed genuinely amused, and when she asked him where Carla was now, he told her not to worry her head about the girl – he'd make sure she was in good hands, and put a stop to all that political nonsense. He brushed aside all further questions, and left the hill house the next day, promising his guests some even better entertainment in the brothels of Girona. Joana had been uneasy, but powerless in the face of Sergi's dismissal.

She looked across at Martin, still studying her with those anxious lines around his eyes. 'So my daughter has lost a boyfriend,' she said, keeping her voice carefully neutral. 'It sounds as though he was no bad loss.'

'But it's not like that, Joana, they were a serious couple, getting married, planning a future together. And that's not all. You see, Carla is pregnant. And with no marriage certificate they'll take the baby away from her. In fact, Sergi is plotting it. I saw him myself in Girona.'

She turned aghast eyes on him, and felt the colour draining from her cheeks. She reached out blindly, and he took her hand in his as he continued talking, telling her how Sergi's henchmen had been keeping watch on Carla, how Carla and her grandmother had hoped to bring the baby into the world hidden in their apartment, how thin Carla was, how desperate, with no news of Luc, and how, yesterday, they had seen Sergi, grim and disdainful, cruising by in his Mercedes with that calculating look in his eye. Gradually it seemed to dawn on him that Joana wasn't responding – hadn't said a word. She looked at him in stricken silence, frozen into physical immobility as her mind reeled. Head and hands were chilled and she thought she might faint.

'Are you all right?' She heard his voice coming from somewhere far away, and as her eyes began to black over she felt two hands come round her shoulders, pushing her head down until she lay across Martin's lap.

'Stay there a moment,' he said, and as he held her in place his hands massaged her shoulders, pinning her against the warmth of his body until the blood came back to her face, and she could sit up again without fainting, though waves of nausea still engulfed her, and the floor seemed to move before her eyes. Martin let her go, and she laid her head back against the sofa, allowing the reeling world to come slowly to rights.

'I gave you a shock, I'm sorry.' Martin's voice was full of contrition, and she shook her head, and made herself look at him. As she met his troubled eyes she felt her own prick with tears, and words came tumbling out that had lain atrophied for twenty-four years.

'Poor Carla,' she started, and as she thought of her daughter the tears spilt down her cheeks. 'My poor Carla. It's such a dreadful thing, that fear, the blind panic that you feel, when no one can help you, and the baby just keeps growing, and you're all alone . . .'

Martin's voice came slowly. 'It happened to you?'

'In 1939, yes. When the civil war was lost. It was a boy from Sant Galdric, Alex, my darling Alex. I was only seventeen, just a girl, and he was my knight in shining armour, but somehow he came under suspicion by the new regime. We never really understood why, because he had never been involved in the war, but you know, people were disappearing all the time back then, just disappearing and you never heard of them again. Or their bodies would turn up weeks later, completely randomly. And Alex . . .' Her voice broke.

'He disappeared too.' The voice was gentle. She nodded, unable to speak.

'And you were pregnant.' He was so matter of fact, so soft-spoken. She nodded again, and as she looked up at his face a sob shook her and the tears took over. He drew her against him, and spoke above her head.

'So Carla?'

'Carla is Alex's daughter. I knew, soon after Alex disappeared, that I was pregnant. I was so scared. And Sergi . . . Sergi had always wanted me, and we made a bargain. He took me and married me, and everyone assumed the baby was his, and I was saved. But then I had to live his life, make my life with him, on his terms.'

She lifted her head and looked at Martin through the haze of tears, willing him to understand, aghast at her own words, her abandonment of reserve. Never had she spoken to anyone like this. Her hand went out to him in supplication, and he caught it and held it, and she saw that he too was crying, why she didn't know, but his cheeks were wet with tears. He looked more appalled even than she felt, and long minutes passed during which neither of them could speak. It seemed to Joana that there was nothing more to say. She'd opened up the door to grief, and now she just gazed blankly on the bleakness she'd exposed.

It was Martin who finally resumed their conversation. 'Carla told me her father hit her,' he said at last, keeping his voice level. 'Did he resent her?'

Joana sighed. 'Things were never easy. But at first he was all right with her. She never looked like him, or even like me, to be honest. She was all Alex, especially as she got older, tall and dark, with a face all angles and expressions. But she loved Sergi when she was tiny, and always tried to please him. He didn't like her back, though, and it showed, and she gradually withdrew from him. That was all right, though – I could paper over the cracks.

'The real difficulty came later. You see, the bargain for Sergi was that he got a wife who could adorn his career, and give him sons to secure his line and cement his future, but the sons never came. He blamed me, of course, and as he always had an aggressive streak we both suffered, Carla and me, whenever he was angry or wanted someone to bully.'

She ran one hand down her arm, as if to feel the bruises. 'Sergi could never in a million years have accepted that he was incapable of bearing children, and yet the evidence was there that it was not me who was infertile. Carla was the proof of that, and he knew it underneath, and it just made him angrier. He got his own back by running me down, bending me more and more to his will. But he still required me to play the role of devoted wife, to smile for his friends and host his parties. In the eyes of the world we were a great couple, successful, fashionable, solidly loyal to the regime.'

She was amazed at how good it felt to let down her guard. She'd never told this story to anyone, and had grown used to her private armour, leaning on it as a prop. This 'cousin' had pierced right through it, though, with his bolt of lightning out of the blue, and now it seemed she couldn't pull the shell back round her.

'You didn't ever feel you could tell your mother?'

'No!' The word spat out from her throat, angrier than she had intended. 'My mother believed like everyone that Carla was Sergi's baby. They all thought I'd sold out when I married Sergi! Well, let them think so! I had to make a new life, and that was that. Later, when it got difficult, well, she was so far away, stuck in that village, praying for me at Mass, no doubt. It was like another world. She could never have understood our lives in Girona, and I wouldn't have swapped all of Sergi's nastiness to go back into that village by then!'

'And Carla?'

'What about Carla?'

'Could you have shared with her? You were both suffering, after all.'

She looked at him with renewed hostility. 'You don't understand! For most of her childhood Carla barely suffered at all from him. He would sometimes strike her, but all fathers would hit their children occasionally. He was hardly around when she was a girl – mostly her early life was just school, girls' parties, music lessons, all that kind of thing. When most of Spain was starving, struggling to find food, she had more than most other girls could hope for, and all I wanted was to keep it that way, keep her innocent and out of it all, and make sure she had a future. But she got prickly as she got older, just at the same time as he was turning against us. She was too intelligent, too direct, too much like her real father, and the two of them began to hate each other. I was stuck in the middle, but she hated me too by then, and wasn't much interested in my opinions. I don't think she needed me to fight her battles for her! She was twice as strong as I'll ever be, and desperate for confrontation.'

She looked out over the veranda towards the hills. 'She

was lucky. She could get away and make her own life. I was in a contract, and had to obey.'

'But she never really got away, did she? Carla has never really been free. Her father had her watched, stopped her marrying, gaoled her fiancé, and now that she's completely vulnerable he's got her trapped!'

Joana winced at the challenge in his voice, and was relieved to see Paula shuffling out with the tray of food and the champagne. She put salad, and rice and chicken in front of Martin, and plonked the bottle on the low table between them, scattering some of the heavy charge in the air. As she headed indoors, Joana grinned at her departing back.

'You'd better get on and eat that,' she told Martin. 'She'll be desperate for her siesta, and wanting to clear the plates quickly! And while you eat you can tell me about Carla. You left her at my mother's place?'

'Yes,' he answered, and told her the story between mouthfuls. 'She's staying indoors, hoping to keep out of your husband's way. We believe that Sergi will try to abduct her – his henchmen saw me with her and then he came by himself to check me out when we were walking together in the street. He has never done that before, Carla says. She hasn't seen him in person since she last visited him and you together. He must wonder if Carla has found herself a new man, and Carla is sure he'll want to remove her from any new friendship which might jeopardise his plans and his control of her. Your mother is sure of it too. The easiest way for him to be sure of removing her illegitimate child is for him to lock her away somewhere.'

He paused to look at Joana, and she bit her lip and

nodded. He continued. 'She's frightened of what might happen at night-time, but we thought that she would be safe by day today if she stayed inside, long enough anyway for me to come here.'

'And she trusted that I would help her?'

Joana couldn't help the little note of appeal that came into her voice. Martin hesitated, and as she watched his face her own hardened in response, and she held up a hand.

'There's no need to answer that. She has no reason to believe in me. Let's just talk practicalities instead. Carla needs to get away immediately from Girona, to somewhere Sergi won't look for her. Well, she can come here. She won't love it – she won't want to be with me, and she has always hated this place, but she'll be safe here. It's the last place Sergi would think of looking for her.'

'Does your husband not come here at all, then?'

Joana laughed a little bitterly. 'As I told you, he came here in August, with some business visitors. Otherwise no. Sergi has discovered far more fascinating company than me now – he had a very cool young woman as his mistress the last time I was in Girona.'

'And are you kind of banished here?'

'In a way,' she answered, after a moment. She almost laughed at herself. Was she going to tell this young man everything about her life? But he made it very easy to talk, somehow.

After a moment she continued. 'Sergi tells the world I have a problem. With this.' She gestured at her glass, and the open bottle of champagne waiting by her elbow. 'He may well be right. But one way or another he has made it difficult for me to be among our old social group. He's done it very cleverly, and everyone believes that I'm here for my health, that he has nothing but concern for me.'

She watched Martin's face for any reaction. It was Uncle Luis who looked back at her, not judging, but just waiting. She felt a little surge of defiance run through her as she drank again from her glass. She'd broken open her cage a little that afternoon, and it felt as though Uncle Luis was applauding her.

'I may yet have a trick up my sleeve that will surprise Sergi, though!' she continued. 'Bring my daughter here, Martin, and we'll talk. She can't have the baby here, but before her time comes perhaps I can change a thing or two. I've maybe accepted Sergi's diktats for just a little too long. It's time I remembered whose daughter Carla really is.'

Alex's face came into clear focus before her, and she wanted to tell him, to reassure him. No one will take your grandchild away, Alex. No one will harm Carla's child. It was like a promise to herself, to the Joana she had once been, before she became afraid.

# Chapter Ten

## Sant Galdric, 1939

*It was the coldest January Joana could ever remember. Above Sant Galdric the Pyrenees were cloaked in snow, deep snow that had driven the shepherds further and further down the mountains to the point where the sheep now huddled in hurriedly fenced areas just outside the village, in dirt fields normally used to grow vegetables. But the ground was too hard this winter for planting vegetables, and, hearing the bleating of the sheep, Joana wondered if they were as hungry as she was. They certainly weren't producing much milk, Uncle Victor said. The little cheese the villagers were eating was sparingly spread on hard bread. But while they had the sheep and last year's flour and potatoes they could still eat, unlike some people in the towns. Franço's armies had cut them off from food supplies, and the winter was hard indeed for the people in the cities.*

*Joana huddled against the church wall, sheltering from*

*the icy wind. There were no village youths in the square this evening, but that suited her. She was waiting for Alex. She hadn't seen him now since Christmas, two weeks ago, and travel was so difficult, but this afternoon he'd arrived home, coming into the village on foot, to spend the long holiday weekend with his family. There would be no feasting for Epiphany this year, but Alex's mother and father were on their own now, with his brother away fighting, and Alex had found a way to be with them – and with her.*

*At Christmas Alex had asked her to marry him. At the thought she hugged herself, enfolding their secret inside her thick woollen coat. They couldn't tell anyone yet. It had been a great thing for his family when Alex was taken on for training by the solicitor in Girona. Until he completed his training they would resist him marrying anyone. And Joana was just a child, or at least that's what they thought of her. She smiled. Alex didn't think her a child. He loved her, he said, for her laughter, her life, and her belief in dreams, and together they were going to make a future, one where she could take Mama and Josep and all of them away from Sant Galdric and into a different world.*

*Night had fallen now in the little village square, and Joana was seriously cold. Supper, such as it was, would be ready at home now, and she could not stay out much longer. Hurry up, Alex, she murmured, and as she did so he turned the corner, his tall, slender form outlined against the dark sky. She came away from the wall like a shot, and he pulled her into his arms.*

*But he was uncharacteristically sober as he drew her through the church doors, out of the night air and into the marginally less cold nave of the church. He sat her down beside him on the hard pew, and cupped her shoulders in his hands so that she looked straight into his face.*

*'I only just made it up here today,* carinyo,*' he told her, 'and God knows how I'm going to get back. I may have to walk all the way to Girona, all thirty kilometres. There's no fuel anywhere, and I was lucky on the way up to get picked up by a carter for some of the way. This may be the last time I can get home for a very long time.'*

*Joana gulped. 'They're coming, then?'*

*'Yes, my love, they're coming, and much faster than anyone thought. Franco's best generals, and an army of hundreds of thousands. They're nearly at Barcelona already, and they'll show no mercy once they take it.'*

*'But we have an army too! They'll defend Barcelona!'*

*'We have no weapons left, Joana. The Nationalists have tanks, and planes, and ammunition, and food, of course. Our men have nothing left to fight with.'*

*'And your brother?'*

*'God knows! We've had no news of him for months. If he's still alive he'll be one of those left fighting in the streets of Barcelona when the attack comes. My father already told me today he doesn't expect to see him again. You know, it makes me so angry in Girona when I hear people saying they just want the war to be over now, no matter who wins. I know they're suffering, but what do they think is going to happen if the fascists walk into the city? Do they think everything's just going to return to normal and we'll all shake hands and be friends? Those bastards of Franco's will murder us all just for being Catalans and for daring to hope!'*

*'My uncle Victor says there could be a truce – a negotiated end,' Joana voiced, but without conviction as she looked into Alex's dark, troubled eyes. He didn't answer, just shook his head, and put his arm around her as she shivered.*

*'You'll be all right here,* carinyo. *They'll be too busy fighting over the cities to worry about tiny villages like this one.'*

*'And you?'*

*'I'll be all right as well,' he said. 'I'm just a clerk, and nobody in Girona knows that my brother fights for the Republicans. They'll have no reason to come looking for me, and I'll just lie low. There won't be any reason to go to work anyway, if the Nationalists take Girona. I can't see anyone worrying about property conveyancing and the like for a while, can you?'*

*He sounded bitter and Joana knew how it had galled him not to be fighting alongside his brother. But his parents had begged him – one son was enough, they'd said, to lose to a brutal Civil War. She raised her hand and touched his cheek.*

*'If no one needs solicitors right now, must you go back to Girona? Could you not stay here until it's all over?'*

*'For how long, though? It may take weeks or it may take months. Nobody knows, and meanwhile the boss keeps up the pretence of being open, and when all this is over we will at some stage have some kind of government, some kind of life, and I'll need my job!'*

*They sat for a while longer in silence, their breath misty in the cold air of the church.*

*'I'll need to go,' Joana said eventually, with a despondency unusual in her. 'They'll be waiting for me at home to eat.'*

*'Me too,' Alex replied, then smiled at her ruefully. 'We'll be all right, you know. We just need to wait and things will come out the other side. You and I have no involvement.'*

*Joana protested. 'My father was a Republican journalist. He was gaoled by the same people who now fight with Franco's army. My Uncle Luis too, and he was a ringleader, so his name was well known. If they come to Sant Galdric looking for Republican sympathisers then my family stands out like a sore thumb.'*

*'Only if they come, and only if someone tells them. What your uncle and father were involved in happened way before the actual war started, and miles away from Sant Galdric as well. When your mother brought you and Josep back here she broke the link with all of that. No, the scores the Fascista will be looking to settle will be much more recent. My parents will be more vulnerable, like others in the village who have a son in the war. But the village will hold together, if needs be. No one will say a word.'*

*Joana shivered again. You really believe that if everyone sticks together we'll be all right? She didn't voice the question – it was useless for now to speculate, and all they could do was hope. There might yet be a negotiated settlement.*

*'Meet me tomorrow, behind the byre,' Alex was saying, and she nodded and kissed him with a fervour that made no concessions to being in church. She would meet him anywhere. It might be their last chance for a long time.*

*In the weeks after Alex's visit little or no news came to Sant Galdric. Nobody was travelling, except for one fruitless journey made by Uncle Victor with a mule and cart to try to get more hay for the sheep. He came back with some meagre sheaves for which he had paid with three valuable livestock, and some news that Barcelona was being fought for street by street, by civilians and military alike. They heard aeroplanes rumbling in the distance, and could imagine the bombardment which must be taking place, both in Barcelona and in coastal towns nearer to Girona. Barcelona had been so grievously bombed in the last year that it was a wonder anything still stood, or so it was said.*

*Alex had left on 8th January. It was nearly three weeks later that they heard the planes that bombed Girona. Oh my God, thought Joana, this is it! Barcelona must have fallen and they're attacking Girona now. The bombs fell with a dull boom, which resonated up the valley towards them and seemed to amplify as it echoed immediately back from the mountains above. The villagers gathered together in the square to listen, in silence, Uncle Victor with his arm round Grandma Aina, and Mama standing erect and calm, with one arm around each of her children. Little Josep, who normally never stayed still, stood as silent as them all in the arc of his mother's arm, his eyes huge as they saw the planes curve round above them after the sound of the bombs had ceased, heading for their base back south.*

*And then the silence was deafening, and all you could do was imagine, and wait, and worry. On 5th February, after five more bombardments, they heard that Girona had fallen, not like Barcelona, where they'd fought for every street corner – this time there was no army left to resist, and the word was the Nationalists had just walked into the city. Joana held her breath and waited for news from Alex. Surely among all the refugees making their way out of the cities he could find a way to walk home? But Sant Galdric wasn't on a route to anywhere and no one came this way – there was no news, no visitors, just silence and hunger, and to her shame Joana found herself longing for something to happen, even though it would almost certainly be bad news. But Alex might come – surely Alex would come.*

*At home her mother continued as patiently as ever to make soup from practically nothing, and to cook rice and potatoes. Straggling refugees finally appeared in the village, thin, hungry and very cold, with stories of a mass flight of the army and thousands of civilians across the border to France. As the village got hungrier and the numbers to feed grew greater, Victor and the other shepherds killed two sheep, splitting the meat between the houses. It was a desperate thing to do – these were female sheep and the life of the village in the future depended on their offspring. Once they'd done this, though, they took the remaining sheep far away from the village, where nobody could find and steal them. There was too much hunger, and too many strangers around whom they distrusted.*

*It was just a few days later, in mid February, that the first victorious troops appeared in the village, just one rattling truck with about a dozen dirtily clad soldiers, waving the Nationalist flag and hooting their horn. People hid, but the soldiers banged on the doors and demanded that everyone come out of their houses, and slowly the villagers did so, grouping again in the square, all together, facing the soldiers, murmuring* sotto voce.

*Joana heard Victor whispering to her mother.*

*'Look, isn't that young Sergi Olivera, old Carla's grandson? What is he doing here among that lot?'*

*'Goodness knows! I haven't seen him in the village for nearly a year. He wasn't a Fascista back then, or at least no one said so! But knowing his father, it shouldn't surprise me!'*

*'His mother would turn in her grave! She was a fine woman.'*

*'Well, and so was the boy, until the mother died and he was left with that rogue of a father. I used to feel sorry for the poor little bugger – but who'd have thought he'd end up with that evil bunch!'*

*Joana looked across at the group of soldiers, armed with a mixture of rifles and revolvers, and there he was in the middle of the group, talking to an older man who looked like the officer in charge. Sergi! Why she knew him! Last summer he'd been among the young men who hung around the square and ogled the girls, and he'd made it clear he liked her more than all the rest. She remembered a comment he'd made that had shocked her at the time.*

*'You'll take some flowering yet, my beautiful girl, but one day you'll be ripe and ready for me to pluck. So don't take any of these village idiots while I'm away. Keep yourself for a real man, and I'll be back!'*

*He'd held her arm and stroked his hand down her back, and she'd been frightened a little by his sheer manliness, but he wasn't seriously threatening, not there in the village square with Alex nearby.*

*Now Sergi was even broader and more muscular*

*than he'd been all those months ago – and he'd become a Nationalist soldier. When had he made that decision, she wondered? Had he decided to join the winning side, enlisting so late? Somehow it didn't surprise her – there was something of the profiteer about Sergi, and anyone that Alex had disliked was not to be trusted.*

*She shrank back behind her uncle. Oh God, Alex, she thought, you told me this wouldn't happen in Sant Galdric! Did Sergi bring those people here? What do they want with us?*

*What they were looking for, it seemed, were runaway Republican soldiers. Half a dozen of the men were dispatched to search the houses, and the rest advanced behind the officer in charge to stand right in front of the villagers.*

*'Right, Olivera, you know these people! I'm sick of going through villages and finding that everyone has suddenly turned into a loyal Nationalist! All these bastard Catalans are filthy Communists, we know that. So tell me who is who here that we should know about.'*

*To be fair to Sergi he looked very uncomfortable as his eyes shifted along the little crowd, and when he caught his grandmother's eye he flinched. The old lady stood stock-still, her eyes gazing at him in despair from behind her thick headscarf, and he dropped his eyes from hers and turned to the officer.*

*'I don't live here,' he explained. 'My father left here years ago, and I just come up on holiday sometimes to see my grandmother. They're pretty quiet-living people here – it's a dump of a village with nothing going for it.*

*They probably don't even know what's been happening out there in the real world.'*

*The officer frowned and tapped his foot impatiently, clearly unsatisfied, and Sergi turned searching eyes and pointed suddenly to someone in the crowd. 'That family,' he called out. 'They have a son fighting for the Communists. That one I know. The son's called Felip, Felip Companys.'*

*'Companys? That's the name of your Catalan chief, isn't it? The one who calls himself your president! President, hah!' the officer spat. 'President of a bunch of monkeys who thought they could stand up against the real Spain! Where's the guy's father?'*

*Joana clutched her uncle's hand as one of their close neighbours was pulled out from the group.*

*'So you're a Companys, eh? Related to that cowardly bastard who's now running for cover in France, are you? No? Well, that's what you say now! But you're a sympathiser, aren't you? You all are! And you sent your son to give him a hand!' The officer's eyes bored into Companys, standing helpless in front of him, and suddenly he punched him, low down in the belly, with the butt of his revolver, so that he doubled up with an agonised grunt. His wife screamed, and ran forward, but the officer brushed her aside, catching her cheek with the edge of the gun without even glancing her way.*

*'Take him away,' he ordered, and from behind him two men leapt forward to grab Companys, and dragged him to the truck, dumping him in the back and jumping in beside him. Small sobs came from the ground where his wife lay.*

*The officer turned to Sergi. 'That can't be all,' he*

*muttered. 'This is the type of village that breeds sloppy anarchists who think they know better than the people who gave them their land and look after them. There must be other Republican supporters here.'*

*Sergi shook his head, and the officer stared him down, and then turned angrily to a man who looked like his deputy.*

*'What about you? You know anyone here?'*

*The man shook his head as well. 'I'm from Barcelona, sir! I don't suppose any of these bumpkins have been near Barcelona in their lives.'*

*The officer paced impatiently around the crowd, his eyes raking over each frightened figure. Nobody moved an inch. Next to her Victor had his eyes fixed on the ground, but Joana couldn't help watching the man's angry, vengeful progress. He caught her eye, and she lowered her head in a hurry, but he stopped beside her and held out his gun to sweep her hair back from her face.*

*'Well, look what we have here!' he leered. 'Who'd have thought this miserable region could produce a beauty like this? What's your name,* belleza*?'*

*'Joana, sir.' She tried to keep her voice steady.*

*'Joana? What kind of name is that?' The anger was back in his voice. 'A Catalan aberration, that's what that is! Call yourself by your decent Spanish name, my girl! Juana, that's what a decent Christian name should be! What are your family names?'*

*She bit her lip and answered him. 'Vigo Garriga, sir. My name is Juana Vigo Garriga.'*

*She saw the deputy beside him start, and touch his*

*superior's arm. 'Now that's odd, sir! An odd combination of names, I mean. Vigo isn't a Catalan name, and I've never met another one around here, but there was a Vigo in Barcelona who worked alongside a guy called Luis Garriga a few years ago. And this girl carries both their names! They ran a filthy, left-wing newspaper, and we crushed it in '34, when we had a right-thinking government in power. I was in the police then in Barcelona, and I remember we arrested Vigo, but we never caught the man Garriga.'*

*'Is that so?' The officer's eyes narrowed. A smile came to his face, and he grabbed hold of Joana's arm and pulled her forward. His face was so close to hers that she could feel the warmth in his frosted breath. 'So, my little beauty,' he purred. 'Do you have a famous little revolutionary for a father?'*

*'My father is dead, sir.'*

*'Perhaps, but that's not an answer! Was he this Vigo we are hearing about?'*

*Joana stared helplessly into the eyes that were raking hers. What could she say? A shiver shook her and her tongue wouldn't work. Suddenly her grandmother stepped out of the crowd behind her.*

*'You are talking about my son-in-law, Señor, and also about my son. My son-in-law is dead, and my daughter with him, and my son has disappeared from our lives, and probably lives some comfortable life in Paris, or London, or somewhere like that. He might as well be dead too, for all he is worth to this family. I brought this child back to the village when they were all gone, to raise her decently in the ways of the Church. I don't care about politics, but I love*

*the Lord, sir, and when those Republicans started killing our priests I renounced my son forever.'*

*Around her Joana could almost hear people holding their breath. She herself cast her eyes to the ground, holding herself completely still as though she could make herself less conspicuous. What would Sergi do? Would he betray them? He knew fine well that her mother was alive and in the group, and he knew that whatever old Aina may have thought of the Republicans she would never really renounce her son.*

*The officer hadn't moved, and he still held Joana by the arm. She heard a movement next to him, and a voice, speaking low. She risked a glance up and froze when she saw Sergi talking into the officer's ear. But whatever he was saying, his words had an unexpected effect. A slow grin came onto the officer's face, and he spoke out almost jovially to Sergi.*

*'Is that so, you young dog? Well, we'll leave her to you, then!'*

*He leered one more time into Joana's face and let her go.*

*'Go give their house a special check, though,' he said to his deputy. 'Olivera, you can go too, and take the girl and the old woman with you. Lover boy or no lover boy, I want them to show you all their correspondence.'*

*Joana looked round for her grandmother. Poor Aina looked as though she was about to faint, so Joana took her arm and supported her as they followed Sergi and the other man to their house. There she and Aina huddled together in a corner as the officer searched cupboards, and pulled out drawers and threw every item of their belongings on the floor. Sergi stayed by them, and when the officer had gone up the wooden stairs to the bedrooms he turned to Joana.*

*'I told them we were engaged,' he said, with a smile of satisfaction. 'I could have lost my job, there! See what I do for you, Joana?'*

*'You let them take Joaquim away! Poor Joaquim Companys!' Grandma Aina was crying now, distressed tears for her neighbour, for the terrible lie she had told against her son, for the violation of her village.*

*'Yes, but that was necessary, don't you see? They wanted someone, and they wouldn't have gone away without taking someone with them, but old Companys' son is a nobody, and they'll soon realise it and let the old man go in a few weeks! What I didn't do, little Joana, is shop the family of that old boyfriend of yours! They've got a son fighting as well, haven't they? Well, I made sure no one found out about him!'*

*Joana could only stare. Did he know about her and Alex? Had it been that obvious even last year when Sergi was here? She caught a breath, more like a sob, and stammered, 'Boyfriend?'*

*'No boyfriend, sweetheart? Well if you're no longer with him, all the better. Will you be grateful to me, little one, when I come back here in a few weeks' time? I'll get away from the regiment for a while, you'll see, and I'll come up to see you. I hope the whole village will be suitably grateful, but you, Joana, you especially!'*

*He pulled a lock of her hair as he spoke, bending her head back a little so she looked straight into his eyes. What he saw there made him frown.*

*'Don't be afraid of me,* belleza. *You are so beautiful I want to kiss that soft mouth of yours, but I won't until you ask me to. I don't mean you any harm. I want you to belong to me, so remember that and forget anyone else you may have been flirting with.' He lowered his voice to a caress. 'Didn't I just save you, sweetheart? Trust me, and all will be fine.'*

*'T-thank you,' was all she managed to say, but he seemed satisfied. The officer came down the stairs. He had her mother's delicate gold necklace in his hand, the one which Papa had given her. It was the only thing of value in the house. He pocketed it without a blink, and with a gesture to Sergi to follow him he left the house.*

# Chapter Eleven

Carla sat in the back of the car with Grandma, in silence, while Martin made semi-awkward conversation with Toni in the front. Toni still didn't entirely trust Martin, it would seem. Was it because he seemed overly friendly with Mama?

She wondered what had happened at the hill house this afternoon to bring about such a change of heart from Mama. 'She didn't know you were pregnant. She didn't know any of what your father had done,' was all Martin would tell Carla.

'And she cared?'

'Yes, she cared. She wants you and the baby safe.'

It seemed an odd way to feel safe, to be going up to her parents' home, where her father might turn up at any time, but even Toni seemed to concur that it was the last place Sergi would visit at this time of year. There was to be a major conference in Girona next month. There was talk of some changes in leadership. Toni had heard from Sergi's other driver that Sergi was having to fight hard to keep his position. He wouldn't leave Girona just now, and certainly not to visit his wife.

Carla wanted to know more. Why was Mama up in the hills? Was there a problem, then, that Papa didn't want to see her? Toni just grunted non-committally. Ask her, was the reply. But Carla struggled to imagine asking her mother anything of the sort.

She leant into Grandma. Thank God Grandma had come with her. But it must be even harder for Maria than for herself. Maria and Joana hadn't met for how many years? Ten? Fifteen? Twenty? The last time they'd really needed a favour and only Maria could ask it? When would that have been? When Uncle Victor had lost his land she knew they'd gone to Joana, but it had done no good. Had Grandma seen her daughter then?

They drove through Sant Galdric in the dark, without stopping. Carla watched Grandma intently, trying to follow her eyes, but there were so few lights on anywhere. Were the houses all empty, or did people just go to bed early here? Grandma's face gave nothing away, and when Carla reached for her hand she gave it a quick squeeze but said nothing.

From the village they snaked through the dark up the hill, to where Mama was waiting. By the time the house came into sight Carla was rigid with nerves. You could see the lights on the veranda from far down the hill. Trees surrounded the house on three sides, but the run up to it had been cleared, so that it was visible for many kilometres from the valley below. It had been built of stone, to look like a landowner's hunting lodge of yesteryear. And yet it was a latter-day folly of her father's, this absurd edifice built deliberately above the village that had spurned him, in imitation of all the people he wanted to be.

The car swung around the house to park at the rear, and there, almost rigid to attention, stood Mama, looking anxious, and apparently just as nervous as Carla. Toni stepped out of the car first, and Joana almost jumped on him.

'Did it go all right?' she asked him. 'You weren't seen? You've been an age!'

'No, we weren't seen, I'm sure of that. But I had to park a long way from the apartment, to be sure, and we waited for Victor to come home, so that he would know what was happening, and that Maria was coming with us.'

There was an understandable stress in Toni's voice. This must be the first time he had acted for Joana in something that could get him sacked by Sergi, if ever he found out. It made Joana an accomplice whom they needed to trust – a new role for them all.

Toni opened the rear door for Maria to get out of the car. Carla sat still for now, just watching. She registered what might have been shock in Joana's eyes. It had been a long time since Grandma and Joana had met, and Grandma had aged.

'My daughter,' Maria said, in her usual gentle tones, and Joana reached forward and kissed her cheeks, punctilious but awkward.

'How are you mother? And my uncle?'

Then Toni came round and pulled open Carla's door, and she had to get out of the car herself. She moved to the front of the car, stiff, edgy, fingers clenched by her side, aware of her gaunt face, her over-thin arms, her huge belly, her worn-out eyes, and stood waiting for Joana's reaction. To her surprise Joana's face twisted, and she came forward in a rush to put her arms around Carla's shoulders, avoiding crushing the tight bump.

The last time I saw her, she wouldn't even look at me, and I could have gone to the devil for all she cared, thought Carla. She stood unyielding, and after a moment Joana withdrew her arms. But she didn't move away.

'Dear Carla,' she whispered. 'My poor child. Come inside.'

They sat in near silence at the dining table as Paula served them, watching Carla with slightly horrified eyes as she heaped far too much stew on to her plate. Grandma sat close to Carla, her eyes scanning this house, which she had never seen, appraising the antique furniture, the gold leaf framed paintings, the thick brocade curtains, which a government official's salary should never have been able to buy, and brought her gaze again and again back to Joana, with grave questions in her eyes that she would not speak.

It was Joana who asked the questions – brisk, commanding questions to fill the silence. They hadn't been visited at the apartment that day? All had been well? They'd brought enough clothes? Maria answered, the briefest of answers to each question, until finally Carla spoke, tense and watchful.

'Martin said you've got some kind of idea of how to

help me, something you want to tell me. Are you going to get Luc out of gaol for me?'

It cut through Joana's small talk, and silenced her for a moment. When she answered, it was equally directly. 'I don't know. I have some information that I've been keeping, and which could damage your father. I'm not sure how to use it, or what effect it might have. I need to think. We can talk about it tomorrow.'

So Mama had already thought she might need some ammunition against Papa? What on earth had brought about such a change of heart? What had happened to that lovely life in Girona? To the dinners and the soirées the Oliveras always graced together?

'Why are you here?' she shot at her mother. 'Why have you stayed up here at the hill house all this time? Martin wouldn't tell me anything. He just said father wanted you to stay here, and told me to ask you about it myself.'

She kept her eyes on Joana, who shifted her gaze, but then looked first at Grandma and then at Carla, and seemed to decide to tell the truth.

'Your father is tired of me, Carla. He has mistresses, and I get in the way. So he leaves me up here.'

'And why do you accept it? You must be bored to tears.' Carla couldn't feel pity. All she felt was a flat kind of curiosity. Joana seemed to be scrutinising the question, turning it over in her head as though she too was looking for the answer.

'Something has gone wrong in your father's life in the last couple of years,' she said at last, 'and he seems to be losing his grip politically. Younger men are coming in, and

Sergi is worried, I know. He's more and more angry at home, and he's becoming increasingly unpredictable. He wants to control everything, even more than ever, as though he needs to prove something to himself. And when he gets angry, he directs it at me. I became frightened of him, to tell the truth. I've been sitting up here for the last few months trying to decide what to do. And feeling sorry for myself, and drinking too much, if you must know.'

She looked an appeal across at Carla and Maria. It was an appeal Carla rejected.

'I've not been having the greatest time myself in the last few months, Mama, if the truth be told.'

Joana flinched, and Martin, who'd been sitting silent on the other side of the table, got up and moved round behind her. He laid a hand on her shoulder.

'You're both his victims,' he said quietly, looking over at Carla. 'And at least you know now just why Sergi has been so obsessed with keeping you under his control.'

Carla watched him. So you're her champion now are you, she wanted to throw at him, but she knew it was unfair. Martin had the same quality as Grandma – he was intuitively caring, and wouldn't refuse anyone his goodwill. Keep your anger for Sergi, she told herself.

She nodded agreement as she answered Martin. 'If my father's political career is under threat then I can see why my relationship with Luc was so worrying,' she said. 'If his adversaries got wind of it they could have a field day using it against him. But Mama, if he's become even more volatile and violent, what will he do to you if you use your information against him?' She shivered involuntarily as she spoke.

'Who said it will be me who uses it? Leave it until tomorrow, my love. As I said, I have some thinking to do, but I am beginning to formulate a plan.'

Grandma rose from her chair looking worn out and frailer than usual.

'I think we should all leave everything until tomorrow,' she said. 'This old lady is tired, and going to bed, if Paula will show me where I'm going.' She turned towards Joana, and placed her hand on her shoulder where Martin's had been just a few minutes earlier.

'We mustn't let you take any risks, though, Joana. I have no idea about your life with your husband, but it seems to me that you already pay a very high price for all this.' She waved her free hand around the ornate dining room. 'The highest price being that you nearly lost our Carla, of course, and your grandchild. But there must be no more prices paid, not by anybody.'

Her voice was as measured and gentle as ever, and Joana hesitated, and then reached up her own hand to cover Maria's, very briefly, before Carla came forward to take Grandma's arm and lead her out to Paula.

'You'll be tired yourself, child,' said Grandma, as Carla leant into her for an embrace.

'Exhausted,' Carla admitted, rubbing her heavy belly. She could barely keep herself upright. 'I'll be up myself in a couple of minutes.'

She returned to the dining room, where Joana was picking up her bag and her evening shawl, preparing to go upstairs. Martin was standing by the door, like an usher in attendance on them all, Carla thought.

'Carla, tell me,' Joana asked, as soon as she came into the room. 'When did your grandmother start wearing that headscarf? Was it after old Aina died?'

Carla nodded. 'I think so.'

Joana sighed. 'It's such a curse, the old habit of going into blacks like that. The old ladies never come out of it once they're there.'

'She doesn't always wear a black scarf, though,' Carla replied. 'She has some flowered ones and white lace ones she wears as well. She just put the black one on today.'

'To come and see me!' Joana sighed again. Carla stayed silent. 'Tell me,' Joana continued, 'how is Uncle Victor? Has he settled in Girona? Does he like his job there?'

Carla thought before replying. 'He never talks about it. I think it's his way of coping. He just comes home each night and shuts the door on Girona, apart from going to the bar sometimes with a few cronies, and I think they're all from the hills around here too, originally.'

She pulled her oversized cardigan around her shoulders. 'Grandma says he only moved to Girona because he lost his land. It was a huge blow to him, she told me. How did he come to lose it? Did Papa take the land away from him? Is that another thing he was responsible for?'

Joana shook her head. 'No, poor Victor lost his land to a company building a quarry. Your father wasn't involved with that project, but he could have helped Victor, perhaps. He always said not, but he couldn't really be bothered, and even back then I'd already lost most of my influence over him. Sergi just said Victor could never make any money on the land anyway, and should do like everyone else and move to the city. There are jobs for everyone now, that's what he says, and everyone can prosper if they dump their old ideas and move with the times.'

'He despised them.' Carla's words were a statement, not a question. 'I remember listening to him when I was a child, talking about the villages as if the people in them were little better than mules.'

'He came from Sant Galdric himself, or at least his father did!'

'Yes, and he wanted it forgotten! And so did you, Mama, so did you, with your city friends and fine clothes and shops. When were you last in the village? What do you know about anyone who lives there now? Oh, it's not an accusation – we've had all those. But Luc used to say that Franco wanted everyone to idolise the old country values, but actually saw the rural poor as sheep to be led by the nose. And because Catalans are rebellious, and still can't be trusted to be his sheep, the government has allowed all the new business partners to walk all over us and our country, from the new seaside playgrounds to our poor, empty villages.'

Carla waited for Joana to disagree, but in fact she smiled at her, wearily, but it was a smile.

'Maybe your Luc is right after all. He talks like Uncle Luis, and like my own father. I used to believe every word they said at one time. Their ideas didn't work, though, and their great Republic fell into chaos. Shall we leave the big issues for tonight, my daughter, and get to bed? We have some more personal battles to fight at the moment, and I need some sleep if I'm to figure out what's best to do!'

They mounted the stairs together, all three of them, and at the top Joana turned and continued their conversation.

'You know, between Uncle Victor and my mother I think it's her I feel for most. Victor led most of his life in his own happy world, and even now that he has to work in Girona his sister has followed him to take care of him. But Mama, well after my father died she spent the rest of her life, all of it, looking after her mother, her children, her brother, scrimping and managing and making everyone's home. She never did anything that she chose for herself. And now she's old . . .' she added, her voice trailing off. 'And wearing that damned scarf . . .'

Carla was astounded. She'd lived over twenty years with her mother without ever hearing her talk about Grandma, not even her name, let alone any compassion. Where were all these confidences coming from?

'But you left her to it!' she answered, indignant. 'You abandoned them all there in Sant Galdric! You never did anything to help her!'

Joana looked at her, and in the gloom of the landing her eyes were unreadable.

'Do you think I don't know?' she said.

# Chapter Twelve

When they came down to breakfast the following morning, it was to be told that Joana had left soon after dawn with Toni in the car.

'Up to something, that's what she was,' Paula grumbled, as she plonked food grumpily on the table. Paula didn't like upheaval, and what with unexplained guests arriving by night, and then her mistress getting up at a time she'd never seen, and calling for Toni, poor Paula was at sixes and sevens.

'She said to tell you she wouldn't be back today, and not to fret, and I'm to serve you the lamb for lunch.' And with that Paula lumbered off, oblivious to the amazed trio she left behind her.

Carla, Martin and Maria were left to gape at each other over hot rolls and home-made jam. Carla couldn't help looking speculatively at Martin.

'Did Mama say anything to you? Do you know where she's gone?'

But he shook his head, and was clearly as bemused as she was. 'I can only guess she's gone down to Girona,' he said. 'After all, where else would she have gone?'

Carla nodded. 'Yesterday she said she had some thinking to do. She had some information she could use against my father, but wasn't sure how best to do so. Well I guess the night brought her some counsel. I just hope she hasn't put herself in danger in any way. My God, that woman can be frustrating! Why can't she share anything with us?'

It was Maria who responded, putting her coffee cup down placidly before wiping the corner of her mouth with her napkin. 'My goodness, but that's good coffee! Your mother's a strong-minded woman, Carla – some might even say pig-headed. Her daughter reminds me of her! But she has thought about whatever she's doing, I'm sure. We can only be patient, and enjoy this coffee, and this view, and wait for whatever she has to tell us.'

The wait should have been stressful, but in the end the day was oddly soothing. They were just a few kilometres from Sant Galdric, and Carla caught her grandmother looking frequently down the valley towards where the village stood hidden from them by the trees and the turn of the hills. Without a car the village might as well be a hundred times more distant. Maria was too old to want to make the journey on foot, and for Carla it was out of the question, even if they weren't supposed to be in hiding.

But the closeness of the village was in the air, and they talked about it, or Grandma did, and Carla and Martin listened. They learnt about their common grandparents, about the girl who'd seemed to have a fancy for Victor, but who had her head turned by the doctor's son from the next village, about the inspirational young teacher who'd come to the village out of the blue, and stayed for three years, long enough to set up a bond with Luis so strong that when he left he took Luis with him, to college in Barcelona.

'Our father hoped that Luis would come back and take over the village school himself,' Maria explained to them. 'But Luis had other, bigger ideas. He couldn't have been happy in Sant Galdric, not forever, but he was good to us all, and visited my mother often enough to stay her favourite!'

And did Victor never find another girl, Carla wanted to know? Not unless you counted a long-standing admiration for that same woman shopkeeper who'd helped Martin find a lift to the hill house the other day.

'But she's a fine-looking woman!' Martin exclaimed. 'What stopped Victor from pursuing that interest?'

'Her husband!' Maria chuckled. 'No, Victor was better single, I think, and adoring the ladies from afar! He's got some set old ways, has Victor, and likes his life just so.'

Carla and Martin walked after lunch along the forest tracks, and above them to a sunny crest where the view fell away before them in endless shades of green. Here Carla didn't walk the way she walked in Girona, urgently, restlessly, driving herself to forget. Here she walked slowly, stopping to examine the late flowers below the cork trees, and following the crickets that jumped across her path. The last time she had walked in the hills was last winter with Luc and his mother and brother. That had been a boisterous tramp over rough ground and through streams, full of action, full of talk. Here she simply meandered, with Martin by her side as though he had always been there, and with Luc, who seemed to walk with them. She even felt the touch of him by her side, and he was beside her all evening.

It was maybe because he seemed so close that she didn't get that awful feeling of losing him as she came out of sleep in the morning. Friday dawned serene and glorious over the hill house. Carla's window framed the sweep of the valley below, and the far summits, hazed peaks of indigo, which the dawn light gradually lit with flame to distinguish them from the sky. She'd slept with her curtains open, so that the dawn woke her slowly, and she lay in a peaceful limbo, watching the advancing light from her bed.

For the first time in months her dreams of Luc receded without leaving her in gut-wrenching dismay. A morning as magnificent as this had to bring something positive, and surely Mama was going to come up with something today.

All morning she and Martin were on the fidget, and by the afternoon Martin was driven to help Grandma roll some wool for knitting, because he was simply unable to sit still. When they heard the car at last, Martin leapt up and shot through the house, leaving the wool lying half ravelled. Carla was about to follow him when Grandma stopped her.

'Sit still, *carinyo*,' she urged her, with some humour. 'We all need to hear what Joana is going to say, and there is no way I'm going to go running anywhere! Or if you must move, just go and ask Paula to bring us some coffee.'

So Carla contained herself, and waited with Grandma

on the veranda. She was pleased that Grandma had worn a flowered scarf today – it would hopefully please Mama. *We need Mama on our side!*

But there was no sign that Joana even noticed as she whisked out with Martin a couple of minutes later, and threw herself into a rattan chair.

'Phew!' she expelled, as she threw an envelope onto the table in front of her, knocking a ball of wool to the floor. 'Well, Carla, there's your evidence!'

She had tense little lines round her eyes, and her hands twitched restlessly, fluttering the air, and creating little corresponding currents of tension in Carla.

Carla reached across the table to look more closely at the envelope, but didn't dare touch it. Joana looked up at her.

'You look a great deal better, my love,' she said.

'I've been catching up on sleep,' Carla acknowledged, and then, after a nervous pause, 'So how was Girona? You saw my father?'

Joana nodded. 'Yes, and what I had seen in his safe was still there, thank God. You see, it came to me the other night, while I was trying to think what to do, that the evidence I had wasn't quite what we needed. I needed more and I had to go to Girona to get it.'

She broke off as Paula brought the coffee, and drank her first cup straight back, proffering it to Paula to be refilled. She took a biscuit too, and ate it hungrily. Carla didn't remember ever seeing her mother so on edge.

'Bring me some champagne, Paula,' she ordered, peremptorily, and Paula grunted and went inside.

'Sergi is being blackmailed,' she continued, after Paula had left. 'You see, I was aware that a man has been coming to see Sergi from time to time that he didn't want me to meet. I saw the man when he came the first time, and I couldn't help being suspicious of his visits. Thankfully Sergi has no idea how aware of his life I am! And he doesn't know I have the combination to his safe either! Well, there was a letter in the safe – the letter the man wrote to ask for his first appointment.'

She looked around at her audience. She certainly had their full attention. 'I'm not saying this is true, but it is alleged that Sergi arranged for one of his political rivals to have a car accident, a hit-and-run affair.' She hesitated, but then continued, 'It was simply accepted as an accident at the time, at least officially. But then . . .' Joana paused again, and when she continued she spoke with some difficulty. 'But then it seems that Sergi had the man he'd employed to do the hit-and-run disposed of to kill off the evidence. That's what the blackmailer says, anyway. The hit-and-run driver had misgivings about Sergi after he'd done his job. Sergi must have frightened him, or somehow given some sign of what he was planning, so the driver left a letter with a friend, with all the details, to be used against Sergi if anything should happen to him.'

'And when the driver was killed, the friend decided to use the letter to blackmail Sergi, rather than give it to the police?' Martin asked.

'Exactly!'

Martin shivered. 'Dangerous, surely, if you knew what Sergi had already been capable of?'

'Not so far, it seems,' Joana answered. 'Sergi was still paying before the summer, and all the evidence of the blackmail is still there.'

'So what's in that envelope is . . .'

'Copies of everything the blackmailer sent to Sergi – his own letter asking for the meeting, and the photostat he made of the driver's evidence against Sergi. I had to go back, you see! I'd written down names and stuff from the letters, thinking that one day this information could be useful, if things kept getting worse with Sergi, but I never really thought of how. And I didn't actually have photostats.'

Carla bit her lip, and held out a hand tentatively towards the envelope. 'Can I see?' she asked, and found that her voice stuck a little.

Joana nodded. Carla waited while Paula shuffled back out with a tray of glasses and the inevitable champagne bottle, and then she reached forward and took the envelope onto her lap. She drew out a number of sheets of thin copy paper, which shook flimsily in the breeze – or was it that her hand shook? I don't want to read this, she thought, but then pulled herself together. Being careful not to let the sheets slip, she flicked through and saw that some were duplicates. Mama had thought to make several copies. There were actually only three pages she needed to read. One was the typed letter from the blackmailer requesting an interview 'regarding the letter enclosed'. He had a pseudonym, and a *poste restante* mailing address, but surely Sergi would have found out quite soon who his blackmailer was? She moved on to the dead driver's letter.

This was handwritten in poor, uneducated script, and

took some deciphering, but its content was detailed and just as chilling as Carla had feared. Was it conclusive enough, though? It was only one man's word, and that man was dead, but there were some facts that could be corroborated, surely? She studied it intently, frowning at the words in an attempt to make them speak to her. Then she shook her head to clear it, and passed the letters to Martin.

'See what you make of those,' she said to him, then turned to Joana. 'There's a lot of accusation in there, but is there really enough factual evidence to pin the hit-and-run on my father?'

Her voice came out tense but muted, and Joana responded in the same tone. 'No, probably not, but there's enough to cause him huge political damage, otherwise he wouldn't have paid up.'

'Why doesn't he just bump off the blackmailer?' Carla asked, and then wondered, appalled, at how easily the thought came to her, and how normal it seemed to imagine her father doing so.

'I don't know. If the guy has any sense he'll have the original letter well hidden, and will hold out the threat that if anything happens to him another party will release the originals to the authorities.'

A sudden wave of revulsion came over Carla, so strong that she felt sick. 'Mama, do you realise that this is my father we're talking about here? He's a cold-blooded murderer, for heaven's sake! He probably killed the driver himself, because if he'd hired someone he would just have set up another potential blackmailer. Did he use a gun do you think, or a knife? Whatever it was it was in complete cold blood. God help me, Mama,' she finished on a horrified whisper. 'You're just his wife, but me, I carry his genes. He's gone from being a power-hungry bully to a calculating killer. And this is my father!'

Martin looked up from his reading of the documents.

'Joana!' he said, urgently.

Joana frowned him down, but he persisted. 'You must tell her now! You can't leave things like this! Surely this is when you have to tell her?'

What did he mean? Carla looked a query at her mother. 'Tell me what, Mama?'

Joana's face was bleached of colour, and suddenly she looked ten years older. She took a quick gulp from her glass, choking a little on the bubbles. Carla looked for help to Grandma. Maria looked just as bemused as she was, but she spoke up for them both, as gently as ever.

'What is it, Joana?' Maria asked.

Joana shook her head violently. 'No, no, I can't!' she cried.

Maria repeated the same words, 'What is it, Joana?' and as she spoke, Joana's face crumpled, and she began to weep.

'Oh God, how to tell you now, after all these years? Do you remember, Mama, way back before I married Sergi, when I was friendly with Alex, Enric the baker's son? He wanted to marry me, but he couldn't tell his family yet, because he was still training. And then when the Civil War ended he disappeared. We never knew why, but we knew he died – his father found that out. And I found out that I was pregnant – with Carla. So when Sergi wanted to marry me I had no choice. I was just relieved.'

Carla took hold of Grandma's hand. Neither of them moved. Grandma's hand didn't even twitch. The afternoon was chilling into evening, and Joana shivered, and drew a hand to wipe her bleached white cheek. Carla watched through a haze as Martin felt for her mother's other hand. Soon we'll all join hands and make a circle, she thought, and suddenly wanted to laugh. The baby moved inside her, pushing against her stomach wall, and she could almost hear it gurgle. Sergi was not her father. He was not her father. Her father was not her father. Could this be true?

'Then he's not . . .' She couldn't finish the sentence.

Joana shook her head and took another gulp of champagne. 'Sergi isn't your father, Carla.'

It was all she said, but it was enough. It made it real. And it explained so much – why he had always been so cold, why he resented her so much. She'd always known he wanted a son, but even worse, the daughter he was lumbered with wasn't even of his own blood. His last words to her came back to her, that day when he'd thrown her out of the Girona house.

'You're a shame to my name and I wish you didn't bear it. But while you're known to be my daughter you'll toe the line or I'll simply make you.'

She carried his name, but not his blood. As the truth of it sank in a wave of something like relief flooded through her. How often had she fantasised that this was the case, that she was not his daughter? As a child she'd woven fairy stories in which she was a changeling, or the baby of some kindly, simple people, who were unknowingly raising Sergi's real daughter. Her fair, elegant, remote mother, her stocky, aggressive father – neither had belonged to her in her dreams, and in the world of fairy tales her tall, dark father, with her own long nose and angular frame, came to find her one day, and she escaped with him through a hole in the garden wall.

She'd outgrown the fairy tale, but her denial of her parents had only increased with the years. She looked across at Joana now, whose frozen gaze watched anxiously for her reaction. She looked nothing like her. So was the dark father of her dreams, whom she'd modelled simply on herself, actually a close image of her real father?

Joana's gaze disturbed her. She felt she ought to be angry, but she was too dazed for anger. Don't demand a response from me right now, Mama, she thought. You've left me without words.

Grandma was looking at Carla as though she'd seen a blinding light. 'Alex Figarola!' she muttered. 'Of course! How could I have been so stupid?'

'You weren't to know, Mama. We never made our engagement public, or even how close we were, and you had so much else to worry about!'

'But you didn't tell me!' Maria's voice was full of grief. 'You just upped and left and announced you were going to marry Sergi, and I never understood, never helped you!'

'I didn't want help! I knew Alex was dead, and I felt dead myself – and Sergi seemed kind then. He knew I was pregnant, and still he wanted to marry me. Why shouldn't I go with him? If I'd told you why, what would it have changed?'

Carla watched as the past was wrenched open between

them, like an old wound exposed. She'd rarely seen her grandmother so distressed – in fact she looked stricken, while Joana's face was bleak but defiant. For Carla, darling *Avia* Maria was her confidant and support, and it was Joana whom she found unapproachable, so she struggled to identify with her mother just now. But who was she to judge? Joana would have been so young – seventeen – and feeling vulnerable, in a time of turmoil and loss. She'd made her choice, and she wasn't now going to go back on it. You made your bed, Mama, and since then we've all had to lie on it!

It was Martin who moved first to ease the strain and patch the wounds. He stood up and poured another glass of champagne, and moved across to put it in Maria's hand.

'When I arrived at your home in Girona,' he told Maria, 'Victor made you take a glass with us all, for my sake. So won't you just take a small glass with us now for Joana's sake? Not for the past, and all the bad times, but for the present, and because we're at least here together?'

Maria looked at him, and down at the glass, and then back up at him in gentle amusement. 'You're trying to make an old lady drink, *estimado* Martí? Well I will! I'll join my daughter in a toast to her daughter, to our Carla, and the miracle that she's here, whoever's child she is. But if you want me to toast in earnest, then let's wait until you've all worked that other miracle, and have brought that poor boy Luc home to be with her.'

The thought of Luc changed the mood, from raw memories and confrontation to sobering thought. Carla gripped her glass hard, as her guts churned in both hope and fear, and the baby kicked a reminder against her stomach wall that time was not on their side.

'Next week!' she said, with determination. 'We have to get him free by next week. But how do we do it? How can we use those letters? Maybe it's time I paid a visit to my supposed father in Girona to show him what we have against him.'

It was Martin who answered, speaking to Joana. 'You took them from his safe, Joana – won't he know that? You were in the house in Girona only this morning, and if Carla turns up at his door tomorrow with this ammunition in her hands he's bound to smell a rat!'

'I don't know that. He hardly registered me passing through, except to warn me not to hang around, because my presence was inconvenient! I told him I'd come down to buy a new coat, because it's getting cold up here, and he was so keen to see the back of me that he gave me money to buy it with.' She hesitated for a moment. 'There's just one other thing I have to tell you though, Mama. Toni found out from Sergi's driver that they went to your apartment last night to look for Carla. They didn't find her, of course, and Uncle Victor wasn't there either.'

Maria had frozen, but relaxed a little at the last words. Carla reached for her. 'Victor will have gone out to the bar, since we've left him alone,' she reassured her. 'You know how he hates being in the apartment on his own!' She shivered, 'But thank God we left when we did or otherwise I'd be in Sergi's hands right now! If I have my way, then after tomorrow he'll leave us all alone for good!'

'How did Sergi take the news that Carla had flown?' Martin wanted to know.

Joana rubbed her cheek, and Carla noticed a bluish tinge that hadn't been obvious before. So Sergi had taken his frustration out on his wife.

'He wasn't a happy man last night,' Joana admitted, ruefully. 'That was when he told me in no uncertain terms to be gone by the time he got back from Barcelona tonight.'

'He was going to Barcelona?'

'Yes, Carla. In a very bad mood indeed.' She drew a breath before continuing. 'I have to say I wondered if he was going to see Josep, since he didn't find you at Victor's.'

Maria's face creased in worry. 'He's gone to Josep?'

Carla's hand was resting on Grandma's, on the arm of her chair. She reached out to take her hand.

'Don't worry too much, Grandma. Uncle Josep is made of strong stuff.' She sighed. 'I just hope my father didn't frighten the children. And who else does he know about among my friends that he might visit and bully? Where is it all going to end?'

'With the letters?' Martin suggested.

'Yes, the letters! We can end it all with those letters, surely. But what do I tell him? Where did I get them from?' Carla asked. 'Just tell me what to say about where I got them from so I don't implicate Mama, and then I'll be down there to see him tomorrow. It's Saturday, so I should find him at home.'

Joana frowned. 'He's got some political rally to attend during the day, but he should be home by early evening. But what are you planning to do exactly, Carla?'

'Why, confront him, of course, and make him release Luc. If he has been prepared to pay a blackmailer because he fears what these papers could do to him, then they must be serious enough to warrant him letting Luc go, especially if I promise him that afterwards we'll disappear and not bother him anymore.'

'You feel you can do it?'

'Oh yes, I can do it! I have to!'

Joana nodded. 'Yes, you're right, and it's probably the only way, but take care. I don't want my husband ruined – he saved me and gave me a life, and I will always owe him – but I don't want you harmed either, *carinyo*, and I know how you two can inflame each other. He sees Luc as a dangerous leftie, I'm sure, and as for you, well I did foist you on him, didn't I?' She sighed. 'Poor Sergi, in many ways. He so needs to be in control, and this whole regime has fostered that side of him. I don't know where his need for power comes from, but it makes him dangerous, I admit, and you – well, you are a very personal thorn in his flesh.'

Carla looked at her mother. 'I'll have the ammunition, though, won't I, Mama? I've never had any ammunition before when dealing with him, and I can promise you I'll be very careful how I use it, and not push him too far. The key person in danger will be you, like Martin says, if Sergi has any suspicion that these documents came from you.'

'I need to come with you Carla,' Martin spoke up suddenly. 'You can't go on your own. And if I'm there, couldn't you just make out that I'm someone who knows his blackmailer, or who knew the dead driver or someone?

You don't have to say anything openly, just imply a connection, and refuse to answer questions. It'll be a game of bluff, anyway, and if he thinks you've had contact with his blackmailer, then he won't suspect Joana of having anything to do with giving you the letters.'

Carla looked at Martin's tense, eager face and knew she would accept his company on this visit. She didn't want to go alone, and she needed support. A week ago she wouldn't have believed it possible to have such powerful weaponry to fire at Sergi, but firing it would not be easy. It took every mental picture of Luc in his prison cell to give her the courage, and make it seem possible.

'Come with me, then, cousin Martin,' she said to him. 'We've thrown enough at you already, and I need you too much to leave you behind this time. Come and help me stay strong and focused, and stop me from reminding him I'm not actually his daughter. He mustn't know I've been told that, because only Mama could have told me. Between us we'll manage not to implicate Mama, and I'll be his hateful, errant daughter, just as I've been for years. But you know Mama, that's the real toast this afternoon. It was the best news you've ever given me. Sergi Olivera may be a nasty murderer without compassion or morals, but he's not my father! He's not my father, and now, by God, he's going to have to give me back my life!'

# Chapter Thirteen

Carla and Martin stood in the shadow of a tree, a little down the road from the house in Girona, waiting in anxious silence for Sergi to come home. It was already nearly dusk, and lights had come on in some of the houses. Martin checked his watch again and again, but they'd been here for a long time, and they knew they hadn't missed Sergi's arrival. The only issue was whether he would come home at all, or whether the event would go on all evening. If so they would have to come back tomorrow.

Maria had come down with them to Girona, and they had left her furiously cleaning up the apartment. There were lingering signs of the visit by Sergi's men. Victor had clearly done his best to tidy up, but it looked as though the contents of all the drawers had been dumped on the floor, and ornaments swept off the sideboard, and poor Victor, as Maria had said, would never really know where to replace things. They helped her as much as they could to put things to rights, but she shooed them aside, because they were getting things wrong, so after a while they left her to it. Victor wouldn't work a full day today, and by the time he came home from work she would no doubt have had everything just so, and fresh food prepared as well. Toni had gone back to the hill house after dropping them all at the apartment. All three of them, Maria, Carla and Martin, would stay in Girona this night.

As they stood watching the street Carla thought how bizarre it was to be walking into Sergi's house, when she had been fleeing him for days. This was the lion's den, and her last memory of it was from just such an evening, pretty much a year ago exactly, when she had faced Sergi's furious ultimatum, and walked out to try to complete her studies on her own.

Would it be different today? It felt different to be arriving with Martin by her side, and the all-important documents in her hand, but the stakes had become so high. Her entire future, and that of her baby and Luc, depended on coming out of this encounter a victor.

She shivered, and Martin put a reassuring arm around her, and as he did so they saw the Mercedes glide by, and come to a halt outside the house. It didn't take long for the gate to open, and for the car to disappear inside. Felip the general handyman must have been on the watch.

They waited a very long ten minutes before they rang the bell on the gate. Carla's head pounded behind overtired eyes, and she was sure Martin must feel the same, but he looked resolute and strong, and she hoped she looked the same.

It helped to be properly dressed for the contest ahead. Joana had brought Carla some new clothes, which she'd bought for her in Girona, maternity dresses that fell in stylish folds around her bump, with matching jackets, and a woollen coat for the autumn evenings. And that morning Joana had trimmed her hair and given it a new style so that it hung in a sweep of curls around her neck. It had reminded Carla of years past, when her mother would style her little girl's hair and dress it with ribbons, an immeasurably long time ago.

It seemed like hours before they heard Felip's plodding footsteps coming round from the back of the house, where he must have retired thinking his work was done. His morose, rather doltish face appeared on the other side of the bars, and he peered through the evening gloom to see who had appeared to disturb his peace.

'Miss Carla?' he gaped at her.

You may well be astonished, she mused. You're Sergi's old retainer, and you may even have been one of those who went to Victor's flat, looking for me. It must be just a little surprising to see me walking voluntarily into his lair!

'Good evening, Felip! Is my father at home?'

He was fumbling with the bolts on the gate, and as it swung inwards he nodded his head furiously. 'Yes, miss. He came in just now. But he has ordered the car in half an hour, and I believe he has some formal dinner or something tonight.'

Joana had been right telling them to lie in wait for him – if they'd come later they could easily have missed him! Well, hopefully he wouldn't have much time to do them any harm in half an hour.

'Right then, Felip, we'll just go on up to the house, then,' she declared, and with a smile at Martin she led the way up the drive. Felip would ring the house bell from the gate, she knew, so their arrival would be well advertised, and either Josefa or Mireia would be on the way to let them in. Indeed, by the time they reached the front door it was opening, and the maid bobbed a surprised curtsy at them as she stood back to let them in.

'Good evening, Mireia.' Carla swept into the house with determined aplomb. 'We've come to see my father. Could you let him know we are here, please.'

'Y-yes, Miss, but Señor Olivera is dressing for dinner at the moment. D-do you want me to disturb him, Miss?' She sounded suitably scared at the prospect.

'I'm afraid so, Mireia – our business is urgent, you see. I think when he knows I'm here he'll want to see us right away, and he won't scold you. Could you just knock at his dressing room and tell him I'm here with a young gentleman?'

Mireia gulped, but nodded and scurried off towards the stairs, leaving them in the elaborate hallway. Carla waved Martin through to the sitting room, where they sat on two leather chairs, side by side, both doing their best to look perfectly nonchalant. Martin looked as short on sleep as she was, but he had a good face for this, she thought – unreadable and composed, apart from the tight look around his eyes. His role this evening was mainly to act as physical support, but she knew he would speak up if he felt the need. He looked across at her now and pulled his rather set mouth into a smile.

'Nice way to spend a Saturday evening! Do you think he'll invite us to his dinner party?'

Carla grinned. Cool card, my cousin, for one so young! A little beat hammered in her chest, and her throat seemed not to want to let her breathe, but as her pulse raced it fed a kind of ebullience that empowered her.

It was very few minutes before Sergi – she could no longer think of him as her father – came striding into the room, but long enough, she thought, for him to have secured the house and warned Felip to stand by. He appeared in his dress trousers and shirt but minus the tie and jacket, and he certainly looked formidable – a force of energy seemed to surround him, and his eyes burnt as they scanned the visitors, his gaze lingering on the line of swollen belly beneath Carla's decorously cut coat, and on Martin, with the same steady focus he'd turned on him that day in the street – Tuesday, that had been on Tuesday, Carla reminded herself, and since then life had changed.

'Well, my little Carla! You've come to visit your father after all this time! But what has been happening to you?' His deep voice filled the room – a purring panther would have felt less dangerous.

Carla took time to scan him in return before replying. They'd played this game before, not too long ago, but this time she was visiting on her terms, and she had taken him very much by surprise.

'Good evening, Papa,' she kept her voice carefully light. 'May I introduce a friend of mine from France who has been visiting us this last while. We just wanted to drop by and offer you a small gift. You see my friend has some interesting connections here in Girona, and he happened to pick up some documents that we thought might be of interest to you. Would you like to see them?'

She held out her hand as she spoke, and Sergi eyed the envelope curiously, but without apparent unease. He took it from her, though, and as he drew out the letters from inside she saw his eyes dilate in quick recognition. Slowly, infinitely slowly, he read through the three pages, although he must know them by heart. When he'd finished he looked up, and the expression in his eyes was stony and hard. But was there a hint of fear there as well?

His voice, though, remained almost mellifluous. 'How kind of you, Carla, to think that I might be interested in this correspondence. But I think your young friend must have mistaken whom they are addressed to, since he is a stranger in these parts. There are some bad people in Girona, as we all know, and he must have fallen upon some of them. It even makes you wonder who our dear French friends are frequenting with here! There is nothing and nobody I recognise in any of what I'm reading here. But you do well to bring these documents here, because they refer to a serious incident, if indeed there is any truth in them, and now I can deal with them as they should be dealt with. And meanwhile I can offer you both the hospitality of this house for a while. I think you have been in need of the right kind of sanctuary, have you not, my daughter?'

The temptation to throw her real parentage in his face was almost overwhelming, but Carla restrained herself. Under no circumstances must she reveal what she knew, because the only person from whom she could have learnt it was Mama. He mustn't know she'd seen Joana. Instead she straightened herself slightly in her chair, and gestured at the letters which Sergi still held in his hand.

'By all means, Papa, do what you need to with these letters. There is no problem, because we have several copies, and we've left them in envelopes with various friends. Let's not beat about the bush anymore! You would like to detain me here tonight, no doubt, but four different people in Girona have copies of these documents, and unless I contact them this evening they will take them to the authorities. Just as honest citizens, of course! And the same applies from here onwards – the documents remain with my friends, and they expect to see me every day, and if I think I am being followed when I go to see them, then I too will release the letters immediately.'

For a moment she believed that Sergi was going to strike at her as so often before. He stood right in front of her chair, his fists not quite flexing, and his eyes bored into hers. Beside her she sensed rather than saw Martin holding himself ready. Long seconds passed. Sergi was not used to being bested, to facing a situation where he wasn't in control. We may already be prisoners now, she thought, and he could call our bluff on this evidence. But how could he dare, when they were so damning that he'd been paying blackmail for them for months? She held his gaze and waited.

'What do you want?' his words came finally, crude and aggressive. 'What is it you want, you little bitch?'

'I want my life back! That's all I want, but to get it back I need my fiancé back. You had him taken away back in

June and you know where he is. I want Luc Serra Torrès released, and then I want to live in freedom. We'll go away and never come back to Girona, and we won't trouble your life, and we will never embarrass you with your friends, but the condition will be that you won't have us followed, and you won't try to control us in any way. As long as we are free the documents will never be used, but the moment we are threatened there are people who will know and who will use them straight away.' She caught a calculating look from him and threw in immediately. 'And it won't be my grandmother or my uncle, you can rest assured of that! Martin has family here in Girona who are completely unknown to you, and even when Luc and I move away they'll be expecting a telephone call once a week. If ever they can't contact us they'll release the letters.'

Sergi shook his head at her in careful bewilderment, having pulled himself back under his canopy of control. 'Carla, I don't know what you are talking about. I know that pregnant women don't always think straight, but in your case I think your condition has seriously disturbed your mind. We don't see you for over a year, and your mother worries herself silly, and then you turn up here heavily pregnant and with these strange stories. You have a fiancé, you say? I hope so, indeed! As your father I am shocked to see you in this condition and unmarried! So where is this young man? You say he has disappeared? My God, too many young men desert their girlfriends when they find they are expecting. It's a shame on our society! What is it that you want me to do, apart from looking after you, my daughter?'

'I want Luc Serra Torrès released from prison in the next two days! And then I want you to leave me and him in peace. It's simple, Papa. You have the keys – use them to open the doors!'

There was another silence and then Sergi looked meditatively at Martin. 'And this young man – you say he's a friend of yours? How does he come into this fantastic story?'

'I'm not sure that concerns you, Papa.'

'Oh, but it does, dear Carla! Foreign visitors to this country are subject to strict controls. If your friend is here on an extended visit, then I assume he has papers to permit him to be here? May I see your papers, young man?'

Carla shot Martin a warning glance, but he was ahead of her.

'Señor Olivera, with all due respect, I don't think my identity or my status is relevant to this meeting.' Sergi made a move towards him, and he sat firm in his seat, and held up his hand. 'You can search me if you wish, but I haven't brought any papers with me this evening. I don't wish you to know my name, or who my family and friends are here, and one set of the documents have been passed on to a further third party whose name even I don't know. So you can't beat the information out of me, if that is your intention. I'm very sorry,' he finished, ironically, and Carla almost laughed at Sergi's galled expression. She added in her own contribution.

'My friend here is returning to France very soon, anyway – his business here is coming to a conclusion, and he will leave the rest to his network here. He has no past here and no future, and nothing you can get hold of, and as I said before, if you try to have either of us followed after we leave here, the documents will immediately be released to the authorities. I'm sure there are some among your colleagues who would be only too pleased to hear what you have become involved with. We've been researching, and we've got some people in mind who we think would love to have these letters.'

The frozen look on Sergi's face told her she had scored a hit with this. He had arranged for an enemy to be disposed of, but that enemy presumably had friends, and allies, and family, and even if his death no longer mattered to anyone, there would be many among Sergi's political rivals who would swoop upon these documents and use them against him. Suddenly she knew they had won.

She stood up, facing Sergi, and as she did so he stepped back, conceding ground.

'We'll be leaving now, Papa. You seem to be dressing for dinner, and if you and Mama have an engagement you won't want to be late. Don't trouble to disturb Mama – her toilette will take her some time, from what I know of her, and we really have nothing to say to one another! Does she know about your deadly activities, by the way? Surely not! Even you wouldn't wish your wife to know that you're a murderer! Well, it isn't my wish to upset her with such things either. Shall we say Monday evening as the deadline for Luc to be released? That should give you plenty of time! I'll know when he is released, don't worry, and I can repeat my promise to you that once he is free we will disappear, and never trouble your life again.'

She held out her hand to Sergi, in a final gesture of sangfroid. She was holding her breath with the pending sense of victory. Martin stood up beside her, close enough so their shoulders were touching, and after a moment Sergi took one more step back and waved them contemptuously towards the door.

'Get out of here, both of you! You've taken enough of my time this evening with your fantasies. I'll see what I can do about this Serra Torrès, since it seems he has knocked you up, you shameless little tramp! That any of your friends should end up in prison should not surprise me, you ungrateful, wayward little whore. You are a worse slut than your mother, and you are no daughter of mine, thank God!'

Carla looked at him in genuine shock – she hadn't expected him to give this information away. But he'd gone beyond pretence now, and in his anger at being bested he just wanted to vilify her. It's a good job you told me yesterday, Mama, she thought, otherwise this might have been a pretty shattering way to learn the truth.

'No daughter of yours? Because you're ashamed of me? Dear Papa, how sad I am to have shocked you so!' Keep the fiction going, she told herself.

'By God, yes, I'm ashamed of you, you little bitch, but nothing you could do would shock me! You're just a dirty leftie's bastard, and you've proved that you have the same loose morals as your mother. Well, I got rid of that father of yours, and if you don't get out of here now I'll do the same to you and this low life you have with you. Go on, both of you, get out of my house and out of my life, and never let me see your face ever again.'

He was so angry now that he was almost out of control, and Carla wasn't sure if she'd heard him correctly. Was he just seeking to inflict shock and damage, or was he seriously saying that he'd murdered her father? Her mind reeled, and she must have looked suitably thunderstruck, because a sneer of satisfaction crossed Sergi's face.

'A-and Luc?' she managed to say.

'Oh, I'll get your lover boy back for you, don't worry! I want you gone, and if he'll take you away he's welcome to you!'

It was clear that Sergi had recovered his *amour propre*. He was lashing at her, and had her stuttering again, and it was this power over others that fuelled him. But it was important that he didn't forget the threat he was under. I mustn't look like his victim, Carla thought, and she managed to pull her shattered thoughts into some focus.

'You already disowned me last year, remember?' she shot back at him, blinking back her tears. 'This is the second time I'm walking out of this house, and I hope never to have to enter it again. Please don't bother coming to the door with us. My friend and I will be happy to see ourselves out.'

She grabbed Martin and headed towards the door, and as they reached it she turned quickly. Sergi was watching her with a look in her eyes that she hoped never to have to see again.

'One more thing, by Monday evening we expect to see Luc not only freed from prison but in Barcelona. I assume he is being held in Barcelona?'

Sergi said nothing. She held his gaze for a second without

flinching. 'No answer? Well, I'll just leave it in your hands, then. I'll look forward to seeing Luc in person by Monday evening!'

She got herself and Martin out of the room as quickly as possible. They emerged from the house to find Felip and Sergi's driver in conference by the gate, which was closed with the bolts across.

'Come, Martin,' Carla said loudly, and they marched towards the gate together. The driver, a big, muscular, military-looking guy whom Carla didn't know from the past, moved forward to stand full-square in front of the gates, but just as they reached him a bell sounded behind Felip, and both men stopped. The bell was clearly a signal, because on hearing it Felip shuffled forward and laboriously pulled open the bolts and swung the nearest gate open. The driver looked up at the house, as if seeking confirmation, but when he saw nothing he stepped aside reluctantly and let Carla and Martin past.

'Thank you,' Carla said. 'Now shut it behind us will you, and bolt it so we can hear the bolts go? We wouldn't like to think you might wish to accompany us along our way!'

They waited outside until they heard the grate of the bolts. The two men moved away towards the house, muttering disconsolately at this thwarting of a capture. And as they did so Martin jerked his head at Carla and they sped off towards the park, not stopping until they were inside the park gates. They had got away! The point was made – no one was to follow them. They were free to leave, and the letters had carried the day. But Sergi had

had his own victory, and his words repeated in Carla's head over and over so she thought she might faint. Martin held her hand, and drew her on, away through the park and away from the sphere of Sergi's influence. And then, when they came near the far park gates he took her in cousinly arms and held her. Her face must have told its own story, because as she collapsed against him she could hear his voice repeating, again and again.

'You're going to get Luc back, Carla. You won. It's the future, remember? The future is what matters! Carla, it's all right, it's all right . . . he just wanted to hurt you. You've won, Carla, and everything is going to be all right.'

# Chapter Fourteen

They couldn't just go straight back to Victor and Maria's apartment. Of one accord they headed through the old streets, aiming for the old city wall. It was now growing quite dark, and Martin took a firm hold on Carla's hand as they climbed up the steep alleyways of the old town, with their uneven cobbles, and an even firmer grip as they went across the ruined Jardí dels Alemanys and up the treacherous steps to the bit of ancient city wall, where they had first walked together just five days ago, although it felt so much longer.

Carla was still feeling shaky, and this night-time stumble around fallen stones and crumbling walls was probably not wise, but she held her stomach and followed Martin, accepting his help with rueful compliance, and stepped gingerly along the stonework in the gloom, holding hard to the stone parapet.

Once at the top they stopped, breathing heavily, and

looked out over the rooftops of the old town, down to the cathedral and beyond. Windows were lit up sporadically all over the town, and a few street lights had just been turned on. The effect of the lights was muted and strangely remote. Carla could almost imagine that the streets were lit by ancient torches, with cloaked medieval priests and townsfolk moving in the shadows to evensong through the alleyways and across the cathedral square.

She turned to Martin and caught the reflection of her own emotion in his eyes.

'Do you feel it?' she asked him.

'The history? Yes, I feel it! What an amazing place this is!'

'They can't take that away from us,' she exulted. 'Whatever people like my father do in their brute ignorance, this view will outlive them, and anyone can come up here – it belongs to the people. It even survived their bombs!'

They walked along as far as they could, to where the wall fell away, and below them were the newer houses, built in the nineteenth century in the gap where the wall was destroyed in a siege.

'You did that!' Carla told Martin. 'You French! It was yet another jumped-up dictator, your Napoleon! His army besieged Girona three times, and in 1809 ten thousand Spaniards starved to death trying to defend this city – the population was decimated and took decades to recover. But you know what? They also managed to kill fifteen thousand of the French besiegers, and Napoleon's army was crippled for a long while.'

'Formidable people, you Catalans! But surely the French didn't demolish all of the wall? The whole side of the city where Victor's apartment is must have been surrounded by a wall once, surely?'

'True! Napoleon only needed a relatively small breach – we did the rest ourselves! In the last hundred years they've pulled down most of the rest of the wall just to allow the expansion of the city, and other bits have just fallen into ruins because Gironese citizens pinched bits of stone here and there for their houses. We're a pragmatic bunch, we Catalans, and try as I might I can't blame everything on you French!'

Martin looked around him, down to the old town on one side, and then to the other side into the now deep blackness of the open hills beyond the new town. Carla wondered what he was thinking. What happened to any city was governed by a mix of politics and simple economics, and it was economics that had the most lasting effect. Franco would eventually die, and Sergi would be replaced, but Girona would keep growing, and people would keep moving here from the villages for work, and no doubt in fifty years time the view from this wall would encompass buildings reaching far towards the surrounding hills.

But the ancient old town would remain – it had withstood Napoleon and Franco, and had its own timelessness, just like those hills. Madrid had been practically razed to the ground by Franco's bombs, and cities like Barcelona had lost major buildings, but hopefully Girona wasn't important enough for anyone to destroy her now.

Carla leant her elbows on the parapet. 'It's horrible to think of all those people starving here 150 years ago. It's not as though they were all soldiers – it was the people of Girona who were stuck inside the walls, completely powerless as two armies fought over their city.'

'The little people were always at the mercy of their overlords, though, weren't they?'

'In Spain they still are!'

'You scored a point for the little people tonight, though.'

Unwanted tears pricked behind Carla's eyes. The meeting with Sergi had been so brutal, so overwhelming, and as the adrenalin faded, she was left now feeling bruised and bewildered. God help them, had he really killed her father? She looked at Martin, longing for reassurance.

'Did we win, Martin? Why doesn't it feel like it? Tell me, did he really kill my father, do you think? You said he was just trying to hurt, but why invent that?'

Martin didn't reply, but just put his arm around her shoulder.

'Please, Martin,' she begged him. 'Tell me what you really think.'

He took a step back behind her so his hands were on her shoulders, and kneaded her tense muscles gently.

'I don't know,' he said. 'He didn't say he killed him, did he? He said he got rid of him, but that's not necessarily the same thing. He may just have set him up – given his name to some vigilante posse, or pointed him out to any group of drunk soldiers looking for game. Then he could just have quietly left them to it. Or he may just have been boasting – he may not have had anything to do with it at all.'

'Well, I think he did.' Carla was sure. 'It just fits. This morning I asked Mama more about my real father, and she told me about his work in Girona, and their plans to make a life as soon as he gained his qualifications. He wasn't involved in the war, and his work was respectable and innocuous. He wasn't someone the *Fascista* would have been interested in, so unless he put himself in the way of trouble, why should anything happen to him? And he wasn't denounced and shot or anything official! Yes, it could have been someone else who actually stuck the knife in him, but Sergi was behind it, mark my words. All he's ever wanted to do is dominate, and win, and have everything his own way, so he killed my father and ruined our lives!'

Her fingers were hurting, and as she looked down she saw that she was pressing them so hard into the parapet that they'd gone white. Martin had stopped massaging her and fallen silent, and they stood for a long time listening to the vague, rather restful sounds coming from the city below them. Gradually her fingers loosened, and the peace of the evening began to have its effect.

'He hasn't succeeded in ruining your life, Carla,' Martin countered, after what seemed like an age. 'You did win this evening, and he only threw all that at you because he couldn't bear you having beaten him so thoroughly. If there's one thing I really am sure of after that meeting, it's that he's going to get your Luc released, and soon, just as you demanded.'

Carla felt a tiny tremor of excitement, just thinking about it, but she'd used up all her brave faces for that night, and was struggling with some long-standing demons.

'Yes,' she sighed, 'I'm sure you're right. My head tells me you're right, but there's a part of me that just can't believe it could be that easy, and that Luc could suddenly just reappear.'

She could hear her own voice and despised herself for sounding so negative, when they'd just achieved so much. Martin took her arm again and pointed her back towards the steps.

'Come on, let's get out of here. The ghosts of Girona are getting to you, my girl. You were magnificent back there, incredibly forceful, and now you're suffering the inevitable reaction. I'm going to buy you a coffee, or something stronger perhaps, somewhere where there are people, and noise. You're not going to start feeling like a victim again now!'

'Can you afford it?'

'I haven't spent a cent, except on bus fares, since I got here, so yes, I think I can afford to buy us a drink! Then we'll go back and reassure Maria and Victor, but not yet. We have just toppled a giant, like in the best fairy tales, and the little people have to feel pleased with themselves for once!'

They made their way down the hill through the ancient stone streets, and along to the Rambla, where Girona society would be meeting this Saturday evening, and Martin led Carla to a trendy-looking bar under the arches. She would only accept a fruit juice, but he insisted on ordering a fancy fruit cocktail for her, complete with straw and a half slice of orange hooked on to the rim. It made her laugh, and she raised her glass to him with a lift of the eyebrows.

'Here's to the little people, then,' she said.

He chinked glasses with her and took a deep draught of beer, giving a little sigh of pleasure. Carla laughed at his expression of deep satisfaction, and sipped her cocktail with an almost playful feeling. Around them the bar buzzed with

Saturday night activity. The young and beautiful of Girona were enjoying the aperitif hour, and Carla felt really grateful for the new, fashionable look Joana had given her that morning, which made her look quite at home among them.

Martin seemed to catch the thought; 'I have to say you don't look like one of the little people,' he commented. He gestured to the surrounding tables. 'You grew up among this lot, didn't you?'

Carla grimaced. 'I did, but I never made it to the position of socialite. I bailed out long before! Sergi would have loved to see me here among them, though. See that table over there and those young girls? That's exactly what my father would have wanted me to be like – there's something very painstaking about their sophistication, don't you think?'

Martin examined the table in question. The two young men were dressed in well-cut suits, and looked like junior executives on a well-prepared ladder to good industry jobs, and their girlfriends could have been twins, with long hair carefully curled to frame their faces, and off-the-shoulder dresses with full skirts, which owed more to the fifties than to the sixties. Their style was kittenish, and would have their fathers' full approval, and their deep-red lipstick could not disguise their highly protected innocence. They listened with becoming deference to the raucous jokes of their companions, and smiled and giggled in all the right places.

Martin grinned at Carla. 'I'd struggle to imagine you in their place, I have to admit. I think your father failed in your education!'

'Maybe because he's not really my father.' Carla sipped her juice through the coloured straw, and studied it with careful attention. 'Tell me, Martin,' she said after a while, 'How come you knew all about my father? How come my mother told you the whole story when she'd kept it so well buttoned up all these years?'

Martin took time to answer, as though he was working out for himself what the answer was.

'It was when I told her about you, about you being pregnant,' he said eventually. 'And about how Luc had disappeared leaving you in such a desperate situation. It was so close to her own experience, and it took her right back to when she was seventeen, and in the same situation. I can't remember when I've seen anyone look so stricken. What was it she said? "It's such a dreadful thing, that fear." I don't think she knew what she was saying, but it was clear she was talking about herself.'

'And she went on to tell you everything?'

'I asked her if it had happened to her, and she broke down.'

Carla looked at him pensively. 'She seems to trust you, though, my mother. She's lowered the barricades with you.'

'I'm new in your lives, Carla – I'm family, but I don't have any part in the history you've lived together. It's easier for you all to trust me, and of course I'm Luis's son as well, and he was everyone's darling, it seems!'

'Does she know that you're like me – that you were Luis's love child? That he didn't even know you existed? That you were taken on by another man as his son? A man who hated you like my supposed father hated me?'

Why am I throwing this at him, Carla asked herself? Her words had come out like bullets – but she wanted to hear him talk about it – he'd lived longer with the knowledge of illegitimacy than she had. Help me, was what she was actually saying.

A cloud seemed to settle on his face, though, as she spoke, and she worried that she'd pushed too far into sensitive territory. She waited, watching his face as it sat in the dark cloud, and after a moment she reached out and touched his hand. He looked up and she smiled at him, and he gave her a smile back.

'It's all right,' he said. 'But I was young and vulnerable when I found out, and unlike you I've got legitimate siblings on both sides who stand on much more solid ground than I do – they don't have to manoeuvre through the same minefield of identity. You know, the similarities between us two are less relevant than the similarity between you and your mother. Whatever happens to you, you know that Luc loves you and that he loves and wants your baby. And your real father truly loved Joana and would have loved and wanted you. The difference is that you're now heading for a happy ending, and your baby will be raised by its real father.'

She looked at him with contrition. 'Do you think Luis would not have wanted you? He loved your mother, surely?'

'He cared about her, I'm sure, but his real love was his wife, and he already had a family he adored. His affair with my mother was a temporary blip in his life at a time when they were both lonely, and the arrival of a child would have caused him terrible complications. No, he wouldn't have wanted me – he would just have felt obliged to be honourable.'

'We want you, though,' she said, reaching for his hand.

'I know. I've felt that acceptance ever since I arrived here. It's what I've been looking for, these last few years.'

'You've succeeded, believe me.'

'Thank you. I feel as though I've finally been entitled to my father since I came here. And, Carla, you could do the same thing if you wanted. If your mother will agree, you could go to Alex Figarola's family and tell them who you are. They lost their son very cruelly back in 1939, and I bet they would be very happy to know they have a grandchild, and that Alex had left a part of himself behind.'

Carla looked doubtful, but Martin was insistent.

'Think how your grandmother received me,' he urged her. 'She was just happy to have a part of Luis in her home.'

'Yes, darling Martin, but you looked at her with those dark-brown eyes and long lashes of yours and she was lost! You play the same trick on everyone! I'm not sure I have your charm.'

'You're the image of your father – that's what your mother says.'

'Poor Papa! Or poor Mama, rather, when she's so beautiful!'

'You're pretty stunning yourself when you're dressed up like this, Carla! And what about your Luc, is he beautiful as well, your fiancé?'

Carla gave a ripple of laughter, and shook her head.

'Oh no! My Luc is a great big lump, as you'll see when you meet him!' A little quiver of excitement shook her. 'God, Martin, I can't believe I may soon have him back! Do you truly, honestly think my ex-father will really have him released?'

'Yes,' he affirmed, raising his glass and tossing off the last of his beer. 'Oh yes, I believe you'll have your Luc back very soon, Carla! I told you, the little people have won this time.'

'Not so little, when you meet my Luc!'

There had been a shower of rain while they were in the bar, and there was an autumnal chill in the air when they emerged. They strolled back through the streets together away from the elegant Rambla towards the much less picturesque streets where Maria and Victor lived. Maria would be anxious, they knew, and Carla felt a twinge of guilt at having stayed out so long, when they'd left her in such anxiety when they set off for the lion's den. But she would forgive them when she heard their news, she knew. Martin delayed them even further by stopping to buy two beers for himself and Victor. A festive mood had come over them at last, and as they came out of the shop Martin took her arm in mute companionship, and she smiled at him, and squeezed his elbow.

'Thinking of Luc?' he teased.

'Mmm!' she grinned. 'And you?'

'Me?' He jumped boyishly to touch an overhanging shop sign, and it rocked and spattered them with a sprinkle of raindrops. He laughed delightedly as Carla protested.

'Me, I'm hungry! We toppled a giant today, and now I want my dinner!'

# Chapter Fifteen

She was driving Josep and Neus mad. She'd arrived on Sunday afternoon and for the hours since she had been prowling around the house, restive and unsettled enough to cause even placid Neus to beg her to sit still for a while. Only Josep's strongest interdiction stopped her from going on Monday morning to stand outside the men's prison, watching the door for Luc to appear. She didn't even know that's where Luc was being held, Josep argued, and if they'd imprisoned him outside Barcelona, as might well be the case, then it could be days before he found his way to her, whatever threats she'd given to Sergi. He might even make his way to his parents' home first. In the meantime, the best place for her to be was here, inside this house, since here was where Luc would come looking for her as soon as he was able to.

Carla refused to think about delays. Luc would be in

Barcelona – she wanted to believe it, it was the easiest thing to believe, and in her troubled dreams that was always where she saw him. But whatever was the reality, Uncle Josep was right, she knew, and she had to wait for Luc here, in the house where he'd left her last. So she acquiesced because there was no choice, but the passive waiting was almost unbearable. Josep was her distraction – there was so much to tell him, so much to ask him as well.

Sergi had indeed visited Josep, it seemed, but he'd failed to intimidate him. Josep had been outside talking to a couple of his neighbours when Sergi turned up with his tough-looking little posse. However mild-mannered Josep might be he was a fit man under forty, used to physical work, and his neighbours were burly men with no love for the authorities. Between them they represented quite a challenge for Sergi's team of four, which included the lumbering, unimpressive Felip.

To avoid a public disturbance Josep had agreed to show Sergi over the house to prove that Carla wasn't there, but the neighbours had kept the rest of the band outside, inviting them to show their official documents if they all wanted to invade the house.

'He had probably been watching the building for a while,' Josep surmised, as he told her the story, 'and there'd been no sign of you leaving the house, so when he came in and all he found were the kids doing their homework he had to accept that this wasn't the place to come looking for you. Neus wasn't even here – she was off at her sister's. I think she was disappointed afterwards that she hadn't been here to give him a piece of her mind. You know my Neus –

she speaks as she finds, and she's been rankling for years at your father's treatment of you!'

Not really her father, though, and when she shared this most recent news with Josep he whistled, and then whistled even more when she told him what Sergi had been up to by way of murder, how his political life had become so complicated, what that was doing to his character, and how Joana was banished to the hill house. And when she told him of Sergi's claim to have eliminated Alex Figarola himself, he just shook his head in horror.

'Dear heavens above, my poor sister!' The words came out in a low hiss. 'It never occurred to any of us back then to suspect that she hadn't gone off with Sergi simply for a better life, and what was said about her in the village doesn't bear repeating. What a monster! What a bloody, evil monster!'

'I know, and I'm not looking forward to telling her of his latest claims. But you know, she did enjoy the trappings of that fancy life,' was Carla's rejoinder. 'She did like the life he gave her, in those early years, and she despised the life she'd left behind, didn't she?'

Josep reflected for a moment, and then slowly shook his head. 'It's maybe not as simple as that,' he answered eventually. 'It's like I told you – she always hated that we had to go back to Sant Galdric after our father died. It's hard to explain the difference now between those two lives. I always assumed she was happy enough when I was a kid – I didn't really think too much about it, I suppose. She was just my big sister. But looking back I can see how much she lost. I can remember times when she would get really angry, and rail at how Mama – your Grandma – had become nothing but a drudge, and insist she wasn't going to have that life herself.'

'Not an easy woman, my mother!' Carla commented, with a wry smile.

'Not easy, no – complex, for sure, and formidable in many ways – but she was always loyal, and caring, and a lot of fun, believe me – she could mimic anyone, and she and I used to get ourselves into hot water together for some of our fooling around. She was ambitious, yes, but her ambitions were for all of us, and not for money, just for a different life. She wasn't always understood in the village, and when she chose Sergi there were many who said it was just typical of her, but for me the cynicism of her choice was a surprise, a real shock. But then she disappeared from our lives completely, and her subsequent behaviour seemed to suggest she'd chosen her path very willingly, so I didn't think much more about it. Now . . . well, now I know why.' He sighed, 'I was right, back then. Poor Joana, she must have been more desperate than I can even imagine.'

'I can!' Carla rubbed her stomach ruefully.

'Yes, well hopefully what you've gone through will help you to understand her better, and stop you judging her so hard. And that monster, that bastard is responsible for all of this suffering! You know, it's a good job I didn't know all this when he came here the other day – I can't tell you what I'd like to do to him!' His hands flexed as he spoke, and little hard lines creased his mouth and eyes. This was a new Uncle Josep, oozing a deep Catalan rage which Carla had never seen in him. But after a few moments his expression lightened, and he said, in a tone of deep gratification, 'But your story is going to end well, Carla! You'll get your Luc back, and by God, you took on Sergi Olivera and beat him at his own game!'

'I couldn't have done it on my own – Martin came with me, and I couldn't have managed without him!'

'Yes, Luis's son! Who'd have thought he'd turn up like that out of the blue? He sounds like a very interesting young man, and he seems to have leapt in to help us all out. I'd like to meet him and shake his hand.'

'He'd like that, he'd love to know you – but you've no need to thank him. Your own mother has him in her care right now, and she's fawning over him as though Luis himself had returned to her! You'd better not visit my grandmother soon, Josep – you'll be nothing to her now compared with our Martí!'

All Sunday evening Carla could think of nothing but Luc. The hours stretched, passing painfully slowly. There's no way he can possibly be released over the weekend, she told herself, trying desperately not to fidget as she waded through piles of Neus's darning just to pass the time. In the back of her mind the fear remained, whatever Martin might think, that Sergi would change his mind, or find a way to get back at them all, and she would find herself back in his net. The confrontation at his house played over and over in her mind, and she found herself repeating her words to him as though she was re-enacting a play. Was this to exorcise the fear she'd felt, she wondered? It would be a long time, she could see, before she would wake up each day in peaceful security.

By Monday she was on hot coals, glued to the window, waiting and waiting. She went outside and walked up and down the pavement until her feet ached, keeping the door to the building always in sight. And when she was too tired to walk any more she returned to her post by the window.

But when he finally came she wasn't looking, having been enticed away to eat with Neus and the boys, home for lunch from school. A tap at the door took them all by surprise, and it was actually Neus, nearest to the door, who answered it, leaving Carla standing by the table, clutching her chair, her gaze fixed painfully on the hall door.

Beyond it she heard voices, Neus and who? A male voice, surely Luc's? It must be! And then the door opened and he was there, thinner, dirty, with a stale smell, his hair shaven short, and a hesitance about him that she attributed to the suddenness of his release, but it was Luc, and she ran to him and his arms came round her, and she clung to him so he couldn't disappear.

They said nothing, nothing but hushed little exclamations, while Neus brought food for him, and then shooed the children out and went to fill a bath for him.

'Look at you!'

'And you!'

'You've got so thin!'

'And you!'

'And how have you been?'

'Fine – and you?'

'Fine.'

Luc was strangely tongue-tied, and his normal exuberance was absent from his eyes. Carla could tell he marvelled to see her, but there was a part of him that struggled. He answered her enquiries stiltedly, and she stopped questioning, and simply sat close and touched him, and he gripped her hand as it grazed his cheek, and brought it down so they touched her belly together.

'The baby?'

'The baby's fine too!'

Later Neus went out to the market and they sneaked off to Carla's room, and there she lay in his arms and studied the furrows around his eyes, and the new strange lines etched around a mouth that had never worried, had always laughed in pleasure at life. Now they lay with their faces turned to each other on the long pillow, and pulled the covers around themselves for comfort, and she talked to him, since for now it seemed he couldn't talk to her.

She told him about the last four months – how she'd looked for him, how she'd longed for him, about staying with Grandma and their worries for the baby, about Martin, Joana, the truth about her father. And he watched her while she spoke, studying her eyes, her mouth, the whole time. When she smiled he smiled, but otherwise he just lay watching, until at last she fell silent.

'Luc,' she whispered finally. 'What have they done to you, my love?'

And then he wept, silent tears that rolled slowly along the ridge of his nose, and dropped onto the pillow beside him.

'Carla . . .' the word was an appeal, and she gathered him to her, too appalled to release her own tears, and held his head to her chest so that his tears soaked her dress.

'I love you, Luc,' she repeated again and again, and the words stayed between them. Long minutes passed by, and eventually his tears ceased, and he lay still, his head held in the crook of her arm. She kissed the shaven head.

'They cut off all your lovely curls!' she said, and deliberately put a smile in her voice.

'I'm an ugly mess.' His own voice was wretched.

'Well, you're MY ugly mess!' She put her hand over his on her belly. 'And his, of course!'

'Hers!'

The words were an invitation, and she almost chuckled with relief. Ever since she'd fallen pregnant he'd been calling the baby Joaquima, while she insisted it was a boy, Joaquim.

'No, dear heart – not hers. This is no girl inside me. I feel it and I know it, and I want my baby boy. I want another Luc.'

'But there's only one Luc!'

'We're making another,' she assured him, and held his hand in place as the baby kicked inside her.

He moved his hand gently over her, the merest stroke to rediscover her, and she reached for him and brought it up to cup her breast. He turned in her arms and his lips found hers, and she had her Luc back at last.

He'd been in solitary confinement for four months. It took all day to get the story from lips that had frozen from lack of speech. They'd kept him in a cell reserved for the most dangerous prisoners, away from the groups of trade unionists and political activists who shared exercise and work routines, and who could have communicated his whereabouts to the outside world. When he asked his guards why he was kept alone they shrugged, and one replied, 'Someone doesn't like you, son, that's all. It happens all the time.'

At first they'd kept him in a cell without a window, under lights he couldn't extinguish, so he had no sense of the passage of time, or day and night, and they visited him at indeterminate intervals to question him – bullying, hectoring interrogation sessions which stopped short of torture, only because, he believed, the interrogators themselves didn't really believe he had anything serious to tell them.

Eventually, he had no idea when, they moved him to his isolation cell, and there he had a window, and could make himself sleep by night and stay awake by day. They allowed him books, but only authorised texts, so he read religious tracts and political essays, and anthologies of poetry by approved writers like Menéndez, which extolled the glories of Spain. He ate three times every day, bad food, but food nevertheless, and he ate it with a grim determination to stay whole and healthy however long this purgatory might last. Every day he was allowed out to exercise for half an hour into a covered yard, and because he had the yard to himself he could run, which he did, and stretch, and push his thinning body to make his muscles work.

'Will I be put on trial for something?' he would ask his gaolers, and they would shrug again.

His only visitor was a chaplain who came twice a week, and let him talk about Carla, until he realised she was pregnant, at which point he got out his prayer book and demanded that Luc join him in a prayer for her endangered soul. He gave Luc paper, and told him to think long and hard and then write down all his sins, but when he came back next time Luc had written love letters to Carla, and a letter to his parents begging their forgiveness for the wasted years of study, which had not yet managed to change this rotten Spain. Typically he'd written out a Lorca poem for Carla, which the chaplain told him to tear up in front of him. Instead Luc had intoned it to him.

'You know the poem, Carla, the one which goes, *I pronounce your name on dark nights, when the stars come to drink from the moon*. It was how I felt, *hollow of passion and music*, and how dared that idiot say that a great poet was wicked just because he didn't like his politics? I told him that Lorca's politics didn't create his genius, but that his genius was beyond the grasp of our politicians. And of course, after that they gave me no more paper.'

And then this morning they had come for him, and taken him to a room where he found his old clothes, and the wallet (empty of course), which he'd taken with him when he was arrested. And once he was dressed they took him to the outside door of the prison and threw him out on the street. There was not a word of explanation, and as he stood in the square in front of the men's prison it was the first time that he actually knew where he'd been kept. He'd made his way more by instinct than design to Josep's house, and as he walked, every rattling bus, every group of chattering children, every car horn sounded in anger, had jarred terribly on ears, which had been kept for so many weeks in almost total silence.

Carla listened to him in appalled silence, letting him tell her in his own way, and at his own pace. He stayed in her room, away from the bustle of the house, and when Josep came home from work he came in to sit with him, shaking his hand with tears in his eyes. Neus brought him her famous bean soup, and he ate propped up on the pillows, with Carla by his side, just as they used to do in his old studio apartment.

Later, when the children had gone to bed, they brought him out of Carla's room, turning off the radio and letting him sit passively while Josep and Neus placidly planned their next day, and Carla brought out the last of the darning. How could a small household have so much darning, she wondered? She accused Neus of neglecting her duties, and Neus grinned, and sent Josep to the kitchen with the remains of their late-evening coffee.

By the following morning Luc was a little better – quiet, horribly subdued, but able to talk. He wanted to go to see his parents, who they knew would have been worrying non-stop since they received Carla's letter, three months ago, telling them their son had disappeared. Luc wanted Carla to go with him, but she had a problem.

'Martin is in Girona,' she told him. 'He needs to go home soon – he has already far outstayed his original plans, and he's worried about his mother, although to be fair she hasn't had the worry or the wait that your own parents have had! But that aside, he won't leave until I come back and he knows what has happened. And there's Grandma, and Uncle Victor, and even my mother – they're all on tenterhooks to know if everything has worked out all right.

I promised I would go straight back, once you were free.'

It was Josep who found the solution. 'Your parents have a phone, don't they? Well call them from the post office, Luc,' he recommended. 'Or if you can't get through then write to them. They'll have the letter within two days. Tell them that you've been freed and will be with them within a week at most, and that you'll be bringing Carla with you, and that you'll be needing to register to get married within no more than two weeks. That will get them excited enough, and they can register your documents, and speak to their local priest, and publish the banns. I assume that's where you are still registered as resident? Good, and your parents will have your birth certificate. Where is your own birth certificate, Carla?'

'It's with Grandma. I took all my documents from my parents' home some time ago – I kind of knew I might need them to be elsewhere.'

'Then you'll have to send it on to Luc's parents from Girona. Terrassa is the easiest and quickest place for you to be married, but meantime there are others you need to see, and I don't think you and Carla should be separated again right now, Luc – you need to stay together. It'll be better, too, if the priest doesn't see Carla's belly until the wedding day, so he can't take some moral stance beforehand and decide not to marry you.'

As he left for work he took Carla by the hand and led her outside with him. An overnight shower had left the air cool, but the clouds were moving away, and another sunny day was promising.

'Take care of that young man, Carla,' was what he

wanted to say. ‘Don’t let him try to do too much too soon. He shouldn’t go away on his own – he needs you to organise things for him just now. He’ll get over it, but he’s been incredibly isolated and under too much strain, and his whole strength has been invested in keeping himself sane. He’s had to use all his reserves, and now that his fight is over he could struggle, especially if he comes under any more pressure. And I don’t think you’ve finished yet with pressure – it will be a while before your lives are simple.’

At the look on Carla’s face he put his arm around her shoulder. ‘Chin up, little niece! You’ve got him back and he’ll be brand new before you know it. He’s far too buoyant a character not to bounce back soon. You just need patience, that’s all.’

Tears pricked the back of her eyes as she hugged him. ‘Thank you! And thank you for what you told me about Mama, as well. We’ll come by here on our way to Terrassa, darling Uncle Josep, if you’ll have us.’

‘We’ll have you, *carinyo*. Kiss your Grandma for me and tell her to come soon to visit us here. That fellow Victor can let her go for a while so she can see her own grandchildren. And Carla!’

‘Yes?’

‘Please tell my big sister Joana I miss her. Tell her Josep would like to see her, and that I have children growing up who have never even met her.’

Carla nodded. ‘I will.’ She stood back as he walked away through the communal garden, tall and fair and lean, much like his father must have been, the journalist father whose legacy he knew he hadn’t been able to match. But he was happy, and serene like Grandma, and where his sister Joana was filled with fretful yearning, he was tranquil in his life, with the gift of making himself liked by everyone he met.

She walked slowly back into the house to join Luc, that other most lovable of men, and found him washing breakfast dishes at Neus's sink.

'Be careful, Aunt Neus, he'll break every good dish you have!' she warned, and he turned and shot her the grin which she knew so well, and which lit up his wayward face. She returned the smile, and thought, we're going to be fine. It will all be all right!

'I'm relatively safe washing up,' he answered. 'It's when I dry that things get broken!'

'Then throw me a tea towel, Aunt Neus, and we'll see if we can get out of your house with our credit still intact. Uncle Josep invited us to stay again on our way to Terrassa, and as we have nowhere else to go and not a penny to our names, I'd hate to see the invitation withdrawn!'

# Chapter Sixteen

'Tell me how long we have to go now, Carla, before the baby is born. I've lost track. I don't even know what day of the week it is.'

They sat on the bus, trundling between Barcelona and Girona. It felt odd to be taking Luc closer to Sergi and his band of thugs, but they had to pass this way. It was already mid afternoon – they'd had to shop for clothes for Luc before they could travel, and then spent a fruitless hour trying to call Terrassa from the overcrowded post office, and then compose a letter instead.

Carla had no real idea of how to progress from here. They had to get away as soon as possible, they had to get married before the baby was born, they had to say goodbye, and move, and her time with *Avia* Maria must be over, because she and Luc remained dangerous guests. They had no money, and she hoped her mother might lend them enough to get away and start out somewhere where no one Sergi knew would ever see them. The road ahead was dauntingly steep, and it would be some time before Luc could carry a full load.

She had him back, though, with his huge hand enveloping hers as they squeezed together on the hard seat.

'I don't know how long exactly,' was her answer. 'I've never even seen a doctor, remember, and I'm working on estimates of dates. I think I've got about five weeks to go. God forbid if the baby decides to come early! We still have to get married, and that may take weeks! You heard what Uncle Josep said – the priest could even refuse to marry us, because I'm such a fallen woman!'

'No, I know the priest by my parents' place. He's young, one of the new school, a campaigner for the Catalan language even – he'll marry us, I'm sure. What do you need for the banns? Two weeks? I'm not an expert at these things.'

'Nor me,' she chuckled. 'It may surprise you to know that I've never been married before! Well, if we don't need to worry about the wedding, all to the good. We've got enough else to worry about!'

She regretted saying it, because Luc's face clouded over. How tired he looked – there was a lassitude hanging over him, which he did everything to disguise.

'Because we have to go into hiding?' he was asking. 'Is that necessary, now that your father has accepted defeat? You don't think we could stay with my parents until after the baby is born, at least, so my father can be around for the birth? You'd find my mother a great help, Carla, and they'd want us to stay.'

'Are you sure? My father will know where they live, you can be sure of that, and he could decide to visit at any time if he changes his mind. You know, if I were your parents I'd be pretty unhappy about my son's choice of bride!'

'Rubbish,' Luc replied, sounding much more like his normal self. He put his arm around her shoulder and gave her a squeeze. 'My parents have lived all their lives under threat from the authorities. Any visit from your father would be no worse than many we had when I was a child! They're quite familiar with bullies, and knowing about him will just put them even more fiercely on your side!'

The idea of a period of peace with Luc in Terrassa to have the baby was very appealing – it was what Luc needed, and the thought of it made the next few weeks seem so much less daunting. Luc's kindly father and mother, with their easy, unconventional view of the world, would offer a safe haven from which to give birth, with medical attention on tap!

She rubbed her belly, and shifted her back on the hard seat, easing herself into a more comfortable position against Luc's shoulder. 'All right then, big fellow, if things look calm in my father's camp by the time we leave Girona, I think it would be wonderful to stay with your parents for a few weeks. If I live quietly I won't meet any of my father's cronies, and later we can move further afield. I'd like to build a life one day a bit further away from his influence.'

'Me too!' Luc was emphatic. 'Believe me, I've no desire to fall into his hands again!'

He dozed then, as the bus rattled its slow way to Girona, and Carla eased his shorn head so that it rested against her. She couldn't get comfortable enough to sleep herself, and resigned herself to stiff shoulders and the inevitable backache by the end of the day. The key thing was for Luc to arrive in Girona in fit condition to cope with her family.

Did it work? It was hard to say. They climbed the stairs to the apartment in silence, but Luc plodded gamely up the stone steps, and smiled at her as she cocked a quizzical head in his direction. She winked and led him inside, hugging her own frisson of excitement.

Familiar smells reached them from the kitchen, and at the table sat Uncle Victor, divesting himself of his work boots. He must have come home only a few moments before them. He looked up, and when he saw Carla with Luc behind her his face split into a slow, broad smile. He carefully placed his boots down by his chair, drew on his slippers, and then advanced towards them and took Carla silently into his arms. Her head was buried in his shoulder, but she was sure his grin was now fixed on Luc behind her, and she manoeuvred herself around enough to catch Luc's widened eyes and diffident smile. Then Victor released her and reached out his hand to Luc.

It was just then that Maria came out of the kitchen, wiping her hands on a cloth. For a moment the whole room seemed to Carla to freeze completely. Victor and Luc were standing completely still, their hands locked but not moving, and Maria had stopped dead in her tracks, her mouth half open. It was so comical that Carla had to comment.

'*Avia*,' she spluttered, 'This is my friendly giant!' and as she spoke she surrendered to a fit of the giggles so strong she had to sit down, clinging to her bump as she held Grandma's astonished gaze.

There was no need to worry about how Luc would get on with Maria and Victor. They sat long into the evening over Maria's fish and aioli, and it was like being with Josep and Neus – uncomplicated and easy-going, and Luc had the gift of making people talk, so that Victor told him about his life as a shepherd and landsman, and more about his job in the factory than Carla had ever heard from him. Production targets were being raised each week as their employer squeezed costs to pay for the building of a second factory. The message they got daily as their rest breaks were cut and their pay rise was axed was that they were contributing to the growth of a greater Spain. Luc let him talk, with just the occasional comment, but it wouldn't be long, Carla thought, before he would be talking about industrial action!

Martin wasn't there. He'd gone up to the hill house two days ago, Maria said, on Sunday morning.

'He was worried for Joana,' she told them. 'He wanted her to know what had happened between you and Sergi, Carla, and that you'd gone down to Barcelona.'

There was a note of concern in Maria's voice. Carla knew that she was worried that Sergi might suspect Joana of having handed the blackmail letter to her. It wasn't likely, she thought, thinking back to the meeting in his house. Joana had been far from his mind. But the merest risk was enough to nag at Maria, and she would be fretting that Sergi might visit the hill house, sore and vengeful after his raw encounter with Carla and Martin on Saturday night.

It was unlikely, Carla was sure. They'd done and said absolutely nothing to link Joana to the documents, and Sergi knew – had even contrived – the terrible relationship between mother and daughter. Why should Joana be involved? Sergi would take any opportunity to get his own back on Carla, but having arranged Luc's release he had other things which must now be occupying his mind. Instinct told Carla that now he would be in his office, bolstering his position ahead of the forthcoming political elections.

Carla's worry was that Martin might talk to her mother about Sergi's revelations. They'd agreed that no one but Carla should reveal what he'd said, and even then Carla wondered what help it could be to Joana to know that Sergi might have killed the man she should have married. Martin wanted her told – he said Joana would have some difficult decisions to make now about her future, and it would help her to make them if she could let go all feeling that she had to be grateful to Sergi for taking her on. He wanted her told, but he wouldn't tell her on his own – she trusted and believed it. But he would be right that Joana would be fretting, on her own at the hill house, and it was like Martin to care. He had an empathy for Joana, and it was curiously reassuring to know that Mama was not on her own at the hill house, waiting for them all.

It seemed Joana had reacted fast to Martin's news. 'She has already sent Toni down here this afternoon,' Grandma told them, 'To check whether you were here. And he told me he'll be back again tomorrow. I hope Sergi doesn't keep too tight a check on Joana's expenditure or the kilometres that car covers – I hate to think how much fuel Toni is using trekking back and forth between Girona and Sant Galdric the way he's doing!'

Carla slept beside her grandmother that night, and wondered whether this would be the last time. Next door she could hear a regular snoring, and wondered how Luc would be sleeping in Victor's bed. From the look of exhaustion on his face as they'd headed for bed she thought nothing would keep him awake, and before she finally dropped off herself she heard a second rumble of snoring join the first, and knew her man was asleep.

The next day Toni arrived just before lunchtime, and this time he was persuaded to stay for lunch. Luc looked better again today, and Carla heard him throwing all his charm at Maria to be allowed to help chop vegetables, before he was pushed forcefully out of the kitchen and sent off to walk off his new-found energy out of doors. Grandma seemed to have quickly got the measure of Luc – her kitchen was way too small for him to be allowed off the leash inside!

So Carla helped her instead until Toni arrived, when she sat with him at the table, cup of coffee in hand. Maria stood close to pour him a second cup.

'Tell me, Toni, how is your mother?' Maria asked. She sounded wistful, as she only did when talking about people from her village. She hadn't been back up to Sant Galdric since she left and closed up the family home, and she must hanker after news of her old friends. Toni's mother was an old protégée of Maria's in the village, and she'd been Paula's predecessor – housekeeper at the hill house until she became unwell and Sergi dismissed her.

Toni's face clouded. 'She gets more and more breathless, and there's never enough money to buy her the medicines which help. I asked your mother, Carla, if *Senyor* Olivera could pay her some kind of a pension, but he'd said she hadn't worked for long enough to get a pension.' His lips tightened at the memory, and Carla thought it must have cost him dear just to ask, only to be shot down.

Toni was continuing, 'She gets by mostly with what I can give her, but the medicines which help the most are expensive.' He sighed. 'She'll be glad you asked after her, though.'

He shrugged off what must be a daily worry, and turned to Carla. 'So you got your fiancé back then, Carla?'

She smiled. 'I did Toni, and in large part thanks to you!'

'And to your mother, it would seem.'

'You're feeling better about Mama now?'

'Getting there,' was the guarded response. 'She has surprised me.'

How strange Toni's life must be, Carla thought, stuck in the hill house with just Paula and Joana for company. It was an upstairs–downstairs relationship, but without enough people to make a life, and they must all just watch each other and revolve in a mesh of suspicion and resentment, in a web that confined and defined them all. Carla thought about Uncle Josep, who had gone from being a boy from the village school of Sant Galdric and had made himself a solid life in Barcelona. His background had undoubtedly set a limit to his ambitions, but Josep had a decent job now, and an independent life that made him happy.

Had it been his mother's health problems that had kept Toni yoked to her parents all these years, and stopped him from taking the risk of making a move? She thought back to when he'd been a boy, and had crept away to join Carla in teenage plotting in the hill house garden, both of them full of plans for the future. He'd been a gifted mathematician, she remembered, but he soon knew more than the local schoolteacher and could go no further, and when Carla had told her mother Joana had just shrugged her shoulders. No wonder Toni had had so little time for Joana. She'd shut her eyes to the people below her for all those years, undeviatingly following Sergi's strict lead, and it would take a long time for her to rebuild all her bonds.

How would Toni react to Luc, she wondered? They were much of an age, but when viewed alongside Luc, Toni seemed unsatisfied and unfulfilled. He had a sweetheart in the village that he could never make up his mind to marry, and a hankering for a better life that he couldn't make happen. How would big, broad, easy Luc strike someone who lived what struck her as life with an itch under the collar?

When Luc came back from his walk he burst into the apartment with his usual energy, wafting the autumn air in behind him. He advanced on Toni with his hand outstretched, and before he knew it Toni had put his own hand in it.

'I've been waiting to meet you,' Luc said. 'You're Carla's friend from old, aren't you? Tell me, was she always such a prickly pear? You knew her as an adolescent, didn't you? Naturally her grandmother thinks she's just wonderful, but I'm relying on you to tell me the truth so I know what I'm getting myself into!'

She might have known that she would be the butt that

he would use to get close to Toni, but how did he know it was necessary? Bingo, Luc, she thought, as Toni smiled and gave a joking answer. She grimaced at them both and got up from the table.

'This bit isn't for me I take it, guys,' she teased, as she went through to help Maria bring plates in from the kitchen. She laid the table around them, and by the time she'd finished they were talking football, and the crucial forthcoming match between Barcelona and Madrid.

'You'll have to forgive me, Toni,' Luc said, 'I'm not really up on what's happening in the team. I've been in gaol for a few months, and haven't had much news. Did you say Barça have signed César Rodríguez as manager?'

Toni nodded vehemently. 'Good news, if he can bring us the same luck as he brought Saragossa! And at least we won't have him playing against us anymore! But tell me more about what the bastards did to you. Did they have you locked up in Barcelona?'

They were away again, and within minutes Luc was talking more freely about his time in prison than since he had been released. Toni kept asking questions man to man, without pussyfooting around, and Maria came out of the kitchen and stood listening, their lunch completely forgotten behind her. When Luc talked about the prison chaplain she crossed herself and muttered, 'Forgive them.' Carla went to her and put her arm around her shoulder.

'He's still with us, *Avia*, and he escaped torture.'

'You don't call that torture, that terrible isolation? God help us, how long might Sergi have left him there? My poor boy, you're a miracle to my eyes!'

Carla winked at Toni. 'So there's another one she's adopted! Don't get above yourself, Luc – my grandmother adopted Toni long before you, and she takes on all kinds of waifs and strays at the drop of a hat.'

'Too right, *Senyora* Garriga! You go ahead and adopt me!' Luc told Maria. 'Don't you let Carla tell you otherwise! I'm a hero, all right – she just doesn't appreciate me.'

Maria clucked in disapproval. 'You're all very frivolous, but you don't fool me. I know what we've been through with poor Carla, and if you've had half of what she has suffered, then there's more on Sergi's plate than I would want to have to account for when I meet my maker.'

She turned back to the kitchen, and flung over her shoulder, 'Above all, your young man needs feeding, Carla, so you come and bring through the rice. And as for you, Toni, you'll eat your lunch with us. We don't have Paula's larder, but it was me who taught your own mother to cook *arroz negro*, so you'll not dare tell me you won't eat mine!'

They ate their meal to the accompaniment of a fund of reminiscences by Maria and Toni about life in Sant Galdric. Carla learnt that the Figarolas, her real grandparents, were still alive, although there was no one else – their other son had never come home from the war either. There was an uncle, though, living in a village not too far away, and he had family, Toni was sure. *Senyora* Figarola had come to Sant Galdric from somewhere nearer to the coast, and she had family she'd left behind there – there was at least one sister who had visited the village, Maria remembered. One day maybe Carla would meet them all!

Carla listened, and took it in, but said little. Being a

Figarola didn't feel very real to her as yet, and her thoughts were on more immediate concerns.

'Never mind me meeting my long-lost relatives,' she said to Luc. 'First you have to meet my mother! She's waiting for us, remember?'

Toni grinned, and Luc cocked an eye at him. 'Should I be scared?' he asked.

But it was Maria who answered, before Toni could speak. Her voice was very serious, and cut through their banter.

'Being scared is what Carla has experienced for the last few months, facing a life without you and her baby. And it's what my daughter faced twenty-four years ago, for the same reasons – a fear she couldn't share and which changed her life. And yet she's been overcoming that fear for the last week to embrace us all again, and to become herself again. So enough joking about my daughter, all of you – we've all had enough of being scared, and the time is now for a little courage and some big hearts. There should be no more them and us, because you know what that actually means? It means that while we sit round this table together we leave Joana in her corner on her own, and it won't do. Do you hear me, Carla? It's what Martin understood, and what you need to understand.'

Carla was silenced. Luc's hand came over hers across the table, and his other arm went round Maria's shoulder next to his.

'I can see why Carla loves you so much, *Senyora*. Big things are happening to us, and if we can all have hearts even half as big as yours, then we're sure to come out right.'

Maria went to shush him, but this time it was Carla who spoke first.

'Uncle Josep said something similar to me, *Avia*, don't worry. He told me I have to give Mama a chance. I won't forget, and as you can see, you can count on the generosity of my big giant here.'

Luc tightened his arm around Maria and smiled his sweetest smile.

'You see?' he said. 'I told you I was a hero!'

# Chapter Seventeen

Martin had made her go to beautiful Besalú on Monday, just like a tourist, for lunch. They'd stood on the remains of the majestic Viejo bridge, which had defended the town for eight hundred years before twentieth-century man had blown away its heart during the Civil War. It was in the final stages of rebuilding now, and almost restored to its former glory.

'This is what they say they're going to do in Girona, to restore the old monuments and buildings,' Joana said. 'But for now what they're doing is more about pulling down everything that's old and building completely new.'

'They'll protect the real old town, though?'

'Oh yes, and maybe one day they'll clean its poor old face and make it look like this,' Joana said, wistfully, looking around at the beautiful yellow stone of Besalú's town walls.

She stood for a long time watching the river Fluvià as

it flowed away below them, its waters low and sluggish now, at the end of this dry summer. Then she took Martin's arm, and they strolled together through the stone gates into the untouched stone streets. They had lunch in a little inn behind the main square, a simple dish of lamb and beans, which they washed down with a rich Tempranillo.

'None of your silly sparkly wine with a dish like this,' Martin had joked, and Joana had rapped his knuckles with her fork, and insisted on ordering some Cava with their *mel i mató* dessert of soft goat's cheese and honey.

It felt like being on holiday. 'I'd love to have gone to the coast,' she said to Martin. 'To Cadaquès. It's so beautiful, and I haven't seen the sea for such a long time. How strange, when we live so near, but once we'd built the hill house, Sergi always wanted to be there in summer, and we would have house guests all the time, especially for the hunting in August. I suppose the last time I was on the coast was near Escala, when we were invited by friends who had their summer home there. That would be three years ago!'

'Bah!' Martin dismissed, 'Cadaquès is full of French tourists nowadays. Give me a place like this any time! I live by the sea, and love it, but your backdrop of hills is so majestic – it takes a lot of beating.'

'Not all year round!'

'No,' Martin conceded. 'Maybe not all the time, or at least, not to live in them on your own. You need to work on that one, Joana. What will you do when Carla and Luc are safe and living their lives somewhere else in Spain? You won't just accept your fate anymore, will you, and imprison yourself quietly on demand? You need better than that.'

His voice of concern wrapped her like a fur coat, and she thought how extraordinary it was that this young man should care about them all so much.

'We're not there yet, Martin,' was all she replied. 'When Carla and Luc are safe, as you say, then you can ask me again, and I'll maybe figure out an answer. For now I just want to see them arrive.'

And so on the Wednesday afternoon she was on the watch, fidgeting around the veranda, listening for the sound of the Mercedes on the track. Martin was outside chopping wood, burying his own fidgets under the cover of exercise.

It was Martin, sharp on the lookout, who gave the call. 'There's the car!'

Surely they must be with Toni! Otherwise he wouldn't be back yet – they'd agreed he would wait in Girona until evening if necessary, in case they arrived. Joana went down the steps from the veranda to stand beside Martin, and together they watched as the Mercedes snaked up the hill towards them. It would pass to the left of the house to stop in the back yard, so they ran round to be there when it arrived.

There were three people inside the car. Carla was beaming from the front seat, and tucked in behind her sat a young man – Luc, this must be Luc! Carla burst from the car as soon as it stopped, and a flash of memory went through Joana of her daughter's unwilling, unbending arrival at the hill house eight days before. This couldn't be more different.

'He's here!' Carla called, unnecessarily, and she pulled open the rear door of the car before Luc could even reach the handle.

Martin moved forward towards the car, but Joana hung back, suddenly very nervous. Before her, Carla was waiting for Luc, who unfolded himself from the back seat and emerged slowly from the car, his eyes taking in all around him. Heavens, what a size! The boy was huge! But he looked strangely abashed for one so big, and on impulse Joana took a step towards him, and Martin stepped back, so that it was Joana whose hand Luc took first.

He was no beauty, she thought, but he had a face that hinted at an interesting personality. Then he smiled, and it lit his eyes, and involuntarily she gave him a smile back. Here was a man who would be kind to her daughter, she thought, with a surge of elation. There would be no hard-edged relationships with Luc.

She turned towards Carla, who was watching her intently. 'What a mountain, *vida meva*!' she said, 'Can we feed him, do you think?'

Carla grinned. 'He eats for two, but he's cheap to run – he'll eat anything you give him, and he just mops up other people's plates when he's hungry! He's so thin, though, after being in gaol. Grandma was trying to feed him up, down there in Girona.'

'Paula will undoubtedly want to do the same – she's already been on a mission to build you up in the last week or so, and now she'll have two to feed. She sourced some chanterelle mushrooms yesterday, so I think you may be in for a feast this evening.' She smiled again at Luc, and found he was watching her with grave, discerning eyes. But there was no disapproval, no prejudged ideas. He just looked as though he wanted to know her, and she squeezed his hand a little before she let it go. She wanted to know him too.

No one wanted to sit still on the veranda, so they all went out for a walk in the last of the afternoon sunshine, tailoring their pace to Carla's as they meandered along the forest tracks, aiming for a clearing on a rise that gave panoramic views of the valley, and of the house behind them. Luc was absurdly solicitous about Carla – he hadn't been present for much of her pregnancy, Joana mused, and must have been caught up in powerless, pent-up worry as he sat in his prison cell.

'Watch Joaquima!' he yelped at one point, as Carla caught her foot on a root. She didn't even falter, and turned on him with her tongue stuck out.

'Joaquim is just fine, thank you!' she answered, and then when she saw her mother's perplexed face she laughed.

'He wants a girl,' she explained. 'But how could a bump this size be anything other than another great manly lump like Luc?'

'It can be anything it likes, as far as I'm concerned, provided you don't call it Joaquim!' Joana retorted, amused.

'Absurd name, isn't it?' Luc agreed. 'A good name for a bump!'

'Have you any names in mind for what may come out of the bump?'

'We've not had much time to talk about it yet, *Senyora* Olivera. I guess we'll wait and see what pops out first, before we commit! Do you fancy Joana for a girl?'

'No way! Do you fancy Luc for a boy?'

It was Carla who answered. 'Not Luc, but a family name, yes. We could name him after grandfather, your father, perhaps – I don't even know his name! I've only ever heard him called by his surname.'

'Yes, I know,' Joana answered. 'Everyone called him Vigo, for some reason. His real name was Juan, which is where my own name came from, but it's not a name he would have needed to see passed on to the next generation. Should you think maybe of Luc's father, instead?'

'Or we could call him Alex.' Luc's words fell into a sudden silence, and Joana drew in a sharp breath. It was astonishing how jagged the knife was every time she thought of Alex. Carla too had frozen, and exchanged a quick look with Martin.

He shook his head at her. 'No,' he mouthed. 'It's all right.'

What on earth was that all about, Joana wondered? Carla was looking at him as though the words had special significance, but only nodded in response. She was such a private, complicated person. Joana looked at Martin, who was still watching Carla's face. He too was so self-contained, even secretive at times. Of all of them, Luc was the only open, straightforward one. She'd only just met this future son-in-law, and already she found him easier than her daughter had ever been. She shrugged in unwonted acceptance. What she couldn't control she wouldn't chafe over, and let's face it, she was just grateful to be included right now in this fragment of their lives.

Later she sat with Carla on the veranda, just the two of them on their own. She wanted to talk to Carla, just to talk normally, like mothers and daughters were supposed to do. With Martin she could talk about anything – about the weather, or food, or more seriously about politics, but simply, with no other agenda. But with Carla the past hung between them, and it blocked all normal conversation. When Martin and Luc were around, Carla would entertain, and amuse, and be amused, but alone with her mother she became, not mute, but guarded. If we can talk the past into history, thought Joana, then maybe things will become easier – our relationship has become stiff from lack of use. So talk, then, you fool, she chided herself. Let's open up the past, if we must.

'Martin tells me you were amazing in the meeting with Sergi,' she said eventually.

Carla gave a little shiver. 'It was the scariest thing I've ever done! And it stayed just as frightening afterwards, because I just couldn't believe we'd actually won, and that he would really get Luc released. He was so menacing – but I was careful to say we would go away and leave him in peace if he let Luc go. I wanted him to feel there would really be an end to all our threats if he just did this one thing.'

'Well you succeeded. He did let Luc go. You did better than I could ever have done – I've never stood up to him, not in twenty-four years. And nor have I ever succeeded in getting the better of him – not even the mildest manipulation.'

'You got him to accept your child, though, didn't you?'

'I don't think I had even the hint of a say in it, looking back! He must have had a fair idea that I wouldn't marry him under normal circumstances, Alex or no Alex, because I was nervous of him, and he was the pariah of our village, so he used my pregnancy to coerce me. And he liked the idea of me having to be grateful to him. All he had to do was give his name to my child and forever afterwards he'd won himself a complaisant wife. But over time that wasn't enough. I've begun to wonder whether his growing anger against me came precisely for that reason. He got me to marry him, but he knew he wasn't my first choice, and that I married him only because there was no other option available. It can't have made him feel too great, underneath.'

'Why did he want you so much, do you think?' Carla asked. 'I mean, I know you were beautiful, but there were other beautiful girls, surely?'

Joana shook her head in shared perplexity, and answered slowly. 'He called me luscious, once. He used to call me his temptress, and yet God knows I was no siren – I may have been pregnant, but he knew I was fundamentally innocent. He seemed to want to devour me, but, do you know, I think what he wanted most was to pluck me out of the village in front of the eyes of his detractors. He wanted to prove that he could walk all over the village that hated him.'

She sighed. 'But for me, he was a saviour nevertheless. Do you know what it would have meant back then, to have a baby without a man to marry you? Well, of course you do know, because you've been frightened yourself. Back in 1939 if a girl got pregnant she and the boy got married. If she had no man who would own her she was damned. And Alex was dead and no one knew how close we had been – I could have been pregnant by a visiting tramp for all I could prove. So Sergi was my saviour. And yours too, Carla, believe me! He saved you from being labelled a bastard, or from being given away!'

A silence ensued, and Joana stretched in her chair. It was six o'clock, and well-trained Paula would shortly appear with aperitifs, and the men would soon be joining them. There was a chill in the evening air, but the sky had remained clear this October, and the sun was setting behind them, casting a reflected glow over towards the east. It occurred to Joana that Carla hadn't made any further comment, and she looked across to find herself being examined. She cocked an eye at her, and Carla pulled herself a little straighter in her chair.

'Mama,' she said, 'Did Martin tell you how Sergi exploded at us at the end of our visit?'

'And called you a whore? Yes, I'm sorry, *carinyo*, you didn't deserve that, but you had already won, otherwise you wouldn't have raised such a reaction. He lost his cool, didn't he? Just like he always does when he doesn't get his own way.'

Carla seemed to be having difficulty continuing, and as she hesitated Martin came through the door from the house. She made a gesture to him and he stopped.

'Mama, I need to tell you what Sergi said when he lost his temper. He called me a whore, yes, but he also told me I was just like you – that you were a whore as well, and that I wasn't his child.'

Joana was surprised. She hadn't thought Sergi would admit this ever to Carla or to anyone – it was information that would hardly help his image.

'And then,' Carla continued, 'he told us that he had got rid of my real father.'

The words hung in the air, strange and oddly formed –

as though Carla had suddenly spoken Spanish to her on this still Catalan evening. Joana turned the words over but they didn't seem to mean anything.

'He said what?' she asked, thinking that if the words were repeated they might acquire some meaning.

Martin stepped quietly towards them and sat on the edge of the sofa, close by Joana's elbow.

'I'm sorry, Mama, but he told us he had Alex Figarola killed, or perhaps even killed him himself. "Got rid of him" were the words he used. I thought at the time he might be trying simply to shock me, but there was something very convincing about what he said.'

Joana looked into the distance. On cue Paula shuffled out, like an extra appearing onstage, Joana thought, bringing a bottle and glasses. Martin stayed close, not touching her, but his arm was so close to hers that she could feel its warmth. Was this what he and Carla had been so secretive about this afternoon? But this wasn't real. Sergi hadn't killed Alex. If he had, then everything that she'd ever believed of him was a lie – all the good things she'd tried to focus on over the years, all her guilt for not giving him sons, all her 'managing' of Carla, and life, and his endless ego, so as to give Sergi his place as king amongst them.

Give me that glass, she wanted to scream at Paula, who was taking so much time serving them. Luc appeared now as well, standing in the shadows of the veranda as though he felt he mustn't approach. There was a bubble around Joana and none of them could join her in it. Outside it the world seemed to be turning quite normally, but inside it she was on her own, completely on her own.

'I had to tell you Mama,' Carla was pleading, her gaze fixed in disquiet on Joana's face. 'You can't go through the rest of your life making your plans as though you have to be grateful to him.'

Why no, thought Joana, I'll do my best not to be grateful. What the hell emotion she was supposed to feel she didn't know, but she knew it wasn't gratitude. Could this be true? Could it really be true? The question turned over and over in her mind as everything she'd believed in evaporated, and the last twenty-four years of her life turned to ashes before her eyes. It hurt physically, in her guts and, sharp as hell in her head, a bulldozer of pain that made it hard to think through what she'd just heard, but which left the image of Alex imprinted crystal clear in front of her, stretched helpless and dying on the ground, with Sergi hovering over him, knife in hand, and that almost lascivious expression on his face.

And the worst thing of all was that now the words had been spoken, the idea implanted, she didn't even find the image difficult to believe.

# Chapter Eighteen

*Sergi sat on the wall by the church, at exactly the same spot where Joana and Alex used to meet, and reached his hand out to Joana. Behind them the square was empty – Sergi's arrival had sent the children scuttling away fearfully from their Easter games. He had been cold-shouldered by the entire village since his arrival that morning, with people drawing back inside doorways to shield themselves from him, and even his grandmother had received him only reluctantly. The word in the village was that she hadn't even wanted to make up a bed for him, and everyone knew how she had done penance in the church every day since his visit with his army troop six weeks ago.*

*Four doors away from her house the Companys family still waited for any news of poor Joaquim, and while his wife might hope daily for his return, the rest of the village were beginning to believe that he would never be seen again. His very name would condemn him to the* Fascista, *and his friends might know that he was no relation of their Catalan President, Lluís Companys, but it was unlikely that any Nationalist would believe it. So the loathing felt for Sergi Olivera was heavy in the air today, and only their respect for his grandmother prevented the men from doing him serious injury.*

*But it didn't seem to bother Sergi. He had sauntered through the village flashing his army stripes, and walked through Joana's door as though sure of his welcome, brushing past an aghast Maria with a dismissive greeting, and now he sat completely at ease in the spring sunshine, examining Joana's overthin frame with a slight frown.*

*'You've lost weight, little sweetheart.' His voice purred at her, and Joana was more nervous of him than ever. His hand beckoned, and she moved towards him in spite of herself. He seized hold of her very gently and pulled her into him, so she stood between his legs, her face just a fingerbreadth from his.*

*'What has happened to you,* meva estimada*? You look unhappy. No, you look more than unhappy, you look as though the world has fallen in on you. Tell me! You know you can tell me anything.'*

*His voice was no longer disturbing, and he spoke with infinite gentleness as he took one of her curls between his fingers. She could feel his warm breath on her cheek. Could she trust him? He seemed to see deep inside her. No one else, not even Mama, seemed to see how distraught she was, how desperate. God, how she needed a friend, but did Sergi want to be her friend? The village didn't fully comprehend what he had done to save her from his officer six weeks ago, but she did. It didn't stop her being afraid of him, but it jumbled up her thoughts so she no longer knew what to think.*

*'Tell me, little Joana,' he repeated, his whisper a caress.*

*She just looked at him, tears blurring her eyes.*

*'My grandmother tells me young Figarola was found dead in Girona. Were you in love with him, Joana?'*

*She lowered her eyes, and he stroked the back of her head. 'Don't worry, little one. Is that why you're so unhappy? But what is it that haunts you? Is it just that you're grieving for him?'*

*She raised her eyes again and he looked deep into them. 'No,' he said. 'There's something more there. You're frightened of something, aren't you? What is it, Joana?'*

*She shook her head, tears rolling slowly down her cheeks. Her arms were trapped between them, and she wrapped them protectively around her still flat stomach. Sergi looked down and a strange light came into his eyes. He reached his arms around her and held her close against his chest, so she could no longer see the expression on his face. He kissed the top of her head and spoke in his most caressing tones, but the triumph in his voice was clear.*

*'Now then,* la meva estimada, *you haven't been too sure about me,* no és*? You're still in love with that young fool who didn't know better than to get himself killed for a foolish Communist regime. And now look how he has left you, facing ruin, if I read things right. But now you will realise who your real friend is.' His hand slid down her back, and just skimmed her thigh through her thin cotton dress.*

*'There's passion in those eyes of yours, Joana. I've always known you're a girl with amorous potential, and I've watched you ripen into a fruit I have to taste.'*

*She still wasn't looking at him, keeping her head buried as his words spelt out her fate. 'It would seem you've already given yourself to him, and now, my seductive little creature, you will give yourself to me, and I will protect you, and take care of his child, and we'll make more children, and you'll know what a real man is like.'*

*His hand pushed below her skirt to stroke her buttocks, and his other hand pulled her head up to face him. What she saw in his eyes was hot desire, and she realised that without saying a single word she had revealed everything to him, and he wanted her, he still wanted her, and her decision had been made for her.*

*'Oh, Alex,' she bled inside as Sergi leant down to kiss her, and fastened greedy, hungry lips on hers . . .*

'Joana, Joana! Wake up, Joana!' A hand was shaking her, and she pulled herself out of the dream and woke up, bathed in cold sweat. A dark face swam before hers, and she gazed at it blindly.

'Alex!' she whispered.

'No, Joana.' Martin's voice cut through her lingering dream, and she came fully awake with a long shudder. Martin was sitting on the side of her bed, one hand on her shoulder, a dressing gown covering his pyjamas.

'Martin?'

'It's all right, Joana. You were having a bad dream – I heard you calling out from down the corridor, and came in to find you calling out, something I couldn't understand, and you sounded so distressed I had to wake you. Are you all right?'

She reached her hand up to grip his. She was still trembling, and she was cold, so terribly cold. She focused on Martin's face.

'Are you all right?' he repeated, troubled.

'I was only a girl, Martin,' she pleaded. 'Only a girl!'

'I know, Joana, I know. Don't worry.'

'Yes, but I was so scared of him!' she whispered. 'He was so overpowering, so domineering, and I could tell he knew he had me beaten. But I told myself all my instincts were wrong, because he was being kind. And I gave myself to him completely, God help me I let him take me right there in the village, like some powerless doll, and he made me his possession.' Her voice broke and she began to cry, and Martin took her in his arms and said nothing, just held her cold body against his warm one while she wept. He wrapped her blankets around her bare arms and over the thin straps of her nightdress, and drew her close to cloak her with his body.

He made no move to touch her beyond this deep enfolding. He was all comfort, all kindness, and she lay inert in the crook of his body, feeling her grief slowly receding as her body warmed. As she drifted eventually back to sleep she felt safe, very safe, and the last thing she remembered was a tiny touch of his lips on the nape of her neck.

She slept without dreams this time, or none that she remembered as she woke, still in semi-darkness, to find Martin asleep beside her. His hair was swept back off his face, his arm outflung, and with his eyes closed his long lashes nestled against the smooth skin of his cheeks. He looked young, untouched, and at peace, more than he had since they'd burdened him with their troubles. She raised herself to rest on her elbow and studied him, remembering that little kiss he'd given her just as she drifted off to sleep.

For some reason she couldn't explain to herself she had never asked Martin anything about himself. Carla and Maria seemed to be on more familiar terms with him, in many ways, but between her and Martin there was a strange kind of empathy, which was more to do with currents of understanding than with the details of their lives. Martin understood her vulnerability, and had cut right through her hard edges from the moment he'd first walked up to the hill house, less than two weeks ago.

And what about her? What did she know about this young creature sleeping before her? To her he was in so many ways the living embodiment of Luis, or was it even of Alex? Intelligent, intuitive, protective but challenging, he was the successful young man who could carry people along with him, and as she looked at him now she felt a biting sense of loss for all she'd exchanged Luis and Alex for. But Luis, you weren't there, my uncle! Where were you to protect us from Franco and all those you'd set us up against? Where were you when they invaded our lives and my Alex was taken?

But Martin was not his father – he wasn't responsible for the past, and something told her that the past must have touched him too. He had a wistful look sometimes, which tugged at her, and when he stood by her in solidarity she felt his need as well as his support. Was he in love with her? She thought perhaps he was. And did she love him? Yes, as she had loved Luis, the miraculous uncle with the winning smile, who had made her believe in herself.

She wondered again about Martin's age. If he was Luis's oldest child then he was twenty-seven years old, but right now he looked younger. How old had Alex been when he died? Just nineteen, if she remembered right. Martin looked a bit like Alex just now, his face elongated in the shadowy, predawn light. The thought of Alex wrenched her gut again, and she slipped out of the bed to go and stand by the window.

There wasn't much to see outside yet, in the gloom, but she gazed down in the direction of Sant Galdric, and for some long minutes she was back there, laughing with Alex over that long summer before it all fell apart, working the fields with Uncle Victor in hitched-up skirts, helping little brother Josep with his homework. A crowd of memories invaded her, and for a time she was unconscious of where she was, in the hill house with her sleeping cousin behind her.

Then Sergi came into her vision, and the marching soldiers, and she was back in that moment in the square, when she'd given up the past and made a pact with the future. She shivered, and came to, suddenly aware of her bare feet on the cold tiles, and the flimsy nightdress with its thin straps. She stroked her hands over the goosebumps on her arms, but made no attempt to move. The cold suited her, and she thought dimly that maybe it would help her think.

Behind her Martin moved in his sleep, and she turned to watch him as he gave a little sigh, and buried his head beneath the covers. He could be Luc, seen like this – just another of the young people for whom she felt responsible. What had she done for them? She'd given them documents that had forced Sergi to set Luc free, but were they really free? Would they ever really be free with Sergi still so powerful?

Sergi was a murderer – she'd known that when she found the documents, much as she might have tried to convince herself that they might not be conclusive. He might not have pulled any triggers himself – he had a group of young thugs around him who formed a kind of posse, eager for advancement and favour, and without a scruple between them. Would it not have been easier, and safer, for Sergi to detail one of them to do his dirty work? He didn't need to say why the driver had to be killed – he could talk some rubbish about him being an enemy of the state, and his chosen vigilante would ask no questions. But it didn't change the fact that he was a killer.

Had he also killed Alex, all those years ago? He didn't have a gang at his command back then, so he would have to have killed him with his own hands. Or would he? Sergi was a manipulator, and back then was primarily concerned with building his own advantage from the chaos of the end of the civil war. Other men were hotheads and dupes and fanatics, and Sergi's entire success had come from knowing how to exploit them. As she thought about it a scenario came to mind of Sergi watching Alex as he left work, speaking a quiet word in the ear of an angry group of Franco's men, on the loose and looking for game in a lawless Girona.

And that's what he could still do to Carla and Luc. He had found the easiest, most painless way to have Luc removed from Carla's life back in the summer, and he had left Carla with her grandmother while he watched her growing pregnancy and made his plans. He would let Carla go now, for fear of the documents she held, but would he really let her disappear completely? He was an angry man, and his anger could burn very cold. Would he be watching when Luc went for his first job, or for his first promotion? Would he track them so that they never quite got the housing they wanted? None of these things could be pinned on him, or would make Carla use the document against him.

She had never before viewed Sergi as malevolent. He had been aggressive, controlling, and so often angry with her and with Carla, but all of this she could understand, and indeed had taken a lot of the guilt for it on herself. She knew he was calculating and power-loving, but so were all his senior colleagues – Franco's regime had encouraged them, pitting official against official, politician against politician, in a policy of divide and rule that shared out the rewards and made sure that no one grew too big for his boots.

Even what he had done to Carla and Luc could be seen, not as malicious, but as him overcontrolling a situation he disapproved of. So what made her think he would act henceforth with cold malice? Only his anger, she thought, that anger that had been growing and that must now be burning even more fiercely after Carla's visit.

Joana moved away from the window and sat at her dressing table, looking steadily at her own reflection in the mirror, grimacing at her face, pinched and pallid in the cold light now filtering in through the window. No more excuses now, she thought. No more protection. I have to take my stand and know whose side I'm on.

She stood up and pulled on a dressing gown, wrapping it tight around her for warmth. Behind her Martin stirred, and she went over to him, shaking him gently by the shoulder until his eyes opened, bleared and bewildered.

'You need to go now, Martin, before the house awakens. You should go back to your room and get a bit more sleep there.' She smiled at him, feeling a kind of tenderness which had been long dead in her. 'I think you need more sleep, *carinyo*, after I woke you up last night. Was I crying out so loud, to wake you down the corridor?'

He shook his head, looking troubled. 'I was already awake.'

'Worrying about us all, as usual?'

He nodded, frowning.

'Don't worry about me, Martin, I'll be all right. And so will Carla, I can promise you that. I'm going to make sure of it.'

He looked a query at her, and she held a finger to her lips and smiled. 'No words just now.'

She moved towards the door and opened it slightly to check that the coast was clear. Martin followed her, and before she held the door open for him she took him in her arms and kissed him on the cheek.

'Thank you, cousin, for what you did for me last night. You brought me compassion, and closeness, and I haven't known that for nearly twenty-five years.'

She heard her voice shaking. That's what comes of living in a cold, hard desert all those years, she thought. When someone brings a little warmth into your life you just can't handle it. But she was handling it better than Martin.

'Don't thank me, Joana,' he said, and then his voice cracked and he couldn't say anymore. He pulled away from her and disappeared.

# Chapter Nineteen

Carla was looking forward the following morning to talking to her mother about her real father. She'd dreamt nightly since last Friday of the dark man who'd visited those earlier dreams when she was a child. She didn't want to talk about Sergi anymore. How many times could they repeat between them that he was a monster who had hijacked their lives? If they talked instead about Alex, would it not give them the chance to give him life and to be more positive?

She'd worried all night about having told her mother what Sergi had said. She'd had to do it, she knew that – Joana was at a turning point, and only the truth would help her to make the right decisions for her future. But knowing this didn't stop her feeling guilty as she remembered Joana's stricken face and subsequent silence last night – all evening as they chatted Joana had joined in mechanically, but tight little lines fretted at her forehead, and she looked fragile as Carla had never known her.

So it didn't surprise her that Joana didn't appear for breakfast, or even later in the morning. She thought her mother might have had a bad night, and hoped that now she was sleeping. But she was impatient to see Joana, nevertheless. Tomorrow she and Luc must leave for Terrassa, and Carla didn't know when she could expect to see her mother again. Their reunion was still fragile, and there was much they still needed to say to try to build bonds for the uncertain future. Not least, Carla wanted to keep the promise she'd made to Uncle Josep in Barcelona, to tell Joana about him, about his life, his wife, the children, and how much he longed to see his lost sister.

Paula came and went about the breakfast dishes with the mute stoicism that seemed to define her, and after breakfast Martin and Luc took a packed lunch and went off together for a long hike up the hill, needing the space and the exercise. Carla went for a rather gentler walk herself, returning to the house just before lunchtime, and was surprised to find that there was still no sign of her mother. She went through to the kitchen and found Paula cleaning silver. A single plate of leftover chicken and salad stood on the sideboard, and on the hob a small pot was steaming with what smelt like boiling potatoes. By all the evidence only one lunch was being prepared today.

Carla looked a query. 'Is Mama not having lunch today, Paula?' she asked.

Paula looked stolidly at the bowl she was cleaning. 'She isn't here, Miss. Toni took her down to Girona early this morning, before any of you were up. She told me not to bother you, but to tell you if you asked that she would be back this afternoon.'

Gone to Girona? Carla was astonished. What on earth had taken her mother to Girona? Her mind shot back to last night, and her revelations to Joana. Surely this sudden trip must have something to do with the news she'd given her? Oh help, she thought, has Mama gone to confront Sergi? I was right to have been worried about having told her, right that she must have had a troubled night – so troubled that she has abandoned caution, it seems. She looked so desolate last night, and there was no way to reach her. A lick of fear went through Carla at the thought of what Joana might be doing. Surely she hasn't thrown everything to the wind?

'Did she say what she was going to Girona for?' she asked Paula, though she was sure that Paula would know nothing. A shake of the head gave her an answer, and she nodded and stepped back, accepting defeat.

'Well, she'll no doubt tell us when she gets back. Would you like some help with the silver, Paula?'

Another shake of the head was the only reply, so Carla took herself off, and after a solitary lunch she tried to keep herself busy while she waited for her mother, or for Luc. She wanted Luc to come back and reassure her again that the things she had told her mother were the things that needed to be told, and that a sane future depended on everything being open, but the guys were taking ages to return.

Eventually she heard them. There was an almighty series of crashing noises behind the house, and the sound of men's voices whooping through the trees. Carla got up and went through the kitchen and out to the back, and there she found Luc and Martin, lying in a heap together in the cleared ground just behind the house, heaving for breath, scratched and covered in pine needles, but laughing like ten-year-old boys.

Carla looked up at the sheer slope above them and realised they'd chosen to come back down from the summit through the trees, rather than by the longer path. A mad act by unruly youths and it was lucky they hadn't broken ankles and knees between them. But they looked renewed and refreshed, and Luc had his old grin back.

They lay for a moment, both flat on their backs, and Luc pointed up at the cloudless sky.

'That,' he said, through heaving breath, 'is the most amazing sight in the world! When you're stuck in a cell and your only exercise is in a covered yard, you long to see the sky. I've been gazing at it non-stop ever since they let me go.'

'And yet we spent most of this summer complaining about how hot it was,' Martin commented. 'It was too hot for walking, and I'm sorry to say we didn't spend much time looking up at the sky! It's amazing what you take for granted.'

'It's good to be able to take things for granted! One day here in Spain we'll be able to take ordinary life for granted, and all we'll have to do is live and put in a decent day's work, and never feel threatened by the police, or nasty-minded profiteers like Sergi Olivera.'

Luc spoke without heat, matter of fact and relaxed as he continued to watch a single tiny cloud crossing the sky, scudding along with the wind.

'That'll come, though, surely?' Martin queried. 'Franco

is getting old and by the time little Joaquima grows up you'll be living in a different country. I only hope I'll still know where you are and be able to find you again one day.'

Luc sat up and grinned. 'We'll manage! As long as we know where you are we'll make sure you know where we are. Who knows, we may need a doctor one day! But you know what we need right now? A shower! Carla is looking at me as though she could never bear to touch me again, and that, you know, is unthinkable! Carla, *vida meva*, will you make coffee for two men who adore you if they promise to present themselves to you clean and free of undergrowth in fifteen minutes or so?'

'Of course, but Luc, Mama has gone to Girona – she was gone before breakfast, Paula tells me.'

She had succeeded in stopping both men in their tracks. Martin froze, and stood stock-still, gazing at Carla with his mouth open and a look of horror on his face. Luc was still sitting on the ground, picking bits of twig and pine needles from his shirt, but at her words he stopped, and rose deliberately to his feet, a very thoughtful expression on his face.

'It seems the news we gave her had a profound effect,' he said, slowly.

Thank you for saying 'we', Carla thought, but it was me who told my mother that her husband killed the love of her life. There was a shadow on Luc's face that reminded her that he had only recently emerged from trauma, strung to the limit, though he hid it well. He didn't need any more worries now, and yet if Joana had indeed gone to tackle Sergi there were implications for Luc and her that must be obvious to anyone. The cold, business-like understanding that Carla had reached with Sergi must be kept on those terms. If he was inflamed, then the beast might go on the rampage, and throw caution to the wind. He would come looking for them then, regardless of any potential consequences to himself.

Uncle Josep's words came back to Carla. What was it he'd said about Luc? 'He's had to use all his reserves, and now that his fight is over he could struggle, especially if he comes under any more pressure.' Luc had been so buoyant for the last couple of days that it was easy to forget. 'It will be a while before your lives are simple,' Josep had said. How true that was.

She looked at the two men, fresh from their hike, happy-go-lucky until three minutes ago, and was vexed with herself. I could have let them have a little longer in the sun, she thought. There was nothing to be gained, after all, by them knowing about Joana's journey until she came back and could tell them herself what she had done, if indeed it was she who came back. Carla suppressed a quick frisson of fear, and rushed into speech.

'Paula tells me that Mama has only gone for a few hours, and will be back this afternoon. I'm hoping she hasn't done anything rash, but actually, knowing Mama, that's unlikely. I shouldn't have told you – she will do her own talking, when she arrives!'

She caught Luc's knowing eyes on her, and made herself smile. 'I've been a little tense,' she told him, putting her arm around him, 'but now you're here I can see I've been a bit stupid. Why don't you go and shower, both of you, like you said, and then we'll have coffee on the veranda while we wait. She won't be long now.'

Luc drew her to him and squeezed her, placing a kiss on her forehead. She raised a hand and stroked his unruly hair out of his eyes.

'Love you,' she said, and he smiled at her.

'Been worried have you, little chamois? Well, that wasn't stupid, because your mother hasn't gone to Girona to buy bread, that's for sure. But we'll wait for her own words, like you say. Can we have some of Paula's cakes with the coffee?'

Over his shoulder Carla watched Martin, who still hadn't moved. For a moment Carla saw through his eyes, and knew that he was consumed with fear for Joana. He was Joana's champion, the medieval knight errant who had put himself at her service. A very gentle, caring knight, but very young, too, thought Carla, and right now he seemed too much alone. She disengaged herself from Luc and went to Martin, putting her arms round him in a very cousinly hug.

'My mother will be fine, Martin,' she assured him. 'She's a very astute woman, and knows her husband very well indeed. She won't be doing anything reckless in Girona. She's due back in an hour or so, and will come in here like a whirlwind, calling for champagne, and refusing to give us her news until she's drunk it.'

He nodded, saying nothing, and for want of any more comfort she could give him, Carla propelled him physically before her towards the house.

'A shower now, *el meu cosí*, because you and my fiancé are a physical disgrace, as well as being reckless lunatics for running down that hill! We all need coffee, but you're not having any in that state!'

They drank their coffee, and despite the worry lines around their eyes Carla thought the two men looked better for their half day away from their daily drama. They kept up light conversation, but all of them must, she thought, now be waiting on tenterhooks for Joana to reappear. She kept her own fears to herself – fears that Joana might not come, or that the car that came up the track might bring Sergi instead. Both Luc and Martin probably had their own versions of these fears anyway.

After a seemingly interminable period of small talk, they heard the car. All of them leapt to their feet, and by the time the Mercedes came into sight they were all three craning over the veranda wall, eyes fixed on the car as though they could see inside it from this distance. But it was Joana – a moment or two longer and that became clear. Her little pillbox hat could be seen outlined in the rear window. Carla breathed again, and led the others on a charge through the kitchen to be in the backyard as the car came round the house and drew to a halt.

It was Martin who opened the car door for Joana, and who took her bag from her as she emerged, smiling and serene, to face the tense little group.

'Well, my dears, it looks as though you've managed to work yourselves up into a nice little frenzy about me while I've been gone,' she said, accepting her handbag back from Martin. 'Shall we go inside? I do indeed have news for you, but I think it would best be told over a glass of champagne.'

Carla began to laugh. Told you so, she wanted to say

to Martin, but it wouldn't be fair, when her words to him had seemed like pure fantasy to herself when she'd spoken them. Mama would always surprise, and if her demeanour now was anything to go by, she was very well pleased with whatever she'd just been doing in Girona.

'Champagne, then, if you will, Mama, but then we need to know what you've been up to. How could you just leave us like that without a word of explanation, and expect us not to fret?'

'Because you'd have tried to stop me. No – no more questions until I have a drink and something to eat in front of me. I've had no lunch to speak of and I'm starving.'

The air was growing cool now, so they went through to the lounge, followed soon by Paula, bringing the drinks tray and some savoury pastries, which Luc and Martin attacked more avidly than Joana. Martin hadn't eaten the cakes with coffee earlier, but now he seemed liberated, and had his eyes fixed on Joana. Well they all did. She had an audience.

And finally she was ready to talk. 'Well, my children,' she said, 'I've done what I probably should have done a long time ago. I've known for many years that Sergi wasn't a good man, but his world was the only world that made any sense, and he didn't seem any worse than any of his colleagues, any of our friends. But after what you told me last night, Carla, it all looked different. I have to say that all my rather fixed loyalty started to seem pretty wretched, and for the first time I found myself looking at him from outside, rather than inside, our marriage, if you see what I mean. It was good to blackmail Sergi and get him to set Luc free, but he's a man who needs to win, and I had a vision of the future that would never really be free of him for Carla and Luc.'

She shifted position on the sofa and took another sip from her glass. No one else moved.

'I'd always felt that I should protect Sergi's position, since that was what gave me and Carla our lives, and it should at least be respected. But last night, suddenly I no longer gave a fig for Sergi's position. On the contrary, I realised that as long as he remains in a position of power he will always use it to follow us and control us all – to think otherwise was a pipedream. So I went to Girona.'

'You didn't go to see Papa!'

'No, Carla, what could I achieve by going to see him? No, Toni and I went to see Pablo Roig.'

'Pablo Roig? But he's Papa's bitterest enemy – the biggest rat in the regional government!'

'Exactly! Sergi stopped Roig from getting promotion once, and Pablo Roig never forgot it. So I took the blackmail documents to him.'

'You did what?'

'Well, I didn't see Roig in person – he's the most untrustworthy man you could imagine, and I wouldn't want him to be able to let Sergi know sometime that his wife had spilt the beans on him. Toni took the documents in to him while I waited outside. Toni has never met Roig, so he can't be connected to Sergi. Toni says he just told Roig he'd picked up the documents and felt they should be handed in to the correct authorities. Roig read the letters through and asked him to wait. He took them away, and when he came back he told Toni he'd done very right, and should just go away now, and take comfort in being a good citizen of Spain.'

'Oh my God! He could have held Toni for questioning! Did you think of that, Mama?'

'No he wouldn't. Roig won't even want it to be known that he handled the documents. He'll have handed them on himself, very quietly. You may want to dispose of a rival, but you don't want his demise to be pinned to you.'

Carla chewed at what Joana had told them, and thought she was right. Her knowledge of the political world Sergi moved in was better than any of theirs, after all – but what a risky situation to have put Toni in, nevertheless!

Joana seemed to read her mind. 'Don't think I forced Toni! Remember your stepfather sacked his mother when she became ill, and has refused her all help since. Toni was a willing accomplice, I can assure you. Ask him for yourself, and he'll tell you.'

Carla looked to Luc to see how he was reacting. He seemed to be more bemused than anything, and she wondered if he had taken in the significance of what Joana had done. A wave of anger and frustration went through Carla as she thought through all the possible implications.

'So you've engineered Sergi's fall from grace, Mama, is that it?' she asked, wanting to be clear. 'Will he be arrested?'

Joana merely nodded, as though she didn't want to say the words.

'But you already said last week that you don't think the allegations in the blackmail documents will be enough to get him ultimately convicted, or even to justify a trial. He'll get out of gaol pretty quickly, don't you think, with all the connections he's got?'

'Possibly Carla, but don't look at me as though you wanted to murder me.' Joana picked up her glass again and looked challengingly back at Carla. 'The point is that he'll have lost his power base, and he won't be able to dog your lives, or blight Luc's career. Don't you realise what he could have done to you? He needn't ever have shown himself openly, but provided he could follow your progress, he could always be there behind every spoilt opportunity, every time you were refused a bank loan, or a house. He may not have been able to influence your academics at Barcelona University, but anyone in government employment, or a bank, or even private employers, could have their view of you coloured by a word from a major regional government department. And he would have done it, believe me, for the sheer pleasure of being able to.'

There was a silence. It was Luc who finally broke it, in a voice which sounded dead, and which pierced Carla to the core.

'That's probably true, Joana, and it might well have made our lives difficult. Instead of that, though, he will now be arrested, and with his connections he'll get himself released in no time. And with or without his power base, he'll believe Carla was responsible for his arrest, and he'll come looking for us – in Terrassa or wherever we go afterwards. And this time he'll have nothing to lose. He won't be looking to bug our lives, but to destroy them.'

# CHAPTER TWENTY

It was almost funny, Carla thought, how she and Martin reacted following Luc's very blunt indictment. Within three seconds she was by Luc's side, standing over him where he sat, in his bleak dismay, and in the same time Martin was next to Joana, a hand on her shoulder as so often before, like a devoted bodyguard. But Joana did not look in the least bit disturbed. She reached her hand up to pat Martin's, and then rose from her chair to cross over to Luc, leaning down and kissing him gently on both cheeks.

'I guess you just have to trust me that things won't happen that way, Luc.' She looked up into Carla's face. 'And you Carla. I haven't done this for revenge, I promise you, and nor have I done it rashly, without thinking through the consequences.'

She turned as Toni came into the room, and Carla was struck by how cheerful he looked. By all appearances he had enjoyed the role he had played this afternoon, and foresaw nothing bad from it either.

'I'm just planning on heading down now, *Senyora*, if that's all right with you?' he said, and Joana nodded approval.

'Have you eaten Toni? Well then, that's fine, and yes, do head off. Toni,' she explained to the others, 'is going back down to Girona. He'll stay over at the Girona house tonight, on the pretext that he has a job to do for me first thing in the morning, and that way he'll be around on the spot if anything happens to Sergi. We don't think they'll hang around too long before arresting him – perhaps tomorrow morning, do you think, Toni?'

'Possibly, *Senyora*, but as you say, they won't wait long. I'll come directly back here when it happens – it'll be seen as quite natural for me to come straight to tell you, anyway. And then I can take you back down with me.'

Carla looked a question. It was clear that the two of them had been making detailed plans during their drive to Girona, but what was now on the programme was beyond her.

It was Joana who answered the unspoken question. 'You see, we've been thinking, and once Sergi has been taken into custody, only a very few people will be able to find out what is happening to him, and I, of course, am one of them. Toni will be seen to come hightailing it up here to get me to help Sergi, and then I can go to see our lawyer. With his help I should be able to get in to see Sergi long before he can call in any of his allies. And Sergi will be wary of trusting any of his political friends anyway, not being sure who has plotted against him, and whatever he may think of me as a companion he's never had any reason to doubt my loyalty. Provided I can stay close to him and the lawyer, we'll know if and when Sergi can hope to be released. But nothing happens quickly here, and I don't think Sergi can even begin to plan an exit from prison for many days – long enough, anyway, for you two to be married and safe. And believe me, he really won't have the resources to find you afterwards. Money won't be enough – he'll be on blacklists everywhere, and won't be able to access the information you need to track anyone down.'

Carla shot another look at Luc, still silent at her side. She could believe herself that for a long time to come Sergi would lack the means to track them if they truly disappeared, but they had hoped to stay in Terrassa for some time, and there he could most certainly find them. He must know very well where Luc's parents lived. How long would it take him to worm his way out of his current dilemma and walk out of prison? It was the unanswerable question, and she didn't have Mama's faith that it would take long enough for them to be safe, for in Franco's Spain you could surely bribe your way out of most things, provided you had access to the right people.

'He has to be locked up first,' she said, suddenly anxious. 'What if they just charge him but leave him free to build his defence?'

'For a charge of murder? And with Roig working against him? No, Carla, they'll take pleasure in detaining him, just for the humiliation. It's their best way of ensuring any political damage is permanent.'

Carla shook her head in frustration. These were political games in a world she didn't understand, and she felt small and vulnerable where her mother seemed to feel empowered.

'We have to get married, that's the only thing that matters right now.' She focused on the one thing that had been her priority now for so many months.

'So should we still go to Terrassa, in your opinion?' It was Luc who was asking, looking at Joana.

'Oh yes, most definitely,' Joana answered. 'Your parents will be worried if you don't turn up soon, and besides, we need to know when the wedding is planned for.'

Carla considered. Mama was right, of course, but she didn't want to leave Girona while things were so much up in the air. She ventured a plan of her own.

'Could we use Toni, do you think, once you're in Girona – even though Sergi's other employees will see he's not there? Surely they'll have other things on their minds, and they'll be looking to you for leadership? Because if so, could he take us to Terrassa and then bring me back?'

She saw Luc frown, and took his hand urgently. 'Think, Luc! Your parents haven't seen you for months, and they must be desperate for you to come home. Let's go up there, and then once we know how plans are developing I can leave you there in your mother's tender loving hands! Just for a day or two while we get a feel for how the land lies in Girona.'

'There's not much you can do,' Joana demurred.

'There's not much I can do in Terrassa either. I promise I'll go up to Terrassa again as soon as we see what that stepfather of mine is up to, and I won't leave Luc until he's ensconced in his parents' sitting room! Look, Luc, we've even got you smartened up before your mother sees you! Paula's put weight on you!'

It was true, and the scabs on his skin were improving, and most of the shadows were gone from under his eyes. He needed lots more loving, and he needed to be free from fear. Well his mother could give him the loving, but nobody could remove the fear until they were clear away from Sergi, and if things looked bad Carla wanted to be on the spot to know immediately.

'You don't think I ought to come back to Girona too?' Luc was asking. 'Otherwise how will I know if things get serious? We may have to move at short notice, and surely Carla and I need to stay together?'

It was Joana who answered him. 'Do your parents have a telephone, Luc? Of course they do, if your father runs a medical practice from home. Well, once I'm in Girona I too will have a phone, so I can let you know what is happening. And just keep remembering, my children, that Sergi is going to have an almighty fight on his hands, and that first fight won't be with you! Believe me, you'll have time and plenty to be married. I wouldn't have done this if I'd been in any doubt of that.'

'All right, Joana, I'll believe you,' Luc answered. 'I want to believe you, and we need to, and I'll have faith in you to take care of your end of things in Girona.' He came up behind Carla and wrapped his long arms right round her bump. 'Just take care of my wife and my child,' he said. 'We've been apart too long, and I want her back as soon as possible.'

'And you'll have her! There's no real need for Carla to come back to Girona at all, but she's as stubborn as a mule, so we won't fight her, and you can work on taking her off my hands in the next few days!'

Luc grinned, and there was nothing left for any of them to say. They were all being carried along in Joana's plans, and her confidence was hard to resist. Toni went off on his mission, treating it like an adventure, and the rest of them were left to bide their time, holed up in waiting, as Luc put it, as he dragged Martin off to the back of the house to play billiards after dinner.

To Martin's protestations that he didn't know how to play, Luc replied that at nineteen years old there were surely more things he didn't know how to play than those he did, but that if he wasn't prepared to learn at his tender age there was something wrong with him.

Carla and Joana were left in the dining room, toying with coffee. Carla felt exhausted, and her bump felt heavier than ever, and she thought her mother must be shattered, having set out so early this morning on such a tricky venture. Joana had a frown on her face, which hadn't been there throughout the long afternoon. Was this a sign of her tiredness?

'Are you all right, Mama?' she asked.

Joana seemed to emerge from a state of abstraction, and smiled vaguely at Carla. 'Oh yes, I'm fine. Tell me, what was it that Luc was saying to Martin just then? Was he really saying he was only nineteen? How can that be if he is Luis's son?'

'Has Martin never told you his story?' Carla found

it very curious, but as Joana shook her head numbly she launched into an explanation.

'Martin isn't one of Luis's legitimate children. He was born later, from a woman Luis had an affair with, and he was brought up like me, as another man's child. He only found out a few years ago and he has struggled with it ever since. So you see, he and I have a lot in common!'

Joana looked startled. 'When was he born?' she asked.

'In 1944, he said – sometime in the autumn, I think, just after France was liberated from the Germans. Uncle Luis didn't even know that his mistress was pregnant – he was killed by the Germans in May that year. Poor Martin was frightened that we would all reject him, I think, when he first came here, until he saw how Grandma welcomed him in, but he was also needing people to make his father live for him.'

Joana reached for the coffee pot and poured herself another cup. She looked rather shocked, and Carla wondered why Martin hadn't shared his story with her, when they were clearly so close.

'Poor Martin,' Joana said, after a while.

'Yes. He helped me a lot, you know, last week after I found out about my real father. He has been dealing with the issues for a good deal longer than I have. Do you realise, we both had fathers who didn't even know we existed? The only difference is that Martin says Luis never really loved his mother, which hurts him. And Luis already had a family, so poor Martin would have been a very inconvenient addition to Luis's life. At least I know my father loved you and would have wanted me, that's what Martin says.'

Joana seemed to pull herself back from a long way away.

'Oh yes, my love, your father would have wanted you!'

'Do I look like him?'

Joana sat up in her chair, and focused on Carla, nodding vehemently. 'Yes, let's talk about your father, because you need to know you're Alex through and through. You look like him, dark, and tall, and with those piercing eyes, but there's more to it than that – he had integrity, and a forceful, challenging brain, just like you. The last time I saw him was just before Barcelona fell, and everyone was hungry and already suffering, and there were so many people who said it would be better just to have everything over, and be done with it. But Alex knew better – he knew Franco would make Catalonia suffer, and that life was going to be even tougher for everyone. But he told me that he and I would be safe if we kept our heads down!'

'You would have been, if it hadn't been for Sergi.'

'Yes, but back then, after the war, all I could see was that Alex had been wrong, and that the future belonged to people like Sergi. I knew I had to abandon all the old dreams when I married Sergi, so I did, lock, stock and barrel. But I couldn't control those dreams in the night hours, and it was a long time before I stopped seeing your father every night in my sleep.'

'I see him too, but I'm never sure if I have him right. I need to see some photos, perhaps – something to make my imaginings more real. She paused for a moment, then continued. 'Martin says I should go to see the Figarola family and tell them I'm their granddaughter. He says they'd be pleased to know their son had left something of himself behind him.'

'That may be true. Do you think it would help you?'

'To have some family on my father's side? Yes, I think it would help me a lot. It would bring him closer, and allow others to talk to me about him and make him real. It's all about reclaiming my father, as Martin says.'

'Yes indeed, as Martin says.' Joana's tone was odd, and it struck Carla that she might feel a bit strange having grown so close to a cousin whom she thought was several years older.

'Only nineteen,' Joana murmured, completely to herself, and Carla took her hand.

'Yes, it's astonishing, don't you think, when you consider everything he's done for us in the last couple of weeks, how he brought us together, and helped me in Girona? He is old beyond his years, kind of like a little wise old man, and maybe it's his quest for Luis which brought him of age before his time. I think he has the gift of friendship, and all of us have felt it. I don't think it matters what age you are if you have that kind of empathy.'

She looked at her mother, and Joana looked up from her coffee cup and smiled, squeezing Carla's hand as it lay in hers.

'Like you, *carinyo*, with that empathy of Alex's! You have the gift of friendship too.'

'When I lay down my bristles!'

'Indeed, but I think you got those from me, not from Alex! Have you forgiven me for what I did today?'

Carla shrugged. 'If Luc has forgiven you, then I have too! I'm worried, but I'll live with it, and like Luc said, we'll trust you to bring us through. Grandma will keep me sane.

Martin says he wants to stay until we know things are all right, by the way. We'll both hang out at Grandma's. If the worst comes to the worst, Luc and I can leave with Martin and find our way into France. At least we're together now, and we can react quickly if we have to.'

'Have faith, my love. I believe you'll have time, not only to get married but to have the baby in Terrassa. And during that time Luc can be looking around for where you're going next.'

Carla was too tired to think about it all too deeply. She held up a hand to cover a yawn, and as she did so she caught Joana doing the same. She laughed.

'Shall we take it one step at a time, Mama? And go to bed? I'm dropping on my feet.'

'And me, child. I think I'm going to sleep tonight.'

'And no bad dreams?'

'Not tonight! I've done with bad dreams. There's too much going on in the present to worry about the past. Shall we leave the young men playing billiards?'

'I think so – they'll be playing for hours, especially if Luc decides he's teaching Martin something. They're just a couple of boys!'

'Yes, just as you say, Carla,' Joana said meditatively, and then gave a tired smile. 'They're just a couple of boys.'

# Chapter Twenty-One

It had taken all of their lawyer's influence to get Joana into the men's prison in the Salt district of Girona, outside visiting times and within not much more than twenty-four hours of Sergi's arrest. The lawyer, Miquel Gibert, had looked after their affairs for many years, and he had received Joana with infinite courtesy on the Friday evening in his office in the old town, delicately making no reference to the very grave charges against Sergi, and talking only of the 'misunderstanding', which they were currently working to rectify.

'So he hasn't been allowed any visitors?' she asked him.

'No, my dear Señora, no visitors apart from myself. Normally newly arrested prisoners are not permitted to see family and friends. This, of course, is to allow time for the necessary interrogations to take place. However, your husband is a man of some importance in this city, and I have been able to secure him better than usual accommodation, and hope to be successful also in arranging for you to visit. Not tonight – I've only just been allowed to see him myself, you know, and he was only arrested this morning.'

'He has only been arrested, not charged?'

'As of this evening no charges have been formally made. But I have had to advise Señor Olivera that he is likely to be charged before the morning.'

Joana accepted with demure gravity his expressions of concern. Yes, she was fine, she assured him, just disbelieving, and worried for her husband. He held her hand for longer than usual as she rose to leave. What mattered now was to keep her morale high, for her own sake and for Señor Olivera's, he urged her. And meanwhile they were surrounded by friends and well-wishers, who would work tirelessly for Señor Olivera's release. She nodded agreement at this polite lie, as he ushered her solicitously to the car.

She wondered whether Sergi would refuse to see her, but at nine o'clock on the Saturday morning she found herself walking along a dank, very smelly corridor in the dirty, disused convent that had served for years as the men's prison in Girona. She was shown into a room, which had nothing but a bare table in the middle, and there on one side of it sat Sergi, looking a little dishevelled but still dressed in his own clothes. Another privilege, perhaps? She heard the door close behind her, and turned to see that the guard had taken up position just inside.

Sergi watched both the guard and her with a closed face, and Joana paused a second to gather herself for the part she had to play, before crossing the little space towards him. He didn't get up to greet her, and his expression was still quite unreadable. Controlling her nerves she took the initiative, pulling out the chair opposite him at the table, and speaking quickly before he could ask her how she came to be here.

'My God, Sergi,' she said, infusing her voice with concern. 'What has happened to you? Toni came back as quickly as he could to the hill house yesterday to tell me you'd been arrested! I couldn't believe it!'

'You've seen Gibert?' Sergi didn't bother to give her a welcome, but his tone was not aggressive.

'Your lawyer? Yes, of course, I went to him first thing, but he hasn't told me anything! He just arranged for me to see you. Sergi what has happened? Is it something political?'

'You might call it that. There's some fabricated letter going around that says I was involved in the death of Ramón Candera. Preposterous, of course, and there's not a shred of real evidence to hold me here. But someone has it in for me, to have dreamt up such a trumped-up bit of nonsense.'

There was a vindictive anger to his voice which boded ill for Carla should he ever catch up with her. He didn't mention her name, though, and Joana thought he wouldn't want his wife to know about that visit to him from Carla and Martin, any more than he would want her to know if he ever managed to take his revenge. He certainly seemed to have no suspicion whatsoever of herself, which was reassuring. He needed to trust her now.

She'd listened enough to the lawyer yesterday to know that the charges against Sergi weren't as trivial as he would like her to believe. In the end, the lawyer had implied, the evidence in those letters would not be strong enough to convict Sergi, just as they'd thought. Too much depended on the word of a dead man, but, nevertheless, Sergi wouldn't want the authorities to dig too deeply into the affair, or into the later death of the driver. He would play the injured innocent with all his usual cool bravado, and work behind the scenes to bring himself clear. He sounded unnerved, though, in spite of himself – she'd never heard him sound so rattled.

'I can't believe it!' she said, and the tremble in her voice was not entirely simulated. 'Surely they can't keep you? Is there anything I can do to help you? We need to get you out of this place!' She gestured around the dirty room. Compared with what he had put Luc through this was surely luxury, but it was an intimidating place, nevertheless.

Sergi looked at her with calculation. 'Oh, they'll let me out. It may just take some time, that's all, and that's what I want to avoid. I have to prove that letter to be the falsehood it really is.'

'How will you do that?'

'Don't you worry your head about that, Joana.' He paused. 'But actually there is something you can do to help.'

She nodded earnestly, but stayed silent. After a moment more of calculation he seemed to come to a decision. 'I want you to go and see Francesco Montilla,' he said.

'Francesco? Your bank manager?'

'Yes, I'll give you a letter for him authorising you to take some cash from my account. You'll need to take out 500,000 pesetas.'

'500,000?' It was an unbelievable sum to take out in one transaction.

'Don't interrupt, Joana! Just listen to me, and follow my instructions very carefully. Get the money, and come to see me again tomorrow morning.' He thought for a moment. 'Don't bring it all here – it's not safe. Just bring me 100,000 for now – it'll do to get the ball rolling, and then I'll tell you what to do with the rest. I may need you to pay some out directly, discreetly of course, but I'll let you know.'

There was tension in the speed at which he spoke, but his voice challenged her to ask any questions, and as she sat in amazement he turned to the guard to say he needed paper and an envelope. The guard opened the door and called to a colleague, and while his head was out of the door, Sergi leant over to Joana.

'Have you got any cash with you? It costs me a fortune to keep these guys happy so I get decent food and stupid things like paper!'

Joana pulled her purse from her handbag and passed over the small amount of cash she had.

'It's all I have. But tomorrow you'll have the money from the bank.'

'No! Put that in a plain envelope and seal it up. I need it intact. But I'll give you the code for the safe and you can take some cash out of there for yourself and bring some to me tomorrow for my personal needs, and bring me some clothes as well. Tell me, has anyone visited the house at all?'

'No, not that I know of. None of the servants has mentioned anything, and certainly nobody has come to the house since I arrived yesterday afternoon.'

He considered for a moment. 'They might, though. I tell you what, Joana, when you go into the safe you need to do something for me. There's an envelope inside, marked Valls, and I want you to take it out of the safe and burn it, all right?'

Joana took care to sound completely bemused. 'Burn it?'

He began to be impatient. 'That's what I said. Just light a match and burn it in the grate. It's not too difficult, is it?'

She shook her head.

'Well do it immediately you get home, and don't go looking at it, do you understand me? I don't think there's anything else that would interest them in the house. Don't put the money from the bank in the safe, just in case – it'll be safer in the car, hidden somewhere. Just don't tell Toni what's inside.'

Someone knocked at the door and passed some sheets of paper to the guard, and Joana waited in silence while Sergi wrote his letter to the bank manager and gave it to the guard to check and approve. Then he sealed it in the envelope and gave it to her.

'You did well coming down to Girona, Joana,' he said to her as she got up to leave. 'I couldn't have trusted old Gibert with something like this. If you're going to take some money from the safe you might as well use some of it to buy yourself a new outfit or two. But make sure you go to the bank first, before it closes.'

So that's me both won over and dismissed, Joana thought, with a certain wry amusement. She looked at him for a moment. Did you really kill Alex yourself, she wanted to ask him, or just kind of fix him up, but of course it was an impossible question to ask. Maybe later, in a few days, if he was happy with what she'd done for him she could negotiate with him a little, and ask him to let her go. While he was here in the prison he had to listen – he couldn't do anything to her, no matter how much her propositions might rile him, and he couldn't walk away.

But for now she thanked him, and pecked him on the cheek, and gave him her most docile, concerned smile as she left the room, clutching the envelope in her hand.

Toni was waiting for her outside in the car, and they drove straight to the bank. It would be open, but would the manager be there himself this Saturday morning? Joana hoped so, because otherwise she would have to track him down at home, and meanwhile Carla and Luc were waiting anxiously at the apartment for news, and for a lift to Terrassa.

There was a part of her that didn't want to hand over any money to Sergi if it was going to bribe people and get him out of gaol more quickly, for after all, the goal was to keep him in there for as long as possible. Joana wasn't quite as confident as she had made herself sound yesterday, to the young people, but her hope was that Sergi would be kept in custody for long enough for Carla's baby to be born in Terrassa, with Luc's father in attendance.

But Joana knew that she had to see through what Sergi had asked her to do. Her role must be to stay as close to Sergi as she could, and to make sure he didn't turn to anyone else for help, so she must get the money and hand it over, just as he had asked. Get the money, then pass by home to raid that safe before going to the apartment to let them all know what was happening. The money Sergi had so dismissively told her to spend on herself would put cash into Carla's hands to take to Terrassa with her. Carla and Luc would need more cash later, to help them start out somewhere new, but to poach money from the safe to that extent would be very visible to Sergi if he got home. One thing at a time – that's what she kept telling herself!

Her mind was racing as they headed to the bank, and she felt like action woman. It made a change from the enforced idle life she'd been living, and she felt as though she'd taken charge again, putting the past behind her and acting for the future. And the action helped to remove Martin from her head as well.

It had shaken her more than she could say to learn how young Martin was. She'd made him her confidant, allowed herself to lean on him as she hadn't turned to anyone for over twenty years, and in her mind he'd been close to her in age – her first cousin, the son of her Uncle Luis. When she thought how closely they'd lain together in her bed it made cold shivers run through her. She'd known he loved her, beyond mere family closeness, and she thanked the heavens for the instinct that had just held her back from him.

She'd had trouble yesterday even speaking to him on the journey to Girona, and he'd obviously been aware of her sudden coldness. Her impulse was to lash out at him, but she knew he didn't deserve it, and the hurt look in his eyes would have been enough anyway to stop her. He would be at the apartment too, with Carla and Luc, and she hoped that maybe all of them being together with Maria and Victor last night would have been of some comfort to him.

But the threat to Carla was more important than

anything that was happening to her, and she shook herself mentally and focused on the task in hand. The car drew up outside the bank, and with some hesitation she went inside. How ridiculous to live a life where she had so rarely even visited a bank! She knew the manager, though – Francesco Montilla and his wife had been regular dinner party guests over the years. How would he react to Sergi's bizarre request?

He was in his office, she discovered. An aloof young clerk took her name through to him, and Francesco Montilla came surging out of his office to greet her and usher her into his sanctuary, calling for coffee as he did so.

'Joana, my dear!' he exclaimed, with a note of surprise he couldn't disguise. 'How are you, dear lady? And the family? Only the other day we were talking about you, Inez and myself, and saying what an age it is since we last saw you!'

He can't have heard about Sergi's arrest, she thought, or he wouldn't be so welcoming. He would change his tune in a moment. And she was right. He read through the letter she gave him while she sipped the little cup of coffee brought by his assistant, and as he digested its contents his eyes flickered over her twice, guarded and measuring. He stayed silent, pretending he was still reading, but Joana thought he was just working out what to say. When he did speak, the gushing welcome had gone from his voice, and he had withdrawn into his official persona.

'This is an unusual request, Señora. Your husband instructs me to give you access to his account, and to hand to you a great deal of money. I gather that he finds himself in some difficulty.'

It wasn't a question – it was as though he didn't actually want to know any more. She could understand why, but her role was to reassure him.

'Sergi has been arrested, Francesco, but he is sure of securing his release before long. You know how the world of public government works. This is just some malicious political manoeuvring.'

The manager nodded, but he must suspect that even if he was released Sergi's career might well be finished. He was no longer someone the Montillas would want to have dinner with, and therefore, neither was she!

But it seemed Sergi's letter was sufficient authorisation for the money to be released, which was what really mattered. The manager left her alone, and soon afterwards a thick package was brought to her, which she signed for, and then the clerk escorted her to her car. As she passed through the lobby of the bank, Francesco Montilla came towards her and took her hand briefly in his.

'You'll go straight home with this, Joana?' he asked, and she noted that he was back to using her first name. His initial shock had diminished and he was now anxious not to alienate a still wealthy client. She smiled and eased her way out, sending best wishes to Inez, and smirking inside at the thought of what he would really be telling his wife that evening. The world of the Montillas was irrelevant to Joana these days.

Those relevant to her were in her mother's apartment, and she was in a hurry to go there now and tell them about what was happening, but first she directed Toni to drive back to the house. She went in through the back door into the kitchen, and found Josefa and Mireia sitting at the table over a late-morning coffee. A smell of baking pastry suggested they were preparing lunch, which she didn't plan to eat here, but one look at their unsettled faces persuaded her that she should at least take coffee with them. The two women had welcomed her like a long-lost hero yesterday, in the upset of the house after Sergi's arrest. She'd deliberately shown herself relaxed and unworried, and they'd seemed to take their tune from her since her arrival. These two had always come to her for orders, and her presence made them comfortable. The men who worked for Sergi outside would be less comfortable. Well that was just tough, she thought! For as long as Sergi remained in gaol and couldn't see his henchmen, she would be mistress here, and they would have to obey her orders. It might prove very useful indeed.

She sat down at the kitchen table, ignoring their surprise at this unprecedented act, and asked Mireia if she too could have a coffee. The girl nodded, almost blushing, and scurried over to the stove where a pot was sitting, not quite on the boil. Josefa stayed put, her arms placidly on the table. She had been with Joana for many years now, and had quietly run this house, producing dinner parties during the better years, and continuing to produce lunch and dinner stoically through innumerable domestic disputes, while Sergi raged and Joana hid. She had occasionally come to work herself with a bruise or two, and Joana suspected that she too had a difficult domestic life, but it was never mentioned between them. The closest Josefa ever came to comment was to recommend Joana to go to bed early. 'Perhaps before the master comes home,' she had suggested more than once, before returning to her own numerous family and her own problems.

Joana guessed that whatever Josefa actually thought of what was happening now, the most important thing for her would be her job and her security, so she spent time reassuring her and Mireia that the master was well and in the process of organising his release.

Coffee over, she went up to her bedroom, and there she counted the money from the bank – more than she'd ever handled. It must be three or four times what Uncle Victor would earn in a year. She wrapped the first 100,000 pesetas back up in the package, put the rest in a large envelope, and took it all through to her bathroom. She wasn't going to keep so much money in the car, but she had her own hiding place where she was sure it would be safe.

Back downstairs she opened up the safe and took out the envelope with the documents. She considered what to do with it. Was there any point in holding on to these documents, since they already had photostats? In this envelope the document with the hit-and-run driver's written evidence was also a copy, but the letter from the blackmailer to Sergi was the original. Clearly Sergi didn't want to risk anyone finding the documents in his house, since it would incriminate him even further, and Joana had to comply with that wish. Would they get a visit from the police, she wondered? If so, why hadn't they been here already?

It was all very confusing, and Joana made the decision to take the envelope with her and consult the others. She quickly took some cash from the safe – enough for her own needs, some more to give to Sergi tomorrow, and as much as she dared for Carla and Luc. There was always a good quantity of money in the safe, but she had to be careful, because Sergi would know how much had gone.

She closed the safe carefully, and took a quick look around the study. If Sergi was unworried about this space being searched, then obviously he didn't have any very political documents kept here. Did his enemies know that? Was that why they hadn't sent anyone to visit? Or were they just content that what they'd already thrown at Sergi was quite enough to finish his political career?

Poor Sergi! A small, but very small, part of her felt suddenly sorry for him as the work of a lifetime lay in ruins in front of him, not because he'd lost it, but because it had been all he ever valued. Was it worth it, then, Sergi, or would a quieter life have left you with fewer enemies and less far to fall? It was a stupid question – Sergi had always been driven, with everything to prove, and there really wasn't any other life she could imagine him living. What a life, though, now she knew more about it! She shivered, and whisked herself quickly out of the study and through the front door to where Toni was waiting.

# Chapter Twenty-Two

Toni had had his coffee too, she realised, so Josefa must have looked after him. He was sitting on the bonnet of the car in the late-morning sun with an empty cup beside him. He leapt up as she emerged from the house, and opened the passenger door for her before disappearing round the back of the house with the cup. Toni had been in a state of high excitement in the last two days, and seemed to be running everywhere.

The journey to the apartment took them through an area of Girona that she couldn't remember ever visiting, narrow and mean and far from her other life. Was this really where her mother had been living for the last few years? It was a district that she knew wouldn't even exist in perhaps ten years' time – such areas would be pulled down to make way for the new Girona. And yet the lives lived here were the norm rather than the exception – people slept and ate and went to work and school, and to all intents was it not the same as the villages, with their run-down houses and hard-working lives? People had gained proper wage packets by coming to the cities, and from all over Spain people were flocking to Catalonia in search of a better life, for here there were jobs, and Girona was going to flourish, everyone knew that. It couldn't come too soon, she thought, as she looked out at the crumbling facades.

Nerves ate at her as they neared the apartment. They were all so united as a family, Victor, Maria, Carla, and now Martin and Luc, but her own place among them was too compromised and complex, and she felt like an outsider. And she would be seeing Victor for the first time in many years. How many she couldn't remember, but she knew that for as long as she'd been married to Sergi, Victor had regarded his niece Joana as a person lost to the world.

She entered the apartment behind Toni, who was her guide. The men were seated around the table already, and she avoided Martin's eyes as she looked around the small space, which reminded her strangely of the main room in the old house in Sant Galdric. She certainly knew that embroidered tablecloth.

Victor got up from the table and came towards them, and Joana watched his grave, gentle face. This was the man who had taught her to play *botifarra*, the card game in which he was the acknowledged champion of the village, and who had taken her triumphantly as his partner in a competition in the village bar – much to Maria's disapproval! He'd mended her pens, and her dolls, and rebound her favourite book with all the care of a professional binder, and all with a twinkle in his eyes, which she remembered with sorrow, for there was no twinkle in him today.

But it seemed there could be acceptance. 'Welcome to our little apartment, Joana,' he was saying to her. 'It's not quite your magnificent mansion, but you'll find your mother's cooking is as good as ever.'

There was something speculative about his voice, but there was a hint of warmth there too. He took her hand and drew her forward, and she wanted to kiss him, but it felt too soon for that. It was a very long time since she'd last kissed Victor.

Carla appeared at the kitchen door, and gave her a worried look. 'So what is happening, Mama?'

Joana gave her a smile. 'Don't worry, *carinyo*, all is just as we expected.'

Carla began to speak again, but Victor interrupted her. 'We are all hoping things are going to be all right, for our little Carla's sake. You can tell us in a moment about what you've found out, Joana, but let's wait until we are all seated at the table together. It seems your daughter and your mother have some treat they want to serve us.'

She ate lunch with them at the little table, tucked between Victor and Carla, and the dish of pork and beans took her way back to her childhood. She wondered if her mother had prepared it deliberately to awaken her memories. It certainly awoke her appetite, and she found herself eating far more than she'd expected, given the state of her stomach. Toni ate with them, which was another novelty for her – she'd never eaten with any of her servants before. He sat next to Martin, and as she looked up and away quickly, she saw Martin put his arm around him briefly, and get a small smile in response.

Maria fussed over them all, serving the food in large bowls, and scolding Luc in particular to eat. He looked a little haggard today, as though he hadn't slept. Where had they all slept, Joana wondered, in this tiny apartment?

Luc looked even more haggard after she told them what she'd been detailed to do for Sergi, and Carla gulped a little when Joana told them about the money.

'So, by tomorrow Sergi will have money to start buying his way out of gaol? Oh help! He'll get himself released, you wait and see, before we have time to get married and get away!'

'No, no!' Joana said. 'Whatever happens, it'll take time. However cleverly Sergi works, the wheels turn slowly in officialdom, and some delicate greasing of palms will be necessary before he can be free to do anything about his anger towards you. Stop worrying and go to Terrassa. If Sergi gets out of gaol I'll phone you, and we can think again.'

'You don't think you should take this opportunity to get away and disappear yourself, since you have all that money at your disposal?' Luc asked. 'It would give you a new start, and it might mean that Sergi would be stuck where he is. He wouldn't have the money to free himself.'

Joana shook her head. 'I thought of that, but it wouldn't work. There's plenty of money left in the bank, and Sergi could find someone else to get it out and pay people off for him. And then what would happen? He'd get free eventually, and come looking for me – much more than he'll ever come looking for you, believe me! He'd be out for vengeance big time! And the money that's there isn't enough to buy me a complete new life – it would only keep me for a year or so, and what would I do after that? No, I have to see this through, and play the faithful wife, and do what I can to hold him in check until you can get away.'

'Martin thinks we should all go to France,' Carla threw in. 'You, and me and Luc – all of us together.'

Joana looked up, startled, and caught Martin's eye. She felt herself flushing, and stopped herself from blurting out a violent no.

She shifted her gaze to Carla. 'Would you want to go to France? Do you think you'd have a better life there?'

It was Luc who answered. 'I think for both of us it would be a last resort, but it does have the attraction that Sergi could never find us there. He could never find you, either,' he added, cocking an eye at her.

But Carla objected. 'No Luc, you know how it is with Spaniards who get out to France! They can't use their qualifications, and because they don't speak the language and don't have proper papers they end up doing manual jobs! And we could never come back – not even to see Grandma, or your parents!'

The two of them had clearly allowed their worries to creep in again since Sergi's arrest, and Joana spoke quickly to stop them.

'Let's not jump guns here,' she said. 'There's no reason at all to think you have to flee the country. We all know Sergi would do you both damage if he could get hold of you, but right now he can't, and even when he first comes out he won't be able to either – not if he has to reach beyond Catalan borders to find you. He'll be struggling to reinstate himself, and trying to get his job back – or any job, come to that! I've seen him, remember, and I can tell you, he's already a fallen man. Go off this afternoon, and see your family, and find out when the priest has scheduled your wedding for, and when you could therefore get away from Terrassa if you need to.'

She took another sip of Maria's appalling coffee, and fished out of her bag the documents she'd taken from the safe. 'And I'll watch over Sergi, and if there is any sign that he's going to get out of gaol too quickly, then we'll use these. I've got the original letter from the blackmailer to Sergi here, which Sergi wanted me to burn, but I haven't. Providing the original to the authorities might just add some weight to the evidence against Sergi and keep him inside for a bit longer if we really needed it.'

'Wouldn't that be dangerous for you? He'd know you must have provided the original to the police,' objected Carla.

Joana chuckled. 'Oh yes, if it comes to that point, then I'll certainly have to run for it, like it or not! I'd have to run with whatever cash I can get hold of, and I'll rely on you to keep me in my old age, Luc! But somehow I don't think we'll need to go that far. Let's not panic, but keep these for me, will you Carla?'

She held out her hand and Carla took the envelope, holding it carefully as though weighing its value.

'I guess it could help, for what it's worth,' she said, at last, though the tension didn't leave her voice. 'It's a shame we don't have the original of the actual hit-and-run driver's evidence! Do you think the police are looking for that?'

'I would guess so. They'll be searching his home and questioning his family. I've been wondering whether that's why they haven't yet bothered with our house, but I guess they must realise that any blackmailer would have kept the key documents well away from Sergi.'

'All right, then,' Carla agreed. 'We go to Terrassa as planned, and we'll work on the basis that Sergi is stuck for long enough for us to get married and get away, and we'll get all our connections working on some kind of decent job for Luc, somewhere far from Catalonia, but still in Spain.'

'I have some family in Asturias,' Luc offered.

'Well that should be far enough!' Joana shot him a smile. 'I can't see Sergi looking for you there!'

'And what happens to you then?' It was Martin who spoke. His tone of deep concern took her aback, and her gaze flew to his troubled face. He was watching her with troubled eyes. How young he looked, and yet he seemed to have aged!

'I'll come out all right,' she answered, trying not to look at him. 'I promise you I'll be all right. I've been thinking, and what I need to do is negotiate with Sergi. He'll be a different man when this is all over – less powerful and perhaps a little bit grateful. We need to come to terms so that I can have a freer life.'

Maria had got up from the table, and came behind Martin to hold him by the shoulder. With her free hand she stroked his wavy hair. For Maria, Martin was another adopted son. My cousin, Joana reminded herself.

Maria was looking over Martin's head towards Joana, with a quizzical expression which Joana couldn't quite pin down.

'We've put this young man through a lot, don't you think, Joana? He's done everything he can for us, surely, and we should let him go back to his mother.'

'I'm fine,' Martin cut in hurriedly. 'Honestly, I'm really fine. You haven't put me through anything at all.'

Joana studied him again, and saw a hint of tears in his eyes. Back to his mother? How old was his mother, she wondered? And then she felt full of remorse. Martin's mother was old enough to have been Uncle Luis's lover, and Martin was his son. It was enough, and whatever his age he was her dear cousin, troubled now and hurt by her rejection when he was worthy of so much more. Why should she feel so humiliated to have bared her soul to a nineteen-year-old, when that nineteen-year-old was Martin, dear ageless Martin, with Luis's eyes.

'Martin, *el meu cosí*, you know how grateful we all are for everything you've done, especially me,' she said. 'If you need to go, then of course we understand, but we'll miss you terribly. I'll miss you.'

He looked at her doubtfully, caught her smile, and returned it. 'Don't listen to my Aunt Maria,' he answered her. 'She worries about my studies, but a few more days won't change things. I'll stay until we know Carla and Luc will be all right, and don't need to bolt for the border with me. Until Carla comes back from Terrassa, at least, and until you've seen Sergi again tomorrow. I'd hate to leave with things so much up in the air.'

'Well, for Sergi things aren't so much up in the air as down in the mud,' Joana commented with a grin. 'And for the rest of us, well things aren't settled, but they will be, and they may not be perfect, but I'm sitting at my Uncle Victor's table, with everyone I most care about around me, and I wouldn't be here if it wasn't for you.'

She looked around for Victor, who had gone across to his beloved radio, and was fiddling with it again, looking for music.

'Uncle Victor?' He looked up. 'Before we send these young people off to see Luc's parents, do you have a little after dinner drink to offer us? A *moscatell*, perhaps? Because when Luc walks out of that door this afternoon we may not see him again for a very long time. Carla will come back to us tomorrow, briefly, but these young people will have to leave Catalonia after their wedding, and Martin will have to go home, and this may be the last time we are all together for longer than I care to think about. I'm not going to get maudlin, because one day I know there will be a reunion, but could we raise a glass, do you think, to the future, and to happy outcomes?'

Victor gave an enthusiastic assent, and within minutes had produced little glasses and an unopened bottle of *moscatell* from the old sideboard. With a unanimous kind of gravity they all stood, and Victor pronounced the toast:

'To all of us,' he intoned, and they all sipped the sweet liquor.

Maria put her hand out to touch Carla's stomach.

'And to the baby, God bless him,' she said.

Carla's eyes filled up, and Luc drew her to him.

'She's a her!' he corrected Maria. 'Although, if I'm honest I don't care, as long as it's a baby! But above all, I'd like to raise a glass to you all, for all you've done for us, and for keeping my Carla safe. I'll take care of her and our baby, I promise you.'

It was Victor who answered him. 'You'd better, my lad! Off with you now to your parents and find out when you're going to make our Carla a respectable married woman!'

Carla grinned through her tears, and Luc kissed the top of her head. 'Respectable? Carla? Oh no, don't wish that on me! What a disappointment that would be!'

# Chapter Twenty-Three

The prison looked no better on the Sunday morning than it had the day before. Toni dropped her there and then went off to Terrassa to collect Carla, who was still refusing to stay away from Girona while things were so uncertain. He'd dropped both her and Luc there early yesterday evening, and told of an emotional reception for Luc from his parents. They seemed like nice people, he'd said – Joana just hoped they would be kind to her daughter.

In the visitor's room at the gaol Sergi was waiting for her just like yesterday, looking more unkempt this time, and as though he hadn't slept well, despite his better-than-average prison quarters. Joana handed him a package of clean clothes, and when the guard wasn't looking she slid the loose cash from the safe across the table to him. He grunted his thanks, and shoved it quickly into his trouser pocket.

'I got the money from the bank yesterday,' she said. The bored guard didn't seem to be listening, but she spoke in a whisper, nevertheless.

'Good. You got the full 500,000 out of Montilla?'

She nodded. 'And I put 100,000 of it in with your clothes. But are you sure it's safe to have so much money in here with you?'

Sergi shrugged. 'I won't have it for long – this first lot is for the police who've been questioning me. But I'll need you to pass the rest to Rafael,' he said, naming an old ally of his, a man somewhat junior to him who had always admired and emulated him. 'He'll know how to use it to reach the right people outside. I'll give you a note to pass to him – he'll be able to get in to see me easily enough here, and after I've told him what to do he can collect the money from you.'

Joana was calculating furiously. Could she delay at all in handing over a note to Rafael? She didn't think so, because she would have to phone him, and Sergi would know afterwards when she'd done so. But whatever happened, Rafael wouldn't get in to see Sergi until tomorrow at the earliest, and then he had to put the cash to use and start work greasing palms.

Could he be trusted to do exactly what Sergi asked? There would be a strong temptation to hold on to some of the cash himself, surely, since Sergi could never be sure if Rafael had paid out exactly what they'd agreed? He would have to offer considerable inducements to keep Rafael on his side. All in all she thought it would be some time before Sergi could win freedom. It was time bought for Carla, and time also for Joana to start her own negotiations.

With this in mind she put as much concern as possible into her voice as she answered him. 'Will Rafael take care of everything for you? Is there anything I can do directly to help you?'

He shook his head impatiently. 'This isn't work for you, Joana – you should know that. Believe me, it's better for you not to get too involved.'

She lowered her eyes, and said quietly, 'I thought I already was involved.'

'Please, Joana, just do what I ask you to. It's very important.'

It was the first time he had said please to her for many years. Joana raised her eyes again and met his uncompromising gaze. Enough for now, she thought, and she gave him an accepting smile, and then rose to leave.

As she came out of the front door of the prison she turned towards the town centre to look for a taxi. She wasn't looking where she was going, and nearly walked into a man who had just crossed the road, heading towards the prison. He apologised, but then shot her a long, interested look which she couldn't quite fathom. He seemed familiar, too, though she couldn't quite place him. Was he a colleague of Sergi's coming to try to gain admission to see him? Perhaps he already had an appointment? The thought chilled her, but then she thought that if he was really a high enough level colleague to win access to Sergi then he should be better known to her. The man was only hazily familiar. Perhaps he was one of Sergi's looser band of henchmen, in which case she might have seen him in passing in the past.

If so he was surely too junior to be visiting. But why was he here?

The question nagged at her on the taxi ride, but then she let it go. She went home and had lunch, and then when she couldn't justify waiting any longer she made the call to Miquel. Any hopes that he might be out for this Sunday were dashed when he answered the phone himself, and by five o'clock he was at the house to collect Sergi's note, eager for news. He was quite clearly stunned by Sergi's arrest, and she surmised that his own political future might be linked to Sergi's fortunes, which would explain how upset he looked as he took the note from her, and how avidly he read it.

'You've seen Sergi?' he asked, though the answer must be obvious. She nodded.

'I've been trying to get in to see him myself,' he continued. 'They say I should be able to see him tomorrow or more likely Tuesday.'

This was good news. If he didn't get his instructions from Sergi until Tuesday, then she could make sure she didn't hand over the money to him until that evening, and he wouldn't even be able to begin to start work until the Wednesday morning, three whole days away. He'd be keen to clear Sergi's name as much as possible, she thought, to reduce the impact of his fall on his known supporters, but after that he'd be wise to step backwards from Sergi's orbit, and find someone else to help him up the ladder.

That evening she visited the apartment again. Carla was there, full of news, with the wedding date set for Thursday. Luc had been right, it seemed, and they'd had the fullest cooperation from the young, modernising priest in Luc's parish. Paperwork that could often take three weeks to organise had been finalised in record time, and there seemed little doubt that the priest fully intended Luc's marriage to take place before any baby could arrive.

But Carla's new good spirits took a knock when Joana told them about Rafael.

'He's seeing Sergi tomorrow or Tuesday?' she fretted. 'So if Sergi really wants to get me he could have a posse up in Terrassa by Wednesday at the latest!'

It took all of Joana's persuasion to convince her that Rafael was not one of Sergi's thugs, and wouldn't be doing that kind of dirty work.

'He could take a note though for someone else!'

'*Calmi*, Carla. Even if he did send some of his henchmen up to Terrassa, which I doubt, they wouldn't have the police with them, and all you would need are enough men to stand up to them. Remember how Uncle Josep stood up to them in Barcelona? That's all you'd need. And Sergi himself won't be out and free to come after you with police friends until after his release and his hoped for return to some power.'

'She's right, Carla,' voiced Victor, from where he sat playing cards with Martin at a little table in the corner. 'Stop fretting over nothing! You've left that young man of yours in good hands, being cosseted like a baby, if what you tell us is right.' Carla grinned in acknowledgement, and Victor continued, 'And by Friday you'll be a married woman. You'll have to work on your cooking skills, but otherwise you'll be all right.'

He cocked his head at Joana. 'Meanwhile, this guy here can't play *botifarra* for toffee, and I need your help. One of you has to help him or take his place, it's up to you, but something needs to be done!'

It was Carla who stepped in to help Martin, while Joana stepped back and sat with Maria to help sort through some odd ends of wool, brought out to make baby clothes. Covertly she watched the so familiar card game, studying her daughter, who was animated and happy as she laughed at Martin's mistakes. It hurt to think of the years of estrangement she had allowed to happen between them, just as it clenched her chest every time she thought of Carla leaving.

And Martin? Don't start any new worries about Martin! He was a bridge-builder, an exceptional person, and he would make a very good doctor, and over time he would forget her, or at least forget how he had felt about her. He had such a bright future. As she watched him, Joana compared it with her own, and felt that clench in the stomach again. Whatever brave face she might put on it, her future looked tough, challenging and ambivalent at best, lonely and confined at worst. She watched the young people and tried not to think about it.

Over coffee it was Martin they talked about. He'd been kicking his heels all day, and had dragged Victor out for a long walk that afternoon, it seemed. Should he leave tomorrow? That was the discussion, and it was hard to imagine what he could still do to help them now. He should return to his studies, Maria insisted. He agreed, with his usual composure, but he looked miserable, and Victor sat with his arm around him, looking not much happier. He would wait until after her next visit to Sergi tomorrow, they decided, just to be sure, and then leave in time to be back in France by evening. It was agreed.

But in the morning Joana didn't make it to the prison. A telephone call came from Miquel Gibert, Sergi's lawyer. Was Joana at home? Would she please be kind enough to receive him immediately? She waited on tenterhooks, and within fifteen minutes he was being ushered into the sitting room.

'Dear lady, can we sit down? I am the bearer of bad tidings – really such terrible tidings!' His suave manner had taken a serious rattling, and his teeth almost chattered together as he continued. 'Señor Olivera – your dear husband – was attacked in his cell this morning. He has been seriously injured – yes, very seriously – and has been taken to hospital.'

Joana could only stare. 'Sergi has been attacked?'

'Yes, Señora, he received such a severe beating that I wonder, really I wonder . . .' His voice tailed off, and he didn't seem to know how to continue.

Joana brought her thoughts into order. 'But who attacked him? Señor Gibert, you told me that I was the only person, other than yourself, who had been permitted to see my husband. So who could have attacked him?'

'I am afraid that it may have been one of the guards. We can't prove anything, of course, and no one is going to admit such a thing. The official story will be that Señor Olivera somehow got out of his room and was attacked by a prisoner. It is not unheard of for one prisoner to attack another violently in this way.'

'But you don't think it could have been so?'

'Really I couldn't say for sure, Señora, but if you ask merely my opinion I would say no. The attack happened at a time of day when prisoners are all locked up, and so far your husband has been kept in solitary confinement. But I was only notified after your husband had been removed to hospital, and there is no way anything could be proved – nor would I even attempt to.'

'And you are sure, Señor, that no one other than you and I has been allowed access to Sergi?'

'As sure as I can be, yes.'

'So tell me, how badly is he injured?'

'I have just seen him.' A look of distaste came over his face, and he took time before continuing. 'He has severe head and body injuries.'

'And unconscious?'

'Oh yes, he is unconscious. I am sorry, Señora Olivera, but I have to warn you – the doctors warn that there may have been some damage to your husband's brain.'

Joana sat digesting what she had been told. In the back of her mind raced the thought that now Luc and Carla would be safe, and she was by no means as distressed as the lawyer clearly expected her to be, but she mustn't show this. She needed to see Sergi, and as she thought of him beaten up and unconscious her stomach tightened and she had no problem showing the right level of distress to Gibert.

'Señor Gibert, can I see my husband? I need to go to the hospital!'

'Indeed, dear lady, I understand, and I will accompany you there, but are you sure you are ready for what you may see?'

He was looking at her as if she were a helpless little girl, and she saw that she could turn this to her advantage.

'Well, I'd like to have my mother and daughter with me,' she answered. 'And we will probably bring my cousin as well, so that I'll have a man with me, Señor, and you will not have to stay with me.'

'Indeed,' he sounded very relieved. 'You need to have your family about you at a time like this. It is what Señor Olivera would wish for you.'

Joana doubted that Sergi would want anything of the sort, but she agreed, and sent Toni to bring Maria, Carla and Martin directly to the hospital. It would be good to have allies.

She gave the lawyer a coffee before they headed off themselves in his car. She listened to his stream of sympathy in silence, and he accepted this as the normal signs of shock and distress. But when they entered the hospital he fell silent, and when they were shown into Sergi's room he stood to one side in an attitude of complete gravity.

Sergi was worse than she'd imagined. She could only see his face, but it was swollen beyond recognition, his eyes and even his eyelids completely invisible behind a wall of angry swellings. His head was wrapped in bandages, but blood had oozed through them on one side of his skull. Gingerly she drew down the sheet which covered him, and his torso was badly bruised, and partially bandaged. His arms had escaped damage, as had his legs, and as she drew the cover back over him she realised that the attack had been carefully directed at his upper half, and particularly at his head.

They had brought Sergi to the private hospital. The room he was in was modern, and he was attached to state-of-the-art machinery, which was presumably designed to keep him alive. A nurse hovered by the door, and within minutes of their arrival a doctor appeared, attentive and courteous, and adjusted the machine before he turned to Joana. Yes, he confirmed, her husband had severe head injuries, plus a punctured lung and some broken ribs. But the most serious damage was to the head, and Señor Olivera was at risk still as his brain continued to swell from the blows he had received. He had a very good chance of coming through, though, and the doctor did not want to distress her unduly.

And if he did pull through? Well, then there would be a very long, slow recovery process, possibly of many months, and the Señora should prepare herself for the possibility of some brain damage.

How much? Well, that was impossible to say for now, but the next few days should reveal more. X-ray results suggested that the parts of the brain responsible for both speech and movement had been affected, but he had seen worse cases. The Señora should prepare herself but by no means despair, since her husband was truly in the best of hands.

'And if he does pull through, the brain damage will be temporary? He will recover?' Joana asked.

'In part at least, Señora. There are many cases of people with such injuries resuming almost normal lives eventually.

We have seen some remarkable recoveries against all expectations, but even after months of recovery your husband may be left slow of movement and speech, and indeed of thought. I wish I could tell you more, but we don't know enough about brain injuries as yet to be able to diagnose long-term effects with conviction, especially when the injuries are so recent. And this was a very strange attack, which was targeted at the head, as though someone wanted to do the maximum amount of damage.'

The doctor shook his head sorrowfully, gave another tweak to the machine and checked various tubes, and then eased himself out of the room, just as Maria and Carla and Martin arrived. Martin stayed in the background as a flood of explanations in Spanish were exchanged, and the lawyer assured Joana of his continued attention to all her needs.

Joana was still reeling from the doctor's reference to the attack being a seemingly deliberate attempt to damage Sergi's brain. But the very thought of such a thing seemed to be hastening lawyer Gibert on his way. His inherently proper nature clearly recoiled from this whole sordid scenario, and he just didn't want to be involved, or at least only from behind the protection of his mahogany desk.

'Come to see me in my office when you are ready,' he told Joana, 'and we will talk about how best you should manage your husband's affairs. For now I will leave you with your family, and would urge you not to distress yourself too greatly.'

He took Joana's hand briefly in his, and manoeuvred himself towards the door with grace, and a respectful bow to Maria and Carla, not actually meeting their horrified eyes. Then he was gone, and Joana was left with Maria and Carla and Martin, whose combined gaze was fixed on Sergi in utter, stunned bewilderment.

'What happened?' Maria whispered.

'Some prison guard or guards have beaten him up, that's what!' Joana whistled. 'God knows why, but it was a vicious attack. You see how they targeted the head specifically? The doctor says he'll have some brain damage, long term, and that it may be permanent.'

Maria was horrified. '*Santa Mare*! Who could have wanted to harm him like this? You mean the guards had something against him? How could they be so brutal?'

'I don't know. Perhaps some official paid the guards to do it?' Joana raised her hands. It was all too sudden, and too brutal.

Carla had gone sheet white, and Joana worried that maybe she shouldn't have come here in her condition. She reached out and took her by the arm. Meanwhile Martin had gone over to stand beside Sergi, and was gazing with almost clinical interest at his swollen face. It was he who spoke.

'Someone wanted to destroy your husband's brain here. Why should any official need to do this to him? Didn't we agree that his career is effectively over? He didn't represent a threat to anyone in government.'

'He had enemies, though.'

'But why put themselves at any risk by arranging this, when he was already down?' He had his eyes still fixed on Sergi, and seemed to be fretting frustratedly at the senseless of it all. 'Was there anyone to whom he was still a threat?' he asked, turning to face the three women.

'Just me.' It was Carla who spoke, in a very small voice, leaning into Joana's arm.

Joana held her, gratified, and gradually the truth dawned on her. 'You, yes Carla, but also the blackmailer! I'm just remembering – I saw a man yesterday going towards the prison, and he looked at me as though he knew me. He was kind of familiar too, but I couldn't figure out who he was. Well, now I remember – it was him I saw when he came to the house for that first meeting with Sergi!' She looked past Martin to where Sergi lay. Oh dear, had Sergi been attacked because his erstwhile blackmailer thought he would now be on his hit list?

Carla made a little frightened sound. 'You think he had some friends among the guards? Someone who could do dirty work for him?'

'I don't suppose we'll ever know, but if that's the case then he's achieved his object, hasn't he, and I don't imagine we'll ever hear from him again.'

Martin backed her up. 'It's over, Carla. I'm sure Joana's right, and it was the blackmailer who organised this, and now he'll be happy.'

Joana shivered, and leaving Carla she took a step forward towards the hospital bed where the shell of Sergi lay. Martin stood to one side, and she had a clear view of her husband. What did she feel? He looked so different, lying there with those bandages covering most of his head, and the tubes everywhere, and that white sheet over him was like a shroud. She shivered again, and Maria came to stand beside her and put a hand on her arm. She leant her head against her mother.

'Poor Sergi,' she said, and meant it. 'Do you know, Mama, I think the person who best understood him was you, or at least you understood where he'd come from and why he was so driven and angry. He always had something to prove, but he was never quite sure he had really proved it, so it drove him further and further, and built that anger in him. What he couldn't dominate he had to hurt. But I don't think he was ever happy. And you know what? I don't think he killed Alex, either. I don't think he felt that powerful in those days, and I think he just said it the other day to hurt Carla, because she had bested him.'

'I hope that's true, *vida meva*,' Maria commented, in hushed tones, her eyes still fixed on Sergi, and the machines that blinked all around him. 'But do you realise that you're speaking about him in the past tense?'

It was true. But somehow Joana was sure Sergi was going to live.

'Yes,' she answered, slowly. 'Because the past is dead – that old Sergi.'

'So you think he'll live?' It was Carla who spoke, her voice doubtful.

'The doctor says there's a chance he may not, but I'd say he'll live, just because it's Sergi! He's a tough cookie. But he'll be ages in here, whatever happens, and the doctor spoke of possible long-term problems in movement and brain function.'

She looked down at him again. 'Do you think he'll be happier, if all that ambition and aggression is gone? I could look after him, you know, if he becomes easier to deal with. He'll need me now.'

Nobody answered her, and they all stood in silence for some minutes, watching Sergi as if a response might come from him. But he seemed more remote the longer Joana looked at him, and eventually she shook herself, throwing off her introspection, and turned to grab Maria by the shoulders.

'You know what, Mama? As I said, whatever happens, Sergi will be in here for a very long time, and do you know what we are now? We're free! Carla and me, and Luc, we're all free! There's no one watching us anymore, and we can do exactly what we want, and my daughter and her husband can live the lives they choose, anywhere they want to be!'

A feeling of elation suddenly surged through her, and she had an urge to twirl her mother round and round, but Maria was still lost in thought, with nothing but confusion written on her face.

'But what will you do now, *carinyo*?' she asked, not understanding.

'Do? Why I, no we, are going to live, Mama! And right now, do you know what we're going to do? We're going to Terrassa, you and I, and Uncle Victor, we're going to go back up with Carla, and I'm going to see my daughter married, that's what. And I'll be the one who buys the champagne!'

'But Joana, how will Victor leave his work?'

'Mama, in my house there are 400,000 pesetas in cash, and in Sergi's accounts there is a great deal more. My uncle can leave his work as soon as he wants to, and at last I'll be able to look after us all properly – not lavishly, perhaps, but decently.'

'And if Sergi regains his faculties?' Typically it was Carla who had this doubt.

'He won't remember anything about what happened to this particular money. It's enough to keep us for many months while we wait to see what happens to him. But the key thing is that from now onwards we live without shadows.' Joana had to stop herself from shouting it, so anxious was she to make them see, and to carry them with her. She reached out her hand, and Maria put hers in it.

'Mama, many years ago I left you all, and since then I've lived a compromised life on Sergi's terms. And I made myself so much believe in it that it's only gradually in the last few months, since I've been incarcerated up there in the hill house, that I've really begun to understand what I'd done to myself, and to Carla, and to all of us. But thank God Carla's life is going to be different. History is not going to repeat itself. Carla has her man and her baby will be born into a different world, and I want us to be there, Mama, all of us together! So come with us to Terrassa, and later I'll look after Sergi properly, I promise you, but let us first be free.'

Maria took her time, then nodded. She shot a look over to where Sergi lay, surrounded by his tubes.

'God help him and pardon him,' she said, and crossed herself. 'But you're right, my daughter. The sun is shining outside this room, and we should all be part of Carla's future.'

Maria turned her gentle smile on Joana, the smile that had pillowed her childhood, and Joana enfolded her in her arms. With one more look over to the body that was Sergi she turned to both Maria and Carla and gestured towards the door.

'Let's get out of here, shall we? The lawyer came before I'd had breakfast, and I need a coffee more badly than I can tell you.'

# Chapter Twenty-Four

Luc's home had been invaded by Carla's family. They completely swamped the house and Luc's gentle parents, and it was hard to believe there could be so many Garrigas in the world. Certainly Carla had never seen them all together before – in fact, she realised, this was the first time they had all been together, ever.

At their head were the older generation, Victor and Maria, and then Maria's children, Josep and Joana, and Josep's wife Neus, and then finally the youngest generation – Josep's three boys, and alongside them Joana's daughter, Carla herself.

And then there was Martin. He might not have the Garriga name, but he had a Garriga father. In fact his father was the absent head of this whole family. But it had taken all of Carla's persuasive efforts to get Martin to Terrassa for the wedding, and he still held himself to one side, shy amongst all the exuberant Garrigas, and unsure of his place in this very Spanish family scene.

'You see all these people here?' Carla said to him on the Wednesday evening, 'Well two years ago I didn't know any of them except my own mother. And until today my mother had never met her brother's wife and children. We've been a broken family, and you're as much a part of this reunion as any of us – even more so, really, when you've played such a large part in bringing us all together.'

Martin smiled, but she wasn't sure she'd convinced him. They were outside in the garden, where Luc's father had laid a treasure hunt for Josep's boys, made all the more exciting for them because it was nearly dark, and the hunt was being conducted by torchlight. With them was Uncle Victor, like a boy himself, yelling in triumph as he unearthed a clue, while their audience was made up of Carla and Martin, and of Luc's father, who had accepted this invasion with the same pleasure and goodwill he'd shown to Carla.

Luc came out from the house and joined them, carefully carrying three beers, and Carla took the opportunity to leave him with Martin, while she slipped into the house to get a jacket, since the night was turning chilly. As she passed through the large, old-fashioned hall she could hear women's voices from the kitchen, where Grandma and Neus were helping Luc's mother to prepare dinner. The men, of course, had nothing to do with preparing food, and through the door of the sitting room Carla could see Joana deep in conversation with Josep, and she smiled at the thought that Joana would find it equally alien to find herself working in a kitchen.

To be fair, though, Joana and Josep had a lot of catching up to do. Brother and sister had met again that afternoon for the first time in nearly twenty-five years, and had stood without words for several minutes, eyes fixed on each other's faces, seeming to soak each other up, noting every detail of the changes wrought by a full generation spent apart. When Joana had left the village, Carla realised, Josep had been a boy of thirteen years old. This sturdy, competent city dweller was a man she didn't know, and possibly wouldn't even have recognised had she passed him in the street.

But Joana had changed less. Carla knew from early photos of her mother that she had looked much as she did now, allowing for some natural aging, and she was not surprised that it was Josep who found it easiest to make the first move towards his sister. It was in Josep's character, anyway. After those silent moments he had stepped forward and taken Joana by the hand.

'So this is little Carla's Mama! Why, I do swear, Joana, that you've grown even more beautiful over the years. Do you still play *botifarra*?'

And after that it had been easy, or it seemed so, though a sort of haze of wonderment seemed to hang over Joana, as she watched Josep with Neus and his boys, easy and funny and masterful, in his role as father and the simplicity of family life. Their oldest boy was about the age Josep would have been when Joana left home, and he looked very like his father. Joana couldn't take her eyes off him.

But in this early evening brother and sister were ensconced in the sitting room, and the world was leaving them alone. Carla could see a beer by Josep's elbow, and a glass on the table in front of her mother whose contents she could easily guess. She slipped by the door without disturbing them and popped her head round the kitchen door.

'Can I do anything?' she asked, but she knew the answer. She had already been shooed out of the kitchen earlier.

'Not at all, my dear,' Luc's mother twinkled at her. 'I'm very ably helped by your grandmother here, and your aunt. In fact, they're leaving me nothing to do, which suits me very well, because I've never been very organised in the kitchen. You go and rest that baby of yours. We don't want any accidents before we get that wedding ceremony over tomorrow.'

Grandma added her voice 'We're doing very nicely here, *carinyo*, and *Senyora* Serra has bought so much food that we are preparing a nice buffet for tomorrow lunchtime as well, which we'll hopefully be able to eat in the garden, if this good weather continues. And we have young Mireia here,' she pointed to Joana's maid, whom they had brought with them from Girona to help Luc's parents handle the influx of people. Mireia was enjoying herself very much, Carla thought, in a house where servants were unknown, and she was therefore treated as an equal human being, a helping hand rather than a subservient one.

'Off you go,' Maria repeated, 'and tell them all outside that we'll eat in half an hour, so the boys had better find that treasure fast.'

Carla acceded graciously, happy enough if truth be told to collect her jacket and then go back to Luc outside. She'd had little time alone with him, and was looking forward to tomorrow evening, when they would finally be given a room together – Josep and Neus's room, with the boys' truckle beds removed, since they would all leave after lunch tomorrow.

This reunion was brief and to be savoured, and the evening meal was therefore long and noisy. Carla took herself off to bed soon after the *moscatell* was produced. Josep was performing a parody of his sister Joana in her younger years, parading up and down the length of the long table, flouncing imaginary skirts and wagging a finger at them in mimicry of Joana's teenage temper. Joana was laughing as Carla never remembered seeing her laugh, and protesting that anyone with Josep as a younger brother was bound to be infuriated more often than not.

Carla passed by Grandma, who was laughing too, and she paused to kiss her before waving a hand at the others.

'You're all very merry, but will you feel so merry tomorrow morning?' she asked them, smiling. 'I'm going to bed now, because if I'm going to face the priest tomorrow I need my beauty sleep first.'

Luc got up to escort her upstairs. 'It's all right, you know, he really is a nice young guy – most untraditional, in the best possible way. He's even in favour of women's education, so you can impress him with your erudition, Carla!'

'I'll believe it when I see it!' Carla retorted. 'I'll rely on Grandma to support me. She's so obviously holy he won't dare to criticise her!'

But the priest was exactly as Luc had described him. He came to the house early next morning to talk Luc and Carla through the service, and he even spoke to them in Catalan, which Carla found almost unnerving from anyone in authority. She answered him in Spanish, stiff in spite of herself, and he held up his hand to stop her.

'We'll do the service in Spanish, *Senyorita*, but here in the house there is no need to be so formal. I come from a village just a few kilometres from here, you know, and we prefer to keep things simple.'

And if anyone told the bishop about him, what would happen then, she wondered? But this house was known to be liberal – a reformist priest could feel safe here.

He left them after talking through their lines with them, and after he'd gone it occurred to Carla that he hadn't at all made her feel conscious of her advanced pregnancy. It was a blessing, but one that was missing later that morning when they walked the short distance from the house to the church. The neighbourhood was at work this Thursday, but a few women had gathered to watch the cortege go by, and Carla could see them muttering at the sight of a bride within so few weeks of giving birth. A couple of younger women even sniggered, and as she caught their gaze Carla felt her stomach tighten, and even had a moment's panic that this was the baby coming.

But it subsided, and she drew herself up and faced the women, holding tight to Luc's arm. People outside their lives had not the least idea of what she and Luc had been through, and now that they were crossing the last hurdle, the opinions of a gaggle of women were irrelevant.

She hadn't dressed as a bride, though. She was dressed in the same tailored dress and coat that she had worn to visit Sergi just two weeks ago. It fitted beautifully over her bump, and she was again grateful for Mama's fine fashion sense. It gave her confidence, and as she walked on past the women she gave them a smile, and inclined her head, in a gesture that discomposed them in a most pleasing way.

They all entered the church together, without formality, and Luc, Carla and Martin advanced to the altar together. To everyone's chagrin Luc's brother had been unable to join them today. His employer had refused him leave of absence, and had brooked no argument, telling him that hundreds of others would be only too pleased to have his job. Luc had sworn angrily, using words Carla rarely heard him use, and had thanked his lucky stars that he was no longer obliged to think of working for 'that bastard', as he called him.

So he had asked Martin to be his best man. Martin had demurred at first, saying it would all be in Spanish, and he was sure to do the wrong thing at the wrong time, but Luc had insisted.

'I'll dig you in the ribs when we need the ring,' he said. 'It's all you have to do.'

So Martin had accepted. He looked a little drowned in the suit he'd borrowed from Luc's father, but he nevertheless brought tears to Maria's eyes.

'My brother Luis has come to my granddaughter's wedding,' she whispered to him, as he stood almost to attention next to Carla, and she held him tight before they entered the church.

In the end Martin produced the ring to order, and the ceremony was over before they knew it, the priest keeping the prayers mercifully brief. Carla held tight to Luc's hand throughout, holding her breath, counting her blessings – she hardly knew what she was doing.

But when he kissed her the cheer that went up in the church was worthy of a much larger crowd, and she couldn't resist looking behind her at all of her family, and giving them a defiant thumbs up. We made it, she wanted to shout.

And then they were back at the house, bearing the priest along with them, for lunch in the garden, on long trestle tables laid out on a terrace newly raked of its leaves. There was a chill in the air, and you could feel that winter was not too far away, but it felt more like spring to Carla. The baby pressed its feet against her stomach – it felt heavier and heavier now every day, with its head pressing down uncomfortably. Come when you like now, she thought, and the relief was so strong she choked up and could barely eat the tapas of anchovies, squid, and *butifarra* sausage and wild cep mushrooms (Luc's father's own fresh gathering from his secret mushroom site in the woods).

They ate pasta, and tender mountain lamb, and when the time came for dessert it seemed Neus had brought up with her from Barcelona a massive wedding cake filled with coconut, almonds, dried pineapple and pecans, cutting off wedges, which she insisted Carla and Luc should feed to each other before the cake was shared out among the rest of the family. Carla had never envisaged that their wedding could be in any way like other weddings, but it turned into a real party, nothing like the opulent, fashionable weddings she had attended with her parents as a child, thank goodness, but full of festive hilarity.

After lunch she walked with her mother in the lovely, ramshackle garden, avoiding damp spots for the sake of

Joana's silk shoes. She repeated to Mama what she had been thinking for the last few hours.

'Well, the baby can come when it wants now. I'm here with Luc's father, and he can call on a midwife when the time comes, so we'll be thoroughly well looked after.' She thought back to the last few months and whistled through her teeth. 'Who'd have believed it! You know, it's only two and half weeks since Martin walked into Grandma's apartment and persuaded me that he should tell you about the terrible mess I was in. Two and a half weeks, and the entire world has changed! This baby will owe its whole future to that moment.'

'Yes.' Joana was unwontedly sober as she answered. 'Thank God for Martin! He has mended the damage I caused. You know, I've never yet said sorry to you, Carla, for letting you go – for allowing my prejudices and false allegiances to damage our relationship so terribly that I didn't even know when you were in the gravest jeopardy.'

Carla put her arm around her mother. 'Well, I was a pretty prickly person to try to love, for a long time, and I deliberately flew in the face of every code you lived by! And the worst didn't happen, did it, and we have mended the damage. Martin could see us all afresh, with an outsider's eyes, and he wasn't weighed down by our history. We'd made a bad and good divide, each of us, forced on us by Sergi, and we couldn't see beyond the barriers he'd built up between us.'

Joana sighed. 'Poor Sergi,' she said, and then stopped in front of a flowering shrub. 'Oh my goodness, look at this! It's a passion flower, and still with some flowers on it, by God, at this season!'

She reached out and touched one of the flowers, flat and open with its white petals and purple-blue stamen. It wasn't the most beautiful flower Carla had seen, but her mother was stroking it almost reverently.

'We had one of these at the apartment in Barcelona when I was growing up. It was your grandmother's pride and joy, and I do remember it still flowered late in the year.'

'Uncle Josep told me about your apartment in Barcelona. You had a garden?'

Joana shook her head. 'Not a garden, but a big balcony, where Josep used to play and drive me mad! And Maria grew jasmine and passion flower in huge pots against the wall. They covered everything, and it felt like a garden.'

She fell into a reverie, continuing almost as though Carla wasn't there. 'They call it the flower of passion, but my Uncle Luis used to call it the flower of hope, because the flowers just keep coming, and new blooms replace the old ones every day. He used to pick the flowers and put them in my hair. That was back in the days of hope, of course. There were no passion flowers later.'

'But there is this one, Mama, and it still has flowers.'

'So it does!' Joana smiled, and reached out to pick two of them, placing one carefully in Carla's hair, and one in her own. 'We are back in the land of hope, it seems!'

Carla touched the delicate flower tucked behind her ear, and kissed her mother on the cheek. 'I know, and today I can really believe in it!'

They headed back to the house, where the men were slowly extricating themselves from the table. They could hear Neus calling for the three boys, who had disappeared after lunch to play a rather violent game of tig at the front of the house, where their noise wouldn't be heard.

'We need to think about leaving,' Josep explained. 'I have to work tomorrow, and the boys have to be at school.'

'Martin is going with you?' Carla asked.

'Yes. Toni reckons we can squeeze him into that great limousine you brought with you, and tomorrow morning we can put him on the train for France.'

The party was breaking up, and as Martin appeared from the house with his travel bag under his arm Carla felt a surge of panic. Josep and his family weren't going out of their lives, but Martin was leaving – really leaving this time.

She looked around for Luc, and he came to her side, and took her hand. Neus reappeared, bearing three reluctant boys along with her, and from the house emerged the other women. Everyone was together, on this terrace, and Carla froze the scene and made her eyes take a photo of it, storing it for future memory. They had photos of the day, taken on Luc's father's old camera, but this was a personal memory in full colour, which Carla captured for herself alone.

Martin came forward to the table, to Carla and Luc. 'I've said goodbye to your parents,' he told Luc. 'They've been very kind, and your father wants to be kept in touch with my studies.'

'We'll do that,' Luc assured him. 'We'll always be in touch now, and you can write to us through either Joana's address or Victor's. And we'll write to you as soon as we have our own address.'

'Where will you be, do you think?'

Luc shrugged. 'Since we can stay, I'll probably look for

a job in Barcelona. It's kind of our city, really.'

Martin nodded, and seemed stuck for any more words. Finally he managed, 'You two will be fine now. Let me know when the baby's born, won't you?'

'We sure will,' Carla replied. 'If Grandma has any say in it we'll probably have to have the baby christened, too, and if that happens we'll make you his godfather!'

'I won't be around much to watch over his or her childhood,' Martin objected.

'We'll have plenty of clucking family around to do that, don't worry. You can be his inspiration to aspire to life on the international stage!'

Martin smiled, and they hugged, with no further words needed. He turned to go to the car, where Maria and Victor were with Josep and his family, waiting to say goodbye to him. But blocking his way stood Joana.

'I have yet to say thank you, *el meu cosí*,' she said to him.

He held up his hand, and the tears that he had been holding back began to fall. Joana took the hand, and held it in hers.

'We love you, Martin. All of us, and especially me. Never forget that, and know that I will always think of you, always remember you and everything you have done for us. And I will follow your career, your life, and expect you back here to see us. You leave a little bit of your heart here with us, and you take away a piece of each one of your family, to live with you in France.'

She kissed him, and he gave way and returned her embrace. 'Thank you,' was all he managed to say, his voice too choked for more, and as he drew away, she took the passion flower from her hair and placed it in his, tucking it carefully behind his ear with a little caress of her fingers.

Two minutes more and he was gone, with all of Josep's noisy crew. Tomorrow he would be back in France, and hopefully he wouldn't get into too much trouble with his university tutors for his prolonged absence. Carla leant against Luc, and he put his long arms around her.

'We will stay in touch with him, you know' he said.

'I know,' she sighed. 'There's just been so much emotion attached to his visit here.' She pulled herself together, and smiled. 'Next time we meet we'll do it without dramas, shall we, and do some ordinary stuff together, what do you think?'

'I can't imagine life being ordinary just yet! But give me time, and I'll become the archetypal accountant, coming home each evening to you and Joaquima, and the five other children you're going to give me, and you'll have my pipe waiting for me, and a pot of *ollada* steaming in the kitchen.'

Carla gave him a punch in the ribs. '*Ollada* my foot! You haven't tasted my cooking yet, dear husband, and you may find that your six children go hungry if you don't cook yourself!'

'Help me, somebody,' Luc sighed, catching Joana's eye. 'I've been misled and now I'm lumbered with a wife who won't cook! What am I to do?'

Joana laughed. 'Don't look at me, Luc! I haven't cooked for nearly twenty years, and I've been a failure in preparing my daughter for marriage!'

'He takes some feeding too, Carla!' It was Luc's mother who threw in the comment.

'That I've seen!' Carla retorted. 'Well, we'll just have to steal Grandma from Victor and have her come to live with us!'

'Or you could learn to cook, *carinyo*,' Maria smiled.

'Or I could learn to cook,' acknowledged Carla. 'But not for six children, mind, and if you get a pipe I'll leave home, Luc.'

'And I wouldn't blame you, Carla,' chipped in his mother. 'Let's get this baby born first, and never mind any more just yet! The cheek of the boy, and he doesn't even have a job yet!'

'Well, if you've got my mother on your side then I'm sunk!' Luc grinned ruefully at Carla. 'Would you accept a modest husband instead, with some small cooking skills and a willingness to survive on sandwiches?'

Carla put her arms around his neck and pulled his head down towards her. 'I don't have much choice either, do I, now that I've married you?' She looked over at Luc's father, who had come out of the house, where he had lit all the lights. It looked cosy inside, and it was getting chilly now outside.

'If you just stay like your father I'll love you forever,' she said, as she kissed the end of Luc's nose, and then led him towards the open door.

# Epilogue

## April, 1964

Carla had been thinking for many weeks now about this trip. A full six months had passed since the events of October – events so dramatic that a little shiver went through her whenever she looked back at them. It would be a long time, she thought, before she would cease having those little, piercing flashbacks.

But for now life had changed completely. She and Luc were married, their baby had been born in wedlock, and life was safe.

It was astonishing what it did to you to feel safe. After six months Carla was beginning to get used to the feeling, and to cease looking over her shoulder all the time. As spring came upon them she had walked the streets of Barcelona, through the flower market, past the cafés with their throngs of courting couples and men doing business Spanish style over the *aperitiù*, and as she pushed the pram between them she felt part of a new order, a happier, hopeful world to which she belonged. Soon summer would be here, and she and Luc and the baby could spend Sundays at the beach, or in Luc's parents' wonderful garden in Terrassa, or just sitting out on their own balcony watching the world of Barcelona passing below them.

But right now she had one more hurdle to cross. She had let all these months go by before making this journey to Sant Galdric, but now she was ready, and the time was right. She was sitting yet again in the passenger seat of the Mercedes, with Toni driving beside her, and Grandma Maria in the back seat cradling the baby. And they were going to visit Enric and Alícia Figarola.

She hadn't known until just after the baby was born that Alex Figarola's mother was called Alícia. It was a name she loved, and which brought her own father Alex to her mind as well, so when – to Luc's eternal delight – their baby had been born a girl, and Joana had told them about the name, they'd made the decision to call their baby Alícia as well.

But until now the child's great-grandmother, Alícia Figarola, didn't even know that the child existed. And the story she needed to learn had to begin long before the baby. The Figarolas didn't even know that their son had fathered a child, and had left behind him his daughter, Carla, who was his image in spirit and form.

Carla drew a long, deliberate breath as apprehension briefly tensed her throat. It was only good news that she was going to impart, and she refused to allow any of the stresses of the past to reinvade her life. Baby Alícia's birth had broken a cycle, and those ruptured relationships, which were the product of war – Uncle Luis dying before Martin was born, and Alex being torn from Joana and her unborn child – these things were in the past. Sergi had waged his own personal war, willed his own private hell on his family, but that was over too, and would never return.

Behind her she heard the baby making the little mewling noise that Luc insisted was singing. Carla turned in her seat to smile at Grandma, who was murmuring little comforts to the child.

'You wouldn't like to sit here in front with Toni, Grandma, so that I can look after the baby?'

'Not at all, *carinyo*!' Maria shook her head, and placed a kiss on Alícia's forehead. 'It's over a month since I visited you in Barcelona, and this little one has changed again. You can have your lovely apartment, with its modern decor and all those fancy gadgets, but I'm going to be the one who makes sure that this little one grows up with more than you young people's modern ideas! She's growing strong, isn't she?' she smiled, gently extricating a lock of her hair from Alícia's podgy grip.

'She's her father, God help her! I hope the Figarolas will recognise my little fair blob as one of their own!'

'How dare she?' Maria was crooning at the baby. 'How dare your mother speak about you like that? You're quite beautiful, *petita* Alícia, and don't you let them be telling you otherwise!'

Grandma Maria had never been busier than in the last few months. It was she who had held the longest vigils by Sergi's hospital bed, and who had control of his nursing room now that he had been returned home. Carla found she couldn't be anything other than sobered and appalled by what had happened to her stepfather. To see him sunken as he was, with such slow movement and minimal recognition returning, made her feel nothing should have to finish this way.

Joana had spent the winter months begging Maria and Victor to give up their apartment and come to stay with her in the Girona house, and with Sergi's transfer home Maria had agreed temporarily. Both she and Victor were staying with Joana for now, but Victor hankered after their little apartment, modest and shabby as it might be. He missed the life of the little café where he met his pals after work twice a week, and he found his bed in Joana's house too soft to sleep properly. He hadn't given up work, either. If he gave up work, he said, then it would be to return to Sant Galdric. But most days he accepted a lift from Toni to the factory. 'I'm becoming lazy,' he would say, but with his usual easy smile.

Maria was happy, for now, in Joana's house, but only because she had care of the sick room, watching over Sergi when the nurses weren't there, and bringing coffee for the nurses when they were. To be useful and surrounded by family was Maria's main wish in life, and Carla had no real concerns about either Grandma or Uncle Victor.

Was Joana as happy? Carla worried about her mother, who was still so tied, and still obliged to play the public game of being Sergi's loyal wife. Joana had the power now, over all their finances, and over Sergi's care, but was she really free? And for now she was busy enough with them all, but what would she do with herself in the longer term?

She seemed to have no interest now in all the fripperies she used to cloak herself in.

Luc would tell Carla not to worry. Joana's life had been blown apart, he said, and she was in a period of re-evaluation, but she was a strong woman and would find her own path. She was happy and busy, and for now just wanted her family around her. But Carla wondered. Something else had changed in her mother. Something had been opened up in Joana back in October that remained exposed, and made her seem vulnerable as a woman, in a way that she had never seemed before. They were women together now, Carla and Joana, but Carla had Luc, whereas Joana was like a solitary flower, and there was a little longing in her eyes, which Carla hoped one day to see disappear. She spent hours thinking through all the eligible men she knew for her mother, until Luc laughed at her and told her to stop trying to play Cupid, because her mother was already Venus.

Sant Galdric came into sight above them, with the mountains behind blanketed under snow for as far as the eye could see. But around the village the ground was green and the trees were blooming. The spring sky was so fresh and clear that the odd little cloud that passed above them seemed like an impertinence. It was a completely different light from the mellow of last autumn, and as they neared the village they passed a fallow field full of poppies and wild irises, which Carla pointed out to Maria with a gesture of mute discovery.

The village hadn't changed from the times when Carla had passed through it before, or at least it was as small and spartan as ever, but it seemed less dusty after the spring rains, and more awake, and she herself was more at peace, and could see the beauty of the old church and the square before it, and the line of little village houses on either side of the square. Seen in this light, Carla could still understand why Joana had found it so hard to be buried here after a childhood spent in Barcelona, but she could also see what it was that made it home for Maria.

You could imagine an earlier village, with a population twice the current size, and the villagers all dancing the *Sardana* together in the square after a wedding or a christening, with their own *cobla* musicians playing the accompaniment. Joana herself had probably danced the *Sardana* with Alex, and Grandma and Uncle Victor in their youth would have undertaken discreet village flirtations under cover of the dance. It was strange to imagine Victor flirting with a village girl, and if he had it would have been a shy affair, she was sure. The brief courtship Grandma had told them about seemed like a blip in an otherwise happy bachelor life. He'd been happiest with his sheep!

The Mercedes drew up alongside the old family house in Sant Galdric. Maria wanted to open the house up again, so that she and Victor could come up here sometimes, and rediscover their village lives. The plan was that on this visit Carla and Maria would stay in the village for a couple of days, so that Carla could get to know some of the village people, and so that Maria could reclaim her home, with the fresh sheets and many cleaning cloths she'd brought with her in the car. Carla would help, of course, but she knew she would be frequently chased outside with the pram.

Maria had some reconnecting to do on her own in her little village home.

Joana would maybe dare to come here some time later, Carla hoped, although she knew her mother needed first to go back to the hill house, and to relearn the beauty of it without Sergi.

So they stopped at the little village house, and went inside to drop off all the bags and trunks that had been loaded into the car. It was a small house, and simple, and the possessions that had been left behind looked lonely in the gloom of the closed shutters. It smelt musty too, and as Toni went round opening windows, Maria patrolled, with little distressed exclamations, picking up little ornaments and dusting them, and placing fresh food in the larder. Carla changed Alícia, and fed her, and thought that before too long the baby would go to sleep. If I am going to brave the Figarolas today, she thought, I want their great-granddaughter awake to greet them.

'*Avia*?' she ventured, and Grandma nodded, and came away from her fussing.

'Yes, my child,' she said, taking Alícia's little hand in hers. 'The time has come. Shall we go and meet your grandparents?'

Toni walked up with them as far as his mother's house, where he stopped. There was a new coat of paint on the front door, so presumably his mother's new pension was being put to good use.

Maria and Carla continued on their way, and as they walked up the street with the pram, Carla looked around her at the shuttered houses, and at the unshuttered ones, which still held village life, and she held Luc's courage to her as they approached the door of her father's home. As she raised a hand to knock at the door, she brought Martin to mind and thought, this one's for you cousin, for telling me to do it. He'd told her again, in his letters, that she should make this journey, and she'd taken her time but now she was here, and she could almost feel him beside her. You're right, dear Martin, she thought. This is the right thing to do, and thanks to you I'm coming home.